The Gift Giving

Favourite Stories by

JOAN AIKEN

Illustrated by Peter Bailey

virago

VIRAGO

First published in Great Britain in 2016 by Virago Press

1 3 5 7 9 10 8 6 4 2

'The Magic of Stories' has been compiled from talks given by Joan Aiken in her lifetime

The stories in this collection first appeared in the following collections:
'All You've Ever Wanted', 'The Pirate Parrot Princess', 'John Sculpin and the Witches',
'Cooks and Prophecies', 'The Lobster's Birthday', 'The Rocking Donkey' –
All You've Ever Wanted, Jonathan Cape, 1953
'More Than You Bargained For', 'The Third Wish', 'Nutshells, Seashells' –
More Than You Bargained For, Jonathan Cape, 1955
'The Boy Who Read Aloud' – *A Small Pinch of Weather*, Jonathan Cape, 1969
'A Harp of Fishbones', 'The Boy with a Wolf's Foot', 'The Lost Five Minutes', 'Humblepuppy',
'A Jar of Cobblestones', 'The Gift Pig' – *A Harp of Fishbones*, Jonathan Cape, 1972
'Crusader's Toby', 'Moonshine in the Mustard Pot', 'The Faithless Lollybird' –
The Faithless Lollybird, Jonathan Cape, 1977
'The Rain Child' – *The Faithless Lollybird*, US edition, Doubleday, 1978
'The Midnight Rose', 'The Dog on the Roof', 'The Gift Giving' – *Up the Chimney Down*,
Jonathan Cape, 1984

The moral right of the author has been asserted

A CIP catalogue record for this book is available from the British Library.

ISBN 978-0-349-00589-8

Typeset in Goudy by M Rules
Printed and bound in Great Britain by Clays Ltd, St Ives plc

Papers used by Virago are from well-managed forests
and other responsible sources.

MIX
Paper from
responsible sources
FSC FSC® C104740
www.fsc.org

Virago Press
An imprint of
Little, Brown Book Group
Carmelite House
50 Victoria Embankment
London EC4Y 0DZ

An Hachette UK Company
www.hachette.co.uk

www.virago.co.uk

The Magic of Stories

Stories are mysterious things; they have a life of their own. Animals don't tell each other stories – so far as we know! Man is the only creature that has thought of telling stories, and, once a story has been written or told, it becomes independent of its creator and goes wandering off by itself. Think of *Cinderella*, or *Beauty and the Beast* – we don't know where they came from, but they are known by people all over the world.

A story is very powerful. If I start to tell you a story, you are almost sure to stop and listen to it. It's like hypnotism – or a small piece of magic. Indeed, stories often have been used for magic, by priests or medicine men. There used to be special stories kept secret and only used on rare special occasions: stories that would heal sickness, or give victory in battle. Storytellers, in primitive times, were treated with great respect, probably given extra large rations of mastodon steak, when the cavemen were all sitting round the tribal fire. In those days, before anything was written down, stories were the means by which important facts were stored and remembered. In a way it is still so. Think how much easier it is to remember that Alfred was the king who burned the cakes than what his dates were; I bet if I stopped anybody in the street and asked them what they knew about King Alfred, those cakes are what they would remember, not which year it happened!

People sometimes ask me: How do you write a story? How do you set about it? How do you get your ideas? And I always say, first you have to have ingredients. You couldn't go into an empty kitchen and expect to be able to cook a dinner. A writer, like a good cook, is always on the lookout for ingredients that might come in handy. Sometimes they are the things you read in the newspaper – the woman who buys a raffle ticket with her last pound and wins a million, the violinist who leaves his Stradivarius in a taxi, the man who trains his dog to bark at Salvation Army bands. Sometimes they come from dreams. I keep a little notebook and write down all these things in it.

I don't really believe there is such a thing as 'a born storyteller', especially when it is applied to me! Storytellers aren't born, they have to learn. It is a craft; like oil painting or ballet dancing, you don't just come to it naturally. A story needs to be carefully built up – like a house of cards – one thing balancing on top of another. And then the end, when you get to it, ought to be a little bit surprising, but satisfying, too, to make the reader think, 'Yes, of course, that's it! Why didn't I think of that?' I can remember exactly the moment when I realized the importance of that surprise, while telling my brother a story on a walk, and I rushed home, and wrote the story down. It was a story about a princess who turned into a parrot. That was when I was about sixteen, and I've never forgotten it. Stories are fun to write! They are, or should be, like a sleigh-ride, and once you get on course, then some terrific power, like the power of gravity, takes command and whizzes you off to an unknown destination.

A very important element in a story is the setting – where it all takes place. Some of the stories I've written have their settings and surroundings so firmly in my mind that I can call them back whenever I want to. 'The Boy with a Wolf's Foot' was written when I travelled back and forth to London every day, along a railway line whose stations all seemed to begin with W. 'The Rain Child' came when I had a job picking apples in a huge series of orchards. 'Moonshine in the Mustard Pot' is a mixture of Paris and the beautiful city of York. My daughter lived for a time in both these cities and I visited her there, and the grandmother in the story is a mix of my daughter and myself. 'A Harp of Fishbones' is purely invention, but I know that mountainside and that ruined city as well as if I had lived there all my life. The stories that have the strongest settings are my favourites. I like to revisit them from time to time, and that is like going back to stay in a house, or piece of country, that one has known since childhood; it is a happy, refreshing thing to do.

Reading is and always will be one of my greatest pleasures, and I love to re-read books and stories that have been favourites for years, and I particularly like to re-visit some of my own short stories, as they too have now taken on that mysterious life of their own. Favourite stories, like unexpected presents, are things that you can keep and cherish all your life, carry with you in memory, in your mind's ear, and bring out at any time, when you are feeling lonely or need cheering up, or, like friends, just because you are fond of them. That is the way I feel about some of these stories.

One of the nicest letters that I ever had from a reader said: 'Your stories are such a gift, they make me feel as though I dimly remember them. I seem to know the characters and places from long ago, like a forgotten dream ...'

Maybe they will feel like that for you too, and become some of your own favourites – after all, where do our stories really come from?

Who knows?

Joan Aiken

Contents

All You've Ever Wanted

Matilda, you will agree, was a most unfortunate child. Not only had she three names each worse than the others – Matilda, Eliza and Agatha – but her father and mother died shortly after she was born, and she was brought up exclusively by her six aunts. These were all energetic women, and so on Monday Matilda was taught Algebra and Arithmetic by her Aunt Aggie, on Tuesday, Biology by her Aunt Beattie, on Wednesday Classics by her Aunt Cissie, on Thursday Dancing and Deportment by her Aunt Dorrie, on Friday Essentials by her Aunt Effie, and on Saturday French by her Aunt Florrie. Friday was the most alarming day, as Matilda never knew beforehand what Aunt Effie would decide on as the day's Essentials – sometimes it was cooking, or revolver practice, or washing, or boiler-making ('For you never know what a girl may need nowadays' as Aunt Effie rightly observed). So that by Sunday, Matilda was often worn out, and thanked her stars that her seventh aunt, Gertie, had left for foreign parts many years before, and never threatened to come back and teach her Geology or Grammar on the only day when she was able to do as she liked.

However, poor Matilda was not entirely free from her Aunt Gertie, for on her seventh birthday, and each one after it, she received a little poem wishing her well, written on pink paper, decorated with silver flowers, and signed 'Gertrude Isabel Jones, to her niece, with much affection'. And the terrible disadvantage of the poems, pretty though they were, was that the wishes in them invariably came true. For instance the one on her eighth birthday read:

Now you are eight Matilda dear
May shining gifts your place adorn
And each day through the coming year
Awake you with a rosy morn.

The shining gifts were all very well – they consisted of a torch, a luminous watch, pins, needles, a steel soapbox and a useful little silver brooch which said 'Matilda' in case she ever forgot her name – but the rosy morns were a great mistake. As you know, a red sky in the morning is the shepherd's warning, and the fatal results of Aunt Gertie's well-meaning verse was that it rained every day for the entire year.

Another one read:

Each morning make another friend
Who'll be with you till light doth end,
Cheery and frolicsome and gay,
To pass the sunny hours away.

For the rest of her life Matilda was overwhelmed by the number of friends she made in the course of that year – three hundred and sixty-five of them. Every morning she found another of them, anxious to cheer her and frolic with her, and the aunts complained that her lessons were being constantly interrupted. The worst of it was that she did not really like all the friends – some of them were so very cheery and frolicsome, and insisted on pillow-fights when she had toothache, or sometimes twenty-one of them would get together and make her play hockey, which she hated. She was not even consoled by the fact that all her hours were sunny, because she was so busy in passing them away that she had no time to enjoy them.

Long miles and weary though you stray
Your friends are never far away,
And every day though you may roam,
Yet night will find you back at home

was another inconvenient wish. Matilda found herself forced to go for long, tiresome walks in all weathers, and it was no comfort to know that her friends were never far away, for although they often passed her on bicycles or in cars, they never gave her lifts.

However, as she grew older, the poems became less troublesome, and she began to enjoy bluebirds twittering in the garden, and endless vases of roses on her window-sill. Nobody knew where Aunt Gertie lived, and she never put in an address with her birthday greetings. It was there-fore impossible to write and thank her for her varied good wishes, or hint that they might have been more carefully worded. But Matilda looked forward to meeting her one day, and thought that she must be a most interesting person.

'You never knew what Gertrude would be up to next,' said Aunt Cissie. 'She was a thoughtless girl, and got into endless scrapes, but I will say for her, she was very good-hearted.'

When Matilda was nineteen she took a job in the Ministry of Alarm and Despondency, a very cheerful place where, instead of typewriter ribbon, they used red tape, and there was a large laundry basket near the main entrance labelled The Usual Channels where all the letters were put which people did not want to answer themselves. Once every three months the letters were re-sorted and dealt out afresh to different people.

Matilda got on very well here and was perfectly happy. She went to see her six aunts on Sundays, and had almost forgotten the seventh by the time that her twentieth birthday had arrived. Her aunt, however, had not forgotten.

On the morning of her birthday Matilda woke very late, and had to rush off to work cramming her letters unopened into her pocket, to be read later on in the morning. She had no time to read them until ten minutes to eleven, but that, she told herself, was as it should be, since, as she had been born at eleven in the morning, her birthday did not really begin till then.

Most of the letters were from her 365 friends, but the usual pink and silver envelope was there, and she opened it with the usual feeling of slight uncertainty.

May all your leisure hours be blest
Your work prove full of interest,
Your life hold many happy hours
And all your way be strewn with flowers

said the pink and silver slip in her fingers. 'From your affectionate Aunt Gertrude.'

Matilda was still pondering this when a gong sounded in the passage outside. This was the signal for everyone to leave their work and dash down the passage to a trolley which sold them buns and coffee. Matilda left her letters and dashed with the rest. Sipping her coffee and gossiping with her friends, she had forgotten the poem, when the voice of the Minister of Alarm and Despondency himself came down the corridor.

'What is all this? What does this mean?' he was saying.

The group round the trolley turned to see what he was talking about. And then Matilda flushed scarlet and spilt some of her coffee on the floor. For all along the respectable brown carpeting of the passage were growing flowers in the most riotous profusion – daisies, campanulas, crocuses, mimosa, foxgloves, tulips and lotuses. In some places the passage looked more like a jungle than anything else. Out of this jungle the little red-faced figure of the Minister fought its way.

'Who did it?' he said. But nobody answered.

Matilda went quietly away from the chattering group and pushed through the vegetation to her room, leaving a trail of buttercups and rhododendrons across the floor to her desk.

'I can't keep this quiet,' she thought desperately. And she was quite right. Mr Willoughby, who presided over the General Gloom Division, noticed almost immediately that when his secretary came in to his room, there was something unusual about her.

'Miss Jones,' he said, 'I don't like to be personal, but have you noticed that wherever you go, you leave a trail of mixed flowers?'

Poor Matilda burst into tears.

'I know, I don't know *what* I shall do about it,' she sobbed.

Mr Willoughby was not used to secretaries who burst into tears, let alone ones who left lobelias, primroses and the rarer forms of cactus behind them when they entered the room.

'It's very pretty,' he said. 'But not very practical. Already it's almost impossible to get along the passage, and I shudder to think what this room will be like when these have grown a bit higher. I really don't think you can go on with it, Miss Jones.'

'You don't think I do it on purpose, do you?' said Matilda sniffing into her handkerchief. 'I can't stop it. They just keep on coming.'

'In that case I am afraid,' replied Mr Willoughby, 'that you will not be able to keep on coming. We really cannot have the Ministry overgrown in this way. I shall be very sorry to lose you, Miss Jones. You have been most efficient. What caused this unfortunate disability, may I ask?'

'It's a kind of spell,' Matilda said, shaking the damp out of her handkerchief on to a fine polyanthus.

'But my dear girl,' Mr Willoughby exclaimed testily, 'you have a National Magic Insurance card, haven't you? Good heavens – why don't you go to the Public Magician?'

'I never thought of that,' she confessed. 'I'll go at lunchtime.'

Fortunately for Matilda the Public Magician's office lay just across the square from where she worked, so that she did not cause too much disturbance, though the Borough Council could never account for the rare and exotic flowers which suddenly sprang up in the middle of their dusty lawns.

The Public Magician received her briskly, examined her with an occultiscope, and asked her to state particulars of her trouble.

'It's a spell,' said Matilda, looking down at a pink Christmas rose growing unseasonably beside her chair.

'In that case we can soon help you. Fill in that form, *if* you please.' He pushed a printed slip at her across the table.

It said: 'To be filled in by persons suffering from spells, incantations, philtres, Evil Eye, etc.'

Matilda filled in name and address of patient, nature of spell, and date, but when she came to name and address of person by whom spell was cast, she paused.

'I don't know her address,' she said.

'Then I'm afraid you'll have to find it. Can't do anything without an address,' the Public Magician replied.

Matilda went out into the street very disheartened. The Public Magician could do nothing better than advise her to put an advertisement into *The Times* and the *International Sorcerers' Bulletin*, which she accordingly did:

AUNT GERTRUDE PLEASE COMMUNICATE
MATILDA MUCH DISTRESSED BY LAST POEM

While she was in the Post Office sending off her advertisements (and causing a good deal of confusion by the number of forget-me-nots she left about), she wrote and posted her resignation to Mr Willoughby, and then went sadly to the nearest Underground Station.

'Aintcher left something behind?' a man said to her at the top of the escalator. She looked back at the trail of daffodils across the station entrance and hurried anxiously down the stairs. As she ran round a corner at the bottom angry shouts told her that blooming lilies had interfered with the works and the escalator had stopped.

She tried to hide in the gloom at the far end of the platform, but a furious station official found her.

'Wotcher mean by it?' he said, shaking her elbow. 'It'll take three days to put the station right, and look at my platform!'

The stone slabs were split and pushed aside by vast peonies, which kept growing, and threatened to block the line.

'It isn't my fault – really it isn't,' poor Matilda stammered.

'The Company can sue you for this, you know,' he began, when a train came in. Pushing past him, she squeezed into the nearest door.

She began to thank her stars for the escape, but it was too soon. A powerful and penetrating smell of onions rose round her feet where the white flowers of wild garlic had sprung.

When Aunt Gertie finally read the advertisement in a ten-months-old copy of the *International Sorcerers'*

Bulletin, she packed her luggage and took the next aeroplane back to England. For she was still just as Aunt Cissie had described her – thoughtless, but very good-hearted.

'Where is the poor child?' she asked Aunt Aggie.

'I should say she was poor,' her sister replied tartly. 'It's a pity you didn't come home before, instead of making her life a misery for twelve years. You'll find her out in the summerhouse.'

Matilda had been living out there ever since she left the Ministry of Alarm and Despondency, because her aunts kindly but firmly, and quite reasonably, said that they could not have the house filled with vegetation.

She had an axe, with which she cut down the worst growths every evening, and for the rest of the time she kept as still as she could, and earned some money by doing odd jobs of typing and sewing.

'My poor dear child,' Aunt Gertie said breathlessly, 'I had no idea that my little verses would have this sort of effect. What ever shall we do?'

'Please do something,' Matilda implored her, sniffing. This time it was not tears, but a cold she had caught from living in perpetual draughts.

'My dear, there isn't anything I can do. It's bound to last till the end of the year – that sort of spell is completely unalterable.'

'Well, at least you can stop sending me the verses?' asked Matilda. 'I don't want to sound ungrateful . . . '

'Even that I can't do,' her aunt said gloomily. 'It's a

banker's order at the Magician's Bank. One a year from seven to twenty-one. Oh, dear, and I thought it would be such *fun* for you. At least you only have one more, though.'

'Yes, but heaven knows what that'll be.' Matilda sneezed despondently and put another sheet of paper into her typewriter. There seemed to be nothing to do but wait. However, they did decide that it might be a good thing to go and see the Public Magician on the morning of Matilda's twenty-first birthday.

Aunt Gertie paid the taxi-driver and tipped him heavily not to grumble about the mess of delphiniums sprouting out of the mat of his cab.

'Good heavens, if it isn't Gertrude Jones!' the Public Magician exclaimed. 'Haven't seen you since we were at college together. How are you? Same old irresponsible Gertie? Remember that hospital you endowed with endless beds and the trouble it caused? And the row with the cigarette manufacturers over the extra million boxes of cigarettes for the soldiers?'

When the situation was explained to him he laughed heartily.

'Just like you, Gertie. Well-meaning isn't the word.'

At eleven promptly, Matilda opened her pink envelope.

Matilda, now you're twenty-one,
May you have every sort of fun;
May you have all you've ever wanted,
And every future wish be granted.

'Every future wish be granted – then I wish Aunt Gertie would lose her power of wishing,' cried Matilda; and immediately Aunt Gertie did.

But as Aunt Gertie with her usual thoughtlessness had said, 'May you have all you've *ever wanted*' Matilda had quite a lot of rather inconvenient things to dispose of, including a lion cub and a baby hippopotamus.

Cooks and Prophecies

'This time we'll have an *entirely* private christening,' said the King to the Queen. 'You remember what a time we had with fairies when Florizel was christened – all of them cancelling out each others' gifts till in the end the poor boy had nothing at all.'

'Very well, dear,' said the Queen sadly. But she loved parties, and in spite of the warning she could not resist inviting just one or two old friends. She did not invite the wicked fairy Gorgonzola.

On the day after the christening she received by post a little note written in red ink on black paper. 'Dear Queen,' it read, 'I was charmed to read about your christening party in yesterday's evening papers. I quite understand that you would not wish to be bothered with an old *fogey* like myself, so I shall not trouble you by calling, but have sent my christening present to the princess by registered post. Yours affectionately, Gorgonzola.'

Filled with alarm the Queen rushed off to the nursery in order to prevent, if possible, the wicked fairy's parcel from being opened. Too late! The head nurse had already undone the paper and string, and was just then opening a dear little gold casket before the baby's wondering eyes.

The horror-stricken Queen saw a small cloud of black smoke rise from the casket and envelop the princess's head. When it cleared away she had become the ugliest baby born in that kingdom for a hundred years.

At that moment, however, a passing bird dropped a prophecy down the Palace chimney. This said:

Seek not Griselda's fortune in her looks
Remember better things are found in books.

This comforted the King, who would otherwise have been inclined to say, 'I told you so,' and he therefore occupied himself by laying out a grand scheme for Griselda's education, for he presumed that this was what the rhyme meant. Though as the piece of paper on which it was written was very sooty, and the writing on it bad, there were some people who insisted that the last word should be read as 'cooks'.

'Ridiculous,' said the King. 'What is found in cooks, pray? Nothing at all. There can be no connection between cooks and my daughter.' And he went on with his neat timetables ruled in red ink, with spaces for Latin, Trigonometry, and Political Economy.

From the age of five poor Griselda was stuffed with these subjects and she hated them all equally. In Latin she could only remember such phrases as 'Give the boy the bread' and 'Each of the soldiers carried his own food'. In mathematics she could only work out the sort of problems in which two men have to pick a given quantity of apples, working at different speeds.

When she was twelve she could stand it no longer, and she went to her father and begged him to let her give up her education and learn cooking.

'Learn cooking?' said the King, horrified. 'Remember you will have to earn your living when we are gone. You won't come into a kingdom like your brother. Do you propose to be a cook, may I ask?'

'Yes,' said Griselda.

'Don't you think it will look rather odd in the advertisements? HRH Griselda. Good plain cooking. Omelettes a speciality. I must say, I should have thought that a daughter of mine could select a better career.'

However, Griselda had made up her mind, and finally she was allowed to learn cooking in the Palace kitchen.

Presently the King and Queen became old and died, and her brother Florizel came to the throne. He was very fond of Griselda and begged her to stay with him, but she decided that the time had come for her to seek her fortune, so she set off one night, secretly and in disguise, in order to avoid any further persuasions and bother. She asked an obliging fisherman to take her across the sea in

his boat, and he left her next morning, alone, but not in
the least downhearted, on a foreign shore.

Some lobster-gatherers met her there and asked her
who she was.

'I'm a Princess,' she said absently.

'Go on,' they cried, laughing, though not unkindly, at
her black boot-button eyes and shiny red cheeks.

'I mean I'm a cook,' she amended.

'That's a bit more like it. Over here for the competition,
are you? You'll find the Palace, third turning on the right
down the road.'

Griselda had no idea what they were talking about, but
she followed their directions and soon came to a handsome Palace. There was a notice on the gate which read:

COOKS!
GRAND COMPETITION

The winner of this Competition will receive
the post of Chief Cook to the Palace together
with half the kingdom (if male) or
His Majesty's hand and heart in marriage
(if female). Further particulars within.

Griselda went inside and found that the competition
was just about to begin. Hundreds of cooks were already
lined up in the vast, spotless Palace kitchen, where all
the cooking utensils were of silver, and the dishes of gold.

A pale, anxious-looking young man was running around dealing out numbers to the competitors. He gave Griselda a number on a piece of paper and pushed her into line. She could hear him saying:

'Oh mercy me, whatever shall I do about supper if none of them come up to standard?'

'Is that the King?' Griselda asked in surprise.

'Hush, they're going to begin. Yes, it is.'

The first event was an apple-peeling competition, which Griselda won easily by peeling twenty-point-four apples in three minutes. Next she won the obstacle race, in which competitors had to go over a complicated course, carrying two eggs in one hand and a frying pan in the other, and finish by making an omelette. She then won two more events in quick succession – the Good Housewife Test (which entailed making a nourishing stew out of an old boot and a cabbage leaf), and the Discrimination Test (distinguishing between butter and marge with her eyes shut).

There began to be some muttering among the other competitors, which increased as she went on with a string of successes. She made a delicious meal from two left-over sardines and some cold porridge. Her sponge cake was so light that when the King opened his mouth to taste it, he blew it out of the window. Her bread rose till it burst the oven. She tossed her pancake three times as high as any of the others, and sprinkled it with sugar and lemon as it fell. In fact there was no doubt at all that she was the Queen of the Cooks, and the King was quite exhausted and pale with excitement by the end of the competition, at having found such a treasure.

'I think we all agree,' he announced, 'that Miss – er, that Number 555 has won this contest, and I have much pleasure—'

However, his voice at this point was drowned by the hoarse outcry from the other angry and disappointed competitors, and it looked as if there was going to be a riot. One of the rejected sponge cakes was flung at Griselda, but it was so heavy that it only got halfway across the room.

The disturbance did not last long, for the King, knowing that cooks generally have hot tempers, had ordered the Palace Militia to be on guard outside, and all the unsuccessful candidates were soon bundled out of doors.

'In short,' said the King, finishing, 'I have pleasure in offering you the job of Palace Cook.'

'And I have pleasure in accepting it,' said Griselda, curtseying.

'As well as my hand and heart in marriage,' he pursued.

'No, thank you.'

'I beg your pardon?'

'It's very kind of you,' said Griselda, 'but I wouldn't feel inclined to marry someone just because he liked my cooking.'

'But it was a clause of the competition,' said the King, outraged.

'Never mind.'

'And then there was a prophecy about it.'

'Oh dear, another prophecy?' said Griselda, who felt that one in her life had been enough nuisance.

'It said:

The girl who weds our king so gay and gallant
Will be a cook of most uncommon talent.

And you can't deny that you are one, can you?'

Griselda couldn't but she did feel that 'gay and gallant' hardly described the pale anxious young creature who stood before her.

'And if you don't marry me you might leave at any time, and then what should I do about my meals?' he said miserably. 'The last cook used to make the cream sauce with *cornflour*.'

'Well, if you don't stop bothering me I certainly shall leave, right away,' said Griselda briskly, 'so run along now, out of my kitchen, or I shall never have dinner ready.' And she shooed him out.

She found that he was a terrible fusser, and always popping into the kitchen to ask if she was sure she had put enough salt in the pastry, or if the oven was hot enough. She found that she was able to manage him, however, for the threat of leaving always quietened him down at once, and things soon settled very comfortably.

But enemies were at work.

The unsuccessful candidates had banded themselves

together in order to get Griselda out of favour. They lurked about the Palace in disguise, and took every opportunity of laying obstacles in the way of her work. They sprinkled weedkiller over the parsley in the gardens when they heard the King ask for parsley sauce, bought up all the rice in the kingdom if he wanted rice pudding, and substituted salt for sugar and cement for flour when Griselda's back was turned.

Griselda, however, was never at a loss. She had with her Mrs Beeton's *Palace Cookery*, and in the chapter on Cookery During Wars and Revolutions she found recipes for rice puddings without using rice, and many other equally convenient hints and suggestions which helped her to defeat the conspirators.

They soon found that their tactics were useless, and resolved upon bolder measures. They went to the witch in the nearby wood and asked her to get rid of Griselda for them – expense no object.

'Griselda,' said the witch thoughtfully, 'I wonder if that would be the baby I had to uglify about twenty years ago? What would you like me to do with her?'

'We thought you might send her to the dragon in the desert.'

'Yes, that would do very well. I seem to remember that there's some prophecy:

When the dragon feels saddish,
Feed him on radish

but I doubt if there's much chance of her knowing that, and it doesn't say what would happen if she did. Very well, you may take it as settled. That will be ten and six, please.'

At that very instant a black, magic cloud swept down on Griselda as she stood making a salad, and carried her into the middle of the desert where the dragon lived. She was rather annoyed, but put a good face on it, and at once began looking for an oasis.

After a couple of hours of walking through sand she came within sight of some palm trees, but was depressed to see the dragon there too, lying in the shade – a vast, green and gold monster.

'Still,' she thought, 'there's room for us both. If I don't annoy him, perhaps he won't annoy me.'

And walking up, she nodded to him politely, said 'Excuse me,' and took a drink at the spring. The dragon took no notice at all.

During the next three or four days, Griselda, who was a sociable creature, found that the dragon enjoyed being read aloud to. He stretched himself out comfortably with his nose on his claws, and seemed to take a lively interest in *Palace Cookery*, which was the only book she had with her. During their simple meals of dates he often looked hopefully at the book, and sometimes pushed it towards her with the tip of his tail, as if asking for more. In fact they grew most attached to each other, and Griselda often thought how she would miss him if she were rescued.

One afternoon she had been reading the chapter on 'Magic Foods, and how to deal with Culinary Spells' when she looked up to see that the dragon was crying bitterly.

'Why, dragon?' she exclaimed, 'don't take on so. Whatever is the matter?'

Feeling in her apron pocket for a knob of sugar or something to comfort him, she found a radish, left over from her last salad.

'Here,' she said, holding it out, 'chew this up – it'll make you feel better.'

Meanwhile at home the young King was having a horrible time. When Griselda vanished he hired first one, then others of the wicked conspirators, but they were such bad cooks that he discharged them all, and was finally reduced to living on eggs, which he boiled himself. His health was shattered, and the affairs of the kingdom were in frightful disorder.

He was sitting down to his egg one day, in gloom, when in walked Griselda, looking very brown.

'My goodness!' he exclaimed, jumping up. 'I *am* glad to see you. They told me you had been eaten by a dragon. Now we can have some decent meals again.'

'Well, I must say, I think you might have sent a rescue force or something,' said Griselda with spirit. 'However, as it happens it all turned out for the best. Look who's with me.' Behind her there was a handsome young man, who came forward and said cheerfully:

'I don't expect you remember me, but I'm your elder brother.'

'Not the one that was stolen by the wicked enchanter?'

'That's right. He turned me into a dragon, and Griselda rescued me with a radish.'

'Well, that is a relief,' said the King happily. 'I was so tired of being King, you can't think. Now you can do all that, and I can live with you in the Palace and eat Griselda's wonderful food.'

'Do you mind his living with us?' asked the new King, turning to Griselda. 'By the way,' he added, 'Griselda and I are married.'

'Of course I don't mind,' said Griselda. 'I'll go and start making supper right away, and you can both come and peel the potatoes.'

So they all lived happily ever after. Griselda stayed very plain, but nobody minded.

John Sculpin and the Witches

One day John Sculpin's mother said to him: 'I *must* wash my hair. Run down to the wishing well and fetch me a bucket of water.'

'All right, Ma,' said John, and he put on his beautiful cap, because it was raining and pouring torrents.

'And whatever you do,' she said, 'don't let a witch get that new cap of yours, because it's just the thing one of the old scarecrows would like and I can't afford another one, let me tell you.'

'How am I to stop her taking it, Ma?' asked John.

'If I've told you once how to get rid of a witch, I've told you twenty times,' said his mother. 'Don't let me hear another word from you. Off with you.'

So John went off, but whether it was from stupidity, or whether he just hadn't been listening, he couldn't for the life of him remember anything his mother had ever said to him about dealing with witches. And that was a pity, because, as it happened, the country round about there was just infested with them.

John went along the road, thinking and thinking, and after a while he met an old woman.

'Afternoon, John,' she said, 'you look fretted about something.'

'So would you be,' said John, 'my Ma's told me the way to get rid of a witch, and I've clean forgotten it.'

'If I tell you, will you give me that fine new cap you're wearing?' she said. John didn't like parting with his fine new cap, but the information seemed worth it, so he handed it over.

'Well,' said the old woman, 'all you have to do is give her a nice bunch of parsley.'

'Of course that was it!' said John. 'I'll forget my own name next.'

He thanked the old woman and went on down the road. The next house he came to was his uncle Sam's, so he went into the garden and picked a nice big bunch of parsley. Then he walked down to the wishing well.

When he came up to the well, there was an old woman sitting beside it in the rain and muttering to herself. John went straight up to her and handed her the parsley, and she took it with a bit of a grunt and vanished; she'd gone to hang it up in her scullery.

John filled his bucket and went home. He put it down with a clank inside the back door and his mother called out to him from the kitchen:

'Did you see a witch?'

'Yes,' said John, 'there was one sitting beside the well, but I gave her a bunch of parsley and she took herself off.'

'That's a good boy,' said his mother, 'there's nothing like that wishing-well water for washing your hair in, I do say. Bring it in here, will you, with the big kettle.'

When John went in, the first thing she said to him was: 'Where's your cap?'

'Oh, I gave it to an old woman,' said John, 'she told me the right way to get rid of a witch.'

'You little misery!' screamed his mother. 'What's the use of telling you anything? You've given your cap to a witch, and not another one do you get till Christmas.'

About a week later John's mother said to him:

'We've finished all the potatoes. You'll have to go over to Maiden's Farm and get a sackful. And *this* time, if you meet a witch, maybe you'll have the sense to give her a bunch of parsley right away.'

So John fetched out his bicycle and pumped up the tyres and found an old potato sack. And before he started he picked nearly a whole sackful of parsley and took it with him over his shoulder. It was about five miles to Maiden's Farm and the whole way, whenever John saw an old woman on the road, he got off and gave her one of his bunches of parsley. He wasn't taking any chances. Plenty of them looked a bit surprised at being given some parsley in the middle of the road, but that made no difference to John. By the time he had reached Maiden's he had been so generous with his parsley that he had none left, and when he got to the farm gate and saw another old woman sitting outside he didn't quite know what to do.

'Haven't you anything for me, dearie?' the old woman asked.

John was a bit embarrassed, so finally he gave her the bicycle pump as that seemed to be the smallest thing he could part with. Then he got his potatoes and went home.

When he came up the garden path his mother called from her bedroom window:

'Got the potatoes, John?'

'Yes, Ma,' John shouted back, 'a whole sackful.'

'But are they good ones?' she said, and came down to see. The first thing she said, when she came into the shed where John had put them was:

'Where's the bicycle pump?'

'Well, you see, Ma,' John explained, 'I'd finished all the parsley, giving it away to old women, by the time I got to Maiden's. So I had to give the pump to the last one. Very pleased with it, she was. You should have seen her.'

'You little good-for-nothing,' screamed his mother. 'What do you think we're going to do without the bicycle pump? Not another penny do you get to buy sweets till you've paid for a new one.'

After that, all the witches in the neighbourhood got to know about John, and they plagued him so much that he never dared stir out of doors without about half a cartload of parsley. So one day his mother said to him:

'I've thought of a plan to get rid of the witches, and for goodness' sake listen to what I'm saying, instead of mooning out of the window.'

Next day she went all round the village saying:

'My John's going to town. Have you any messages you want done?'

By the time she got home she had a list of messages as long as her arm, and all the witches knew that John was catching the 9.18 train into Tabchester the next day.

The porter always used to say that he'd never seen such a sight as there was that day. The station wasn't very big, and it was crowded from one end to the other with witches, all waiting for the 9.18 to come in. Some of them bought tickets and some didn't. John came a bit late with his shopping basket and list. He went and had a private talk with the porter, who was also the station master, and the guard, and the engine driver. Presently the porter (whose name was Mr Sims) went off and brought along the train. It wasn't a very big one, for it only went as far as Tabchester. There was no one else in it but John and the witches.

When the train began to move, John got up and made a little speech.

'Ladies,' he said, 'I didn't think I could bring enough parsley for all of you, so I've arranged a little treat for you, and you'll find it in the dining-car at the end of the train.'

So he went along the corridor to show them the way, and all the witches came pushing along behind him, rubbing their hands.

At the end of the train the corridor bent round, and there was a door to join on to another coach, if one should ever be needed. So John stood at the corner, and as each witch came round, he pushed her through the door and off the end of the train. And that was the end of her. All except the last. For the last but one, when he pushed her through the door, gave a kind of squeak, and that warned the one after her. So, quick as a wink, she changed herself into a bluebottle, and when John looked round, he thought he must have finished them all.

He went into the town and did all his errands, and when he got home he and his mother had a good laugh, thinking about all the witches.

But the last witch went home in a frightful temper, thinking how she could be revenged on John.

One day she put on a tweed cap and a false moustache and got on her bicycle and went off with a box on her back. And when she came to John's mother's cottage, she knocked at the front door and asked if they wanted to buy any toothbrushes. John's mother didn't recognize her and she bought a new toothbrush for John. But the witch had poisoned this toothbrush, so that when John brushed his teeth with it, he would drop down dead on the spot.

But you know what boys are, even if the witch didn't. John never brushed his teeth in a month of Sundays. The first night he gave the brush a bit of a rub along the scullery draining-board, to make it look used, and then he stuck it up on the shelf, and that was that.

Next morning his mother called:

'John! Whatever have you been doing on the draining-board? It's all black.'

John came and looked, and sure enough, the board looked as if something like a black stain had been rubbed along it.

'I'm sure I don't know,' he said, 'unless it was my new toothbrush?'

He took it down and looked at it. Just then a fly came and settled on it, and the next minute it fell off on to the floor, as dead as a doornail. John and his mother looked at each other.

'A witch did that,' said his mother. 'You must have left one of them out, and she's got a spite against you. I'll be on the lookout for her the next time she comes selling things to me, the artful old besom.'

A few days later the witch saw John coming down the road as well as ever. So she ground her teeth and began to think out a new way of getting rid of him.

Next morning she came riding up to the cottage in the uniform of a district nurse.

'Morning, Nurse,' said John's mother, 'there's no one ill here, I'm thankful to say.'

'Oh, I heard your little boy was ill,' said the witch.

'It's more than *I* heard,' said his mother, 'but you can see for yourself.'

For John came round the corner with a bundle of faggots.

'Oh dear yes, he's terribly ill,' said the witch. 'I can see it by the way he walks. You must put him to bed at once. I'll give you some medicine for him.'

John's mother was a bit worried at that, and she hustled him into bed. That afternoon the witch came back with a little red bottle of medicine.

'You give him that,' she said, 'and we'll have no more trouble with him.'

John's mother poured it into a glass, but you know what boys are. The minute her back was turned he poured the whole glassful into a jam-jar full of honeysuckle on the wash-stand.

Ten minutes later she came back.

'Good gracious, John!' she said, 'whatever's happened to that honeysuckle? It's all black and shrivelled.'

'It must have been the medicine,' said John, 'I poured it into the jar.'

'That's that witch again,' cried his mother. 'I'll lay for her the next time she comes pretending to be the district nurse. But the next time I catch *you* pouring your medicine down the sink or anywhere else, there'll be trouble.'

A week later the witch saw John cycling through the village, and she nearly burst with rage. She thought and thought, but she simply could not think of anything nasty enough to do to him. While she was thinking, however, she nearly plagued the lives out of John and his mother in small ways. For they'd wake up in the morning to find nothing but giant vegetable marrows growing in the garden, or the fried potatoes would turn to lumps of coal in their mouths, or the tap would start running in the middle of the night, and they would come down to find the kitchen flooded.

'It *is* so distressing,' said John's mother to a friend of hers. 'You never know whether you are on your head or your heels.'

'There's only one thing to do when a witch starts plaguing you like that,' said her friend, 'you ought to pour a bucket of water over her, that's been taken from a running stream less than seven minutes before. Then she turns into a black cat.'

Well, in the next three days John was fairly exhausted. He spent the whole of his time running backwards and forwards to the stream with buckets. And, of course, the witch never turned up.

But on the fourth day a smart young man came up the garden path, selling fine new dishmops. He had a whole bunch of them in one hand.

'Aha,' said John to himself, 'I've got you now.' He stood behind the door with his bucket and waited for the young fellow to knock.

But as a matter of fact the young man was a real salesman, and if John had looked out again he would have seen the witch herself, sneaking up behind him, with a carrier bag full of scorpions, which she meant to put in the copper to surprise them. John never looked, though, and when a knock came at the door he popped out and flung the whole of the bucket over the young man, and then ran for his life. It was lucky he did, too, for the man was in a terrible temper when he picked himself up.

The first person he saw was the witch, who was laughing enough to split her sides. Of course he thought she had thrown the bucket, and he gave her such a clout with his dishmops that he knocked her spinning into a clump of nettles. Then he took himself off, muttering such things under his breath that John's mother's black spaniel turned quite white to hear them.

But John and his mother were looking out of the side window to see what happened, and when they saw the man go off, and that he hadn't turned into a black cat, they thought that something must have gone wrong, and the spell hadn't worked. So without waiting to see more they packed up all their belongings in the tablecloth and cleared out as fast as they could go.

The witch went home, grumbling and cursing, and after that, she wasn't nearly so lively about making herself a nuisance to people.

John and his mother settled down in a different part of the country where there weren't so many witches; which they might as well have done at first.

The Lobster's Birthday

Early one fine summer morning, two persons might have been seen making their way somewhat furtively across the fields from the village of Tillingham to Slugdale Halt. Every now and then they glanced cautiously behind them as if they almost expected to be pursued and taken back. Their names were Gloria and Harold. Gloria was a lobster. It was her birthday, and she had persuaded Harold, who was a horse and an acquaintance of hers, to take her into Brighton for the day. The difficulty was that their employer did not approve of days off; he never took one himself, and did not see why other people had to go gadding away, spending money, when they might just as well have stayed quietly at home and behaved themselves. Consequently Gloria and Harold had to leave very early, as they had gone without permission, and were still afraid that Mr Higgs might see them from some window as he stood drinking his early morning tea.

When they reached the station, which was in a cutting, Harold heaved a sigh of relief.

'Thank goodness we can have a bit of a breather,' he said. 'Mr Higgs can't see us here.' He sat down on the station seat, which sagged under his weight. Gloria seated herself primly beside him. She carried a large wicker basket, and wore a festive spotted scarf.

'Dear me, I'm ever so warm. The weather is quite oppressive, isn't it,' she said. Then she looked reprovingly at her companion and exclaimed 'Harold! Put your shoes back on. What will people think of you! I declare I'm quite ashamed of you.'

'All very well to talk,' mumbled Harold. 'You made me wear these confounded shoes. Knew they'd be too tight in this weather.'

However, Gloria insisted that he must put them on again, and he finally did so with many protests, and hobbled off to buy two cheap day returns to Brighton.

At length the little train came in sight, and Gloria immediately began to fuss, running up and down the platform, retying her veil, rearranging everything in her basket and clamouring that she had lost her gloves, while Harold stood expressionlessly in one spot and tried to look as if she had nothing to do with him. When the train stopped she cried: 'Oh, Harold, we must find a non-smoker. You know I can't stand cigarette smoke.' Without saying a word, Harold opened the nearest door and pushed her in. She subsided in a heap on the seat with her things all round her. Harold slumped down in the opposite seat and at once pulled a paper from under his arm and became absorbed in the racing news.

When Gloria had collected herself a little she began to chatter. 'Harold, do you think we could have the window down a little? This smoke gets in my eyes terribly. Do you think these people would mind?'

There were two other people in the compartment, a man and a woman, who both had their eyes shut. However, the man murmured 'Not a bit, go ahead', without opening his eyes, so Harold opened the window a few inches.

'Now I think when we get there, I'll go right away and buy my new hat,' Gloria went on. 'What sort of a hat would you like me to have, Harold?'

'Don't mind a bit,' said Harold, his nose in the paper.

'I like a nice *fancy* hat,' said Gloria happily. 'Not too big, you know, but striking. What they call flair, a hat's got to have, if it's going to suit me. Mrs Ellis was telling me about a place right on the front, called *Natty Hats*, it is. I thought I might go there first.'

'All right,' said Harold, 'but I'm not going in one of those places. I should feel a fool. I'll go and have my hair cut while you get yourself suited.'

The woman asleep at the other end of the compartment, who had stirred a little at the mention of hats, now opened her eyes and let out a shriek.

'Percival!' she exclaimed. 'Pull the communication cord

at once. There's a horse in the carriage!' Then she saw Gloria and screamed again.

'Pray calm yourself, madam,' said the horse patiently. 'I am quite harmless, I assure you.'

But the woman kept exclaiming, and would have pulled the cord herself if her husband had not stopped her.

'Don't make a fool of yourself, Minnie,' he said crossly. 'Bad enough to have to travel with horses and riff-raff without becoming a laughing-stock. Sit down, do, for heaven's sake.'

'I shall write to *The Times*,' his wife kept protesting. 'They ought at least to have No Horses carriages. As for lobsters, there ought to be a law against their travelling in trains. Pushing in where they're not wanted. What business have lobsters in trains?'

Gloria gave her a spiteful look. 'Some people seem to think they own the whole railway,' she said to Harold. 'They might like to know that other people, who have quite as much right to travel, only want to keep themselves to themselves, and wouldn't demean themselves by intruding.'

Harold looked anxiously at the woman. 'Madam,' he began.

'Don't speak to me,' said the woman vigorously. '*Don't* speak to me or I shall scream, I know I shall.'

'But madam,' Harold began again.

'Percival, *will* you tell this person not to molest me. If you utter a single word more to me I shall have you given in charge the moment we get to Brighton.'

The horse shrugged his shoulders and settled back to his paper. Gloria drew herself up coldly, and looked out of the window. The woman gave them a baleful glare, while her husband tried to dissociate himself from the whole affair.

Twenty minutes later the train arrived in Brighton. During the whole of this time the woman had kept Harold and Gloria under constant observation, as if she expected one of them to throw a bomb the minute her back was turned.

When she stood up to collect her things together she let out a cry of horror. 'Percival! My knitting! The wool has fallen out of the window.'

'That is what I have been trying to tell you, madam,' said Harold calmly. 'It fell out at Bishopsvalley Halt, fifteen minutes ago.'

As Harold and Gloria left the platform they looked back and saw her standing at the very furthest extremity, furiously winding, while ten miles of wool came slowly towards her.

They took a bus down to the front, and Gloria went at once into *Natty Hats*.

'And hurry up,' Harold called after her. 'I want a cuppa. I didn't have my tea this morning on account of you and your blessed treat.' Gloria ignored him and walked haughtily through the door. Madame Arlene at once glided forward to serve her.

'Mademoiselle required a hat?'

'Something nice and fancy,' said Gloria, her eye roaming greedily round the display stands.

'But Mademoiselle is rather short and has – ahem – rather a *bright* complexion. Would not something more simple – we have here a black velvet beret with diamond clip, price fifteen guineas?'

'Now, now,' said Gloria, 'none of your taste for me, thanks. I want something nice and bright, with feathers.' Madame Arlene brought out several other hats, but none of them seemed quite what she wanted, and she was presently aware of Harold, looking very cross, strolling up and down outside. He had had his hair cut and looked very military.

'Oh well, I'll leave it, thanks ever so,' said Gloria, and scuttled out. 'No need to make me conspicuous,' she scolded Harold. 'You could have waited a bit further along, couldn't you?'

When they had had a cup of tea, however, sitting in deck-chairs, good humour was restored, and Harold suggested that they should go on the pier before Gloria looked at any more hats. So they paid their money and clicked through the turnstile.

Gloria had her fortune told by the Seer from the East – Put One Penny in and Learn the Secrets of the Stars. She put in a penny and pulled out a piece of paper which said, 'You will be your own fate today'. 'Stupid things they tell you, don't they,' she said, tossing it into the sea. Then she suddenly squealed 'Oo! Look, Harold! Over there!'

She was pointing to the display stand of a shooting gallery. Among the prizes offered were some feather dusters, with red handles and gay red-and-purple feathers.

'Just what I want for my hat! They might have been made for me. Oh, do have a go and win one of them, Harold,' she urged him. Harold rather unwillingly went over to the booth.

'Eight shots for half a crown,' said the man, looking at him suspiciously. 'Never heard of a horse shooting before.'

'I don't suppose you often see horses on the pier at all,' Harold replied coldly. 'I'll have eight shots please. How many bullseyes to win a prize?'

Three, the man told him. Gloria was teetering about behind him in such a state of excitement that he made her go away – he said the sound of her claws on the iron treads made him nervous. So she went and stood round the corner clutching her basket feverishly. As a matter of fact, Harold had never shot before, but he often took part in a game of darts, and he was very anxious not to let Gloria down, so he aimed with great care.

'Eight bulls,' said the proprietor. 'Blimey! On the halls, are yer? What'll you have for your prizes?'

'I'd like two of those dusters, please.'

'Better make it three for luck,' said the man cordially. 'Any time you want to give a display, just let me know and I'll fix it up for you.'

Harold took Gloria the trophies and she squeaked with

pleasure. 'Three! Harold, you are a dear!' She was about
to embrace him, but he backed cautiously away. She stuck
the feathers on her head and rushed off to find a mirror
and admire herself.

After this they began to feel hungry and found a sheltered seat where they could eat their sandwiches – grass
for Harold and mayonnaise for Gloria. Then Harold
wanted to sleep, but Gloria began to fidget and suggested
they should go for a trip in the *Skylark* to see the Seven
Sisters.

'All right,' Harold agreed. 'I can sleep in the boat as
well as anywhere else, I suppose.'

Off they went. Gloria had never been in a boat before, and sat bolt upright, giving little cries of pleasure and excitement at everything, and taking care that everyone could see and admire her beautiful plumes. Alas! As they went further out to sea the wind freshened, and a sudden gust whisked all three off her head and overboard.

'Stop the boat!' shrieked Gloria. 'My hat!'

'Sorry, miss,' said the owner. 'Should have fastened it on better. No hope of getting it now.'

'Harold!' she cried in despair. 'My hat!' But Harold was nearly asleep, and only grumbled 'Expect me to dive after it? Did you ever hear of a horse swimming?'

Poor Gloria took a last frantic look round and then dived in herself. She managed to seize two of the feathers, and then the propeller of the *Skylark* struck her on the head and she knew no more. Harold had fallen into a blissful doze, and never noticed that she was no longer beside him.

Presently a girl who was swimming near the shore espied a lobster floating near her.

'Coo! Here's a bit of luck,' she said. 'This'll do nicely for supper.' She towed the unconscious Gloria in to land and popped her into a beach bag with some sun-tan lotion, dark glasses and peppermint creams. 'I'll just get my things on and pop into Arlene's, and then I'll be stepping home. Mum will be pleased.'

As soon as she was dressed, she went into *Natty Hats*,

where one of the assistants was a friend of hers. Business was slack just then, and she began gossiping with this girl. Meanwhile the powerful fragrance of the peppermint creams partly revived Gloria and she crawled out of the bag in search of fresh air and lay weakly down on a large straw cartwheel hat. By and by a woman came into the shop and began trying on hats.

'How much is the straw?' she inquired.

'Five guineas, madam,' said the assistant, without turning round.

'Very well, I'll take it. You needn't bother to wrap it, I'll wear it. Rather attractive and original, don't you think, Percival?' she said, turning to her husband. He merely shuddered, but she took no notice and put down five guineas on the cash desk. Then she and her husband left the shop and began strolling along the front.

Meanwhile the *Skylark* had put back to shore, and its owner woke up Harold, who stumbled up the beach in a dazed condition, without noticing that his companion was not there. He walked along the front, and soon noticed a commotion ahead of him. The warm sunshine was reviving Gloria, and she began waving her claws about and putting herself to rights before she became aware that she was on a moving platform. People gazed admiringly at this remarkable hat ornamented with a live lobster, and soon a small crowd was following, while the woman who had bought it still walked underneath quite unconscious of what was happening.

Harold saw them coming towards him, and his eyes bulged. 'Gloria!' he said. 'What are you doing up there?'

'Oh!' shrieked the woman. 'It's that horse again. Take it away. Everywhere I go today it's nothing but horses, horses.'

'But, madam,' said Harold, always polite, 'you have my partner on your hat. If you will excuse me one moment, I will assist her to alight.'

'Harold, where am I?' said Gloria faintly.

'Do you mean there is a real lobster on this hat?' cried the woman underneath. 'This is a gross swindle. I paid five guineas for it. I shall take it back to the shop and complain.'

At this moment the representative of the *Brighton Guardian* arrived.

'Please stand still for a moment while I take some pictures,' he begged them. 'This will be quite a sensation. Dashing Dowager Displays Live Lobster on Hat. May I congratulate you, madam. You are the fortunate winner of our Original Headgear Competition. Your prize is a Rolls-Royce and a free pass to the Magnificent Cinema every night for the next five years. May I ask where you obtained this novel creation?'

Much mollified by this news, the woman told him that she had bought it at *Natty Hats*.

'This will mean a boom for Arlene,' said the reporter. 'Why, here she comes now.' In fact Arlene, her assistant, and the assistant's friend were hastening along the front, having just discovered that the lobster had been stolen.

'Good afternoon,' the reporter greeted them. 'You will be pleased to learn that your creation here has just won the Original Headgear Prize. Can you tell me if you have any other ideas in the same line – a salad hat, perhaps, or a calves' foot toque?'

While the explanations were going on, Gloria beckoned to Harold.

'Do you think you could lift me down,' she whispered weakly. 'I feel a little faint.'

He did so quietly, without anyone noticing. 'Let's get out of here while they're all talking,' he muttered. 'It's nearly time for our train, and Mr Higgs won't like it at all if we get our names in the papers.' Gloria nodded, and he cantered off up a side street, carrying her on his back. By the time their absence was noticed they were well away. Madame Arlene offered to replace the bare straw hat by another, and everyone parted happily, except the girl who had hoped to have lobster for supper.

Gloria and Harold stopped to have a refreshing cup of tea on their way to the station, and after all only just caught their train. They flung themselves into the last carriage, and only realized after the train had started that they were again in the same compartment with Percival and his wife. She was now wearing a very gorgeous hat, covered with red bouncing cherries.

She gave Gloria and Harold a haughty look and then

decided to ignore them. Harold was feeling tired and longing to be back at home and to go quietly to bed. Gloria
was still a little faint after her experiences, and insisted on
leaning out of the window, in spite of the notice warning
her not to.

'You know I can't stand the cigarette smoke,' she said
reproachfully.

When they were nearing Slugdale Halt she took out her
pocket mirror to adjust her red feathers.

'Oh! They've gone!' she cried in dismay. 'Where are my
beautiful feathers?'

'They fell off at Bishopsvalley Halt fifteen minutes ago,'
said Percival's wife acidly. Gloria shed a few tears, and
then cheered up.

'Oh well, I suppose I was fated not to have them,' she
said philosophically. 'It looks that way. And anyway, who
ever heard of a lobster wearing a hat?'

She gave Percival and his wife a dazzling smile, and let
Harold help her out of the train. They strolled off across
the fields towards Tillingham Village and the Horse and
Lobster Inn.

The Parrot Pirate Princess

The King and Queen were quarrelling fiercely over what the baby Princess was to be called when the fairy Grisel dropped in. Grisel, that is to say, did not drop in – to be more accurate, she popped out of one of the vases on the mantelpiece, looked round, saw the baby and said:

'What's this?'

'Oh, good afternoon,' said the King uncomfortably.

'We were just putting you on the list of people to be invited to the christening,' said the Queen, hastily doing so. She had presence of mind.

'Mmmmm,' said Grisel. 'Is it a boy or a girl?'

'It's a girl, and the sweetest little—'

'*I'm* the best judge of that,' interrupted the fairy, and she hooked the baby out of its satin cradle. 'Well, let's have a look at you.'

The baby was a calm creature, and did not, as the Queen had dreaded, burst into loud shrieks at the sight of Grisel's wizened old face. She merely cooed.

'Well, you can't say she's very handsome, can you? Takes too much after both of you,' Grisel said cheerfully. The baby laughed. 'What are you going to call her?'

'We were just wondering when you came in,' the Queen said despairingly. She knew that Grisel had a fondness for suggesting impossible names, and then being extremely angry if the suggestions were not taken. Worse – she might want the baby called after herself.

'Then I'll tell you what,' said Grisel, eagerly leaning forward. 'Call it—'

But here she was interrupted, for the baby, which she still held, hit her a fearful whack on the front teeth with its heavy silver rattle.

There was a terrible scene. The King and Queen were far too well-bred to laugh, but they looked as if they would have liked to. The Queen snatched the baby from Grisel, who was stamping up and down the room, pale with rage, and using the most unlady-like language.

'That's right – laugh when I've had the best part of my teeth knocked down my throat,' she snarled. 'And as for you – you—' She turned to the baby who was chuckling in the Queen's arms.

'Goo goo,' the baby replied affably.

'Goo goo, indeed. I'll teach you to repeat what I say,'

the fairy said furiously. And before the horrified Queen could make a move, the baby had turned into a large grey parrot and flown out of the window.

Grisel smiled maliciously round the room and said: 'You can take me off the christening list now.'

She went, leaving the King and Queen silent.

The Parrot turned naturally to the south, hunting for an island with palm trees, or at least a couple of coconuts to eat. After some time she came to the sea. She was disconcerted. She did not feel that she could face flying all the way over that cold grey-looking water to find an island that would suit her. So she sat down on the edge to think. The edge where she sat happened to be a quay, and presently a sailor came along, said 'Hullo, a parrot,' and picked her up.

She did not struggle. She looked up at him and said in a hoarse, rasping voice: 'Hullo, a parrot.'

The sailor was delighted. He took her on board his ship, which sailed that evening for the South Seas.

This was no ordinary ship. It was owned by the most terrible pirate then in business, who frightened all the ships off the seas. And so fairly soon the parrot saw some surprising things.

The pirates were quite kind to her. They called her Jake, and took a lot of interest in her education. She was a quick learner, and before the end of the voyage she knew the most shocking collection of swear words and nautical phrases that ever parrot spoke. She also knew all about walking the plank and the effects of rum. When the pirates had captured a particularly fine ship they would all drink gallons of rum and make her drink it, too, whereupon the undignified old fowl would lurch about all over the deck and in the rigging, singing 'Fifteen men on a dead man's chest, Yo, ho, ho and a bottle of rum,' and the pirates would shout with laughter.

One day they arrived at the island where they kept their treasure, and it was all unloaded and rowed ashore. It took them two days to bury it, and the parrot sat by, thinking: 'Shiver my timbers, but I'd like to get away and live on this island!' But she could not, for one of the pirates had thoughtfully tied her by the ankle to a tree. She sat swearing under her breath and trying to gnaw through the rope, but it was too thick.

Luck, however, was with her. The second day after they had left the island, a great storm sprang up, and the pirates' ship was wrecked.

'Brimstone and botheration and mercy me!' chorused the pirates, clinging frantically to the rigging. They had little time for more, because with a frightful roar the ship went to the bottom, leaving Jake bobbing about on the waves like a cork.

'Swelp me,' she remarked, rose up and flew with the wind, which took her straight back to the island.

'Well blow me down,' she said when she got there. 'This is a bit better than living on biscuit among all those unrefined characters. Bananas and mangoes, bless my old soul! This is the life for me.'

She lived on the island for some time, and became very friendly with a handsome grey gentleman parrot already there, called Bill. Bill seemed to know as much about pirates as she did, but he was always rather silent about his past life, so she gathered that he did not want it mentioned. They got on extremely well, however, and lived on the island for about twenty years, which did not change them in the least, as parrots are notoriously long-lived.

Then one day, as they were sharing a bunch of bananas, a frightful hurricane suddenly arose, and blew them, still clutching the bananas, out to sea.

'Hold on tight!' shrieked Bill in her ear.

'I am holding on,' she squawked back. 'Lumme,' Bill, you do look a sight. Just like a pincushion!'

The wretched Bill was being fluffed out by the wind until his tail-feathers stood straight up. 'Well you're not so pretty yourself,' he said indignantly, screwing his head round to look at her. 'Don't half look silly, going along backwards like that.'

'Can't you see, you perishing son of a sea-cook,' squawked Jake, 'it stops the wind blowing your feathers out – have a try.'

'It makes me feel funny,' complained Bill, and he went back to his former position, still keeping a tight hold on the bananas.

'Mountains ahead – look out!' he howled, a moment or

two later. They were being swept down at a terrific speed towards a range of hills.

'Is it the mainland?' asked Jake, swivelling round to get a glimpse. 'Doesn't the wind make you giddy?'

'Yes. It's the mainland I reckon,' said Bill. 'There's houses down there. Oh, splice my mainbrace, we're going to crash into them. Keep behind the bananas.' Using the great bunch as a screen they hurtled downwards.

'Mind last week's washing,' screamed Jake, as they went through a low belt of grey cloud. 'I never in all my life saw anything to beat this. Talk about seeing the world.' They were only twenty feet above ground now, still skimming along, getting lower all the time.

'Strikes me we'd better *sit* on the bananas if we don't want our tail feathers rubbed off,' said Jake. 'Oh my, look where we're going.'

Before Bill had time to answer, they went smack through an immense glass window, shot across a room, breaking three vases on the way, and came to rest on a mantelpiece, still mixed up with the bananas, which were rather squashed and full of broken glass.

'Journey's end,' said Jake. 'How are you, Bill?'

'Not so bad,' said Bill, wriggling free of the bananas and beginning to put his feathers to rights.

Then they were both suddenly aware of the fairy Grisel, sitting in one corner of the room, where she had been knocked by a vase, and glaring at them. She picked herself up and came and looked at them closely.

'It's you again is it?' she said. 'I might have known it.'

'Pleased to meet you,' said Jake, who had no recollection of her. 'I'm Jake, and this is my husband Bill.'

'I know you, don't you worry,' said Grisel. Then Jake suddenly remembered where she had seen Grisel before.

'Oh lor – don't you go changing me into a princess again,' she cried in alarm, but hardly were the words out of her beak, when, bang, she was back in her father's palace, in the throne-room. She looked down at herself, and saw that she was human once more.

'Well! Here's a rum go,' she said aloud. 'Who'd have thought it?' She glanced round the room and saw, through a french window, the King and Queen, a good deal older, having tea on the terrace. There was also a girl, not unlike herself. She went forward to them with a very nautical gait, and hitching up her trousers – only it was a long and flowing cloth-of-gold skirt.

'Hello Pa! Pleased to meet you!' she cried, slapping the King on the back. 'Shiver my timbers, Ma, it's a long time since we met. Not since I was no longer than a marline spike. Who's this?'

They were all too dumbfounded to speak. 'Hasn't anyone got a tongue in their head?' she asked. 'Here comes the prodigal daughter, and all they can do is sit and gawp?'

'Are you – are you that baby?' the Queen asked faintly. 'The one that got taken away?'

'That's me!' Jake told her cheerfully. 'Twenty years a

parrot, and just when I'm beginning to enjoy life, back I comes to the bosom of my family. Shunt my backstay, it's a funny life.'

She sighed.

The King and Queen looked at one another in growing horror.

'And this'll be my little sissy, if I'm not mistaken,' said Jake meditatively. 'Quite a big girl, aren't you, ducks? If you'll excuse me, folks, I'm a bit thirsty. Haven't had a drink for forty-eight hours.'

She rolled indoors again.

'Well I suppose it might be worse,' said the Queen doubtfully, in the horrified silence. 'We can *train* her, can't we? I suppose she'll have to be the heir?'

'I'm afraid so,' said the King. 'I hope she'll take her position seriously.'

'And what happens to *me*?' demanded the younger sister shrilly.

The King sighed.

During the next two months the royal family had an uncomfortable time. Jake obviously meant well, and was kindly disposed to everyone, but she did make a bad crown princess. Her language was dreadful, and she never seemed to remember not to say 'Stap my vitals' or something equally unsuitable, when she trod on her skirt. She said that trains were a nuisance.

'You don't want to traipse round with the drawing-room curtains *and* the dining-room tablecloth pinned to your tail. I'm used to flying. Splice my mainbrace!' she would cry.

She rushed about and was apt to clap important court officials and ambassadors on the back and cry 'Hallo! How's the missus, you old son of a gun?' Or if they annoyed her, she loosed such a flood of epithets on them ('You lily-livered, cross-eyed, flop-eared son of a sea-cook') that the whole Court fled in horror, stopping their ears. She distressed the King and Queen by climbing trees, or sitting rocking backwards and forwards for hours at a time, murmuring 'Pretty Poll. Pretty Jake. Pieces of eight, pieces of eight, pieces of eight.'

'Will she *ever* turn into a presentable queen?' said the King despairingly, and the Queen stared hopelessly out of the window.

'Perhaps she'll marry and settle down,' she suggested, and so they advertised for princes in the *Monarchy's Marriage Mart*, a very respectable paper.

'We'll have to think of Miranda too,' the King said. 'After all she was brought up to expect to be queen. It's only fair that she should marry some eligible young prince and come into a kingdom that way. She's a good girl.'

Eventually a Prince arrived. He came quite quietly, riding on a fiery black horse, and stayed at an inn near the palace. He sent the King a note, saying that he would be only too grateful for a sight of the Princess, whenever it was convenient.

'Now we must really try and make her behave

presentably for once,' said the Queen, but there was not much hope in her voice.

A grand ball was arranged, and the court dress-makers spent an entire week fitting Jake to a white satin dress, and Miranda obligingly spent a whole evening picking roses in the garden to put in Jake's suspiciously scarlet hair.

Finally the evening came. The throne-room was a blaze of candle-light. The King and Queen sat on the two thrones, and below them on the steps, uncomfortably but gracefully posed, were the two princesses. A trumpet blew, and the Prince entered. The crowd stood back, and he walked forward and bowed very low before the thrones. Then he kissed Miranda's hand and said:

'Will you dance with me, Princess?'

'Hey, young man,' interrupted the King, 'you've made a mistake. It's the other one who's the Crown Princess.'

Jake roared with laughter, but the Prince had gone very pale, and Miranda was scarlet.

'I didn't know *you* were the Prince of Sitania,' she said.

'*Aren't* you the Princess, then?' he said.

'Have you two met before?' the King demanded.

'Last night in the Palace gardens,' said Miranda. 'The Prince promised he'd dance the first dance with me. But I didn't know, truly I didn't, that he was *that* Prince.'

'And I thought you were the Crown Princess,' he said. There was an uncomfortable silence. Jake turned away and began humming 'Yo ho ho and a bottle of rum'.

'Your Majesty, I am sorry to be so inconvenient,' said the Prince desperately, 'but may I marry *this* princess?'

'How large is your kingdom?' asked the King sharply.

'Well, er, actually I am the youngest of five sons, so I have no kingdom,' the Prince told him, 'but my income is pretty large.'

The King shook his head. 'Won't do. Miranda must have a kingdom. I'm afraid, young man, that it's impossible. If you wanted to marry the other princess and help reign over this kingdom, that would be different.'

The Prince hung his head, and Miranda bit her lip. Jake tried to put her hands in her white satin pockets, and whistled. The crowd began to shuffle, and to quiet them, the Royal Band struck up. And then Jake gave a shriek of delight, and fairly skated across the marble floor.

'*Bill*, my old hero! I'd know you anywhere!' A burly pirate with a hooked nose and scarlet hair was standing in the doorway.

'Well, well, well!' he roared. 'Looks like I've bumped into a party. You and I, ducks, will show them how the hornpipe ought to be danced.' And solemnly before the frozen Court they broke into a hornpipe, slow at first, and then faster and faster. Finally they stopped, panting.

'I'm all of a lather. Haven't got a wipe, have you, Jake?' Bill asked.

'Here, have half the tablecloth.' She tore a generous half from her twelve-foot train and gave it to him. They both mopped their brows vigorously. Then Jake took Bill across to where the King and Queen were standing with horror-struck faces.

'Here's my husband,' said Jake. The Court turned as one man and fled, leaving the vast room empty but for the King and Queen, Jake and Bill, and Miranda and the Prince.

'Your husband? But you never said anything about him. And here we were, searching for Princes,' the Queen began.

'I don't think you ever asked me for *my* news,' said Jake. 'And now, if you'll excuse us, we'll be going. I've waited these two months for Bill, and a dratted long time he took to get here. Told him my address when we were parrots together, before all this happened, and a nasty time I've had, wondering if he'd forgotten it. But I needn't have worried. Slow but sure is old Bill,' she patted his shoulder, 'aren't you, ducks?'

'But—' said the Queen.

'Think I really stayed here all this time learning how to be a lady?' Jake said contemptuously. 'I was waiting for Bill. Now we'll be off.'

'But—' began the King.

'Don't be crazy,' said Jake irritably. 'You don't think I could stop and be queen *now* – when all the Court have seen me and Bill dancing like a couple of young grasshoppers? You can have those brats –' she nodded towards Miranda and the Prince, who were suddenly looking hopeful. 'Well, so long, folks.' She took Bill's hand and they went out.

And now, if you want to know where they are, all you have to do is go to the island where they lived before, and directly over the spot where the treasure was hidden, you will see a neat little pub with a large signboard: *The Pirate's Rest*, and underneath: *By Appointment to Their Majesties*.

The Rocking Donkey

There was once a little girl called Esmeralda who lived with her wicked stepmother. Her father was dead. The stepmother, who was called Mrs Mitching, was very rich, and lived in a large but hideous house in a suburb with a dusty, laurelly garden, an area, and a lot of ornamental iron fencing.

Mrs Mitching was fond of opening things, and getting things up. The things she opened were mostly hospitals, or public libraries, or new by-passes, or civic centres, and the things she got up were sales of work, and bazaars, and flag days. She was in fact a public figure, and was very little at home. When she was, she spent her time receiving callers in her fringy, ornamented drawing-room.

'How is your little girl?' they would sometimes ask. 'Is she still at home, or has she gone to boarding school?'

'Oh, she's at home,' Mrs Mitching would reply, 'but she has her own play-room you know, so that we needn't

disturb one another. I don't believe in grown-ups bothering children all the time, do you?'

Mrs Mitching could not afford school for Esmeralda, as
she needed all her wealth for opening and getting up. She
always took Esmeralda along to the openings, in a white
muslin dress, painfully starched at the neck and wrists,
because people liked to see a child on the platform. But
for the rest of the time Esmeralda had to manage in her
old brown dress, much too short now, and a torn pair of
gym shoes. She had her meals in the kitchen, and they
were horrible – bread and margarine, boiled fish and
prunes.

But the most melancholy part of Esmeralda's life was
that she had nothing to do. The play-room which Mrs
Mitching spoke of was a large dark basement room, shad-
owed by the laurels which overhung the area. There was
nothing in it at all, not even a chair. No one ever came
into it, and it would have been thick with dust had not
Esmeralda, who was a tidy creature, once a week borrowed
a broom from the housemaid's cupboard and swept it. She
had no toys. Once, Mr Snye, the man who came to cut
the laurels, had given her a length of garden twine, and
she used this as a skipping rope, to keep herself warm.
She became a very good skipper, and could polka, double-
through, swing the rope, and other fancy variations, while
if she felt inclined to do plain skipping she could go on
almost all day without a fault.

There were no books to read in the house, and she was

not encouraged to go into Mrs Mitching's rooms or outside, because of her shabby clothes, though she sometimes took a stroll at dusk.

One day Mrs Mitching was to open a jumble sale. She was being driven to it by the Mayor in his Rolls-Royce, so she told Hooper, the housemaid, to bring Esmeralda by bus, dressed in her white muslin, and meet her at the Hall. Then she went off to keep an appointment.

'Drat,' said Hooper. 'Now what am I to do? Your muslin's still at the laundry from last week.'

'I'll have to go as I am,' said Esmeralda, who quite liked openings. At least they made a change from wandering about in the basement.

'I don't know what Madam'll say,' said Hooper doubtfully, 'but I should catch it if I didn't take you, sure enough.' So they went as they were, Esmeralda in her old brown dress and shoes.

When Mrs Mitching saw them she gave a cry of dismay.

'I can't let you be seen like that! You must go home at once,' and she hurriedly left them, before anyone should connect her with the shabby child.

Hooper had set her heart on a violet satin pincushion she noticed on one of the stalls, so she pushed Esmeralda into a corner, and said, 'You wait there, I shan't be a moment. It won't matter, no one will know who you are.'

Esmeralda stood looking quietly about her. An elderly gentleman, Lord Mauling, making his way to the platform,

noticed what seemed to him a forlorn-looking little creature, and stopping by her he took a coin from his pocket
and said: 'Here, my dear. Buy yourself a pretty toy.'

Esmeralda gave him a startled look as he went on his
way, and then stared at the coin she held in her hand.
It was a shilling. She had never had any money before
and was quite puzzled to know what she should buy with
it. Almost without realizing what she was doing she
began to wander along the stalls, looking at the different things offered for sale. There were books, clothes,
bottles of scent, flowers – all the things she saw seemed
beautiful, but she could not imagine buying any of them.
Then she came to the toy counter. Toys! She had never
had one. The only time she ever touched a toy was sometimes when Mrs Mitching opened a children's ward at a
hospital, and she would present a ceremonial teddy-bear
to a little patient. She gazed at dolls, puzzles, engines,
without noticing that most of them were shabby and
second-hand. Then at the end of the counter she saw
what she wanted; there was no hesitation in her mind,
she knew at once.

It was a rocking donkey – grey, battered, weather-
beaten, with draggling ears and tangled tail. On the side
of his rockers his name was painted – 'Prince' – it hardly
seemed the name for someone so ancient and worn. And
the price ticket pinned to his tail said '1/–'.

'I'd like the donkey, please,' said Esmeralda timidly
to the lady at the stall, holding out her coin. The lady

glanced from the coin to the ticket and said, 'Good gracious. Can this really be going for only a shilling? Surely they mean ten? Mr Prothero,' she called to a gentleman further down the room, but he was busy and did not hear.

'Oh well,' she said to Esmeralda. 'You take it. You won't often get a bargain like that, I can tell you.' She took the coin, and lifted the donkey down on to the floor.

'How will you get him home?' she asked.

'I don't know,' said Esmeralda. She was lucky though. As she stood hesitating with her hand on Prince's bridle, someone familiar stopped beside her. It was Mr Snye, the man who cut the hedges.

'You bought that donkey?' he said. 'Well I'm blest. That'll be a bit of fun for you, I reckon. Like me to take it home for you in the van? I've got it outside – been bringing some flowers along for the platform.'

'Oh, thank you,' Esmeralda said. So he shouldered Prince, nodded to her and said, 'I'll be home before you are, like as not. I'll just leave him in the shrubbery for you.'

Esmeralda went to find Hooper, who had bought her pincushion, and they caught their bus home.

As soon as dusk fell, and no one was about, she slipped up the back steps and half dragged, half carried Prince from his hiding-place down through the basement passage to her play-room. She put him in the middle of the floor, and sat down beside him.

It was a strange moment. For as long as she could remember she had had no company at all, nothing to play with, and now here, all of a sudden, was a friend. She felt sure of that. She put an arm over his cold smooth neck, and he rocked down and gently touched the top of her head with his nose.

'Prince,' she said quietly, and almost wondered if he would reply, but he was silent. She combed out his tangled mane and tail, and sat with him until the room was quite dark and it was time to put herself to bed.

As she went to her tiny room upstairs it occurred to her that he might be cold, alone in that dark basement. She took one of the two blankets off her bed, slipped down again in her nightdress, and tucked it over him. Back in bed she tried to settle, but could not; it was a chilly night and one blanket was not enough to keep her warm. Also she could not help wondering if Prince felt lonely and perhaps homesick for wherever he had come from? So presently she was tiptoeing back to the play-room with the other blanket. She made a sort of nest for the two of them, and slept all night on the floor, curled up between his front rockers, so that if she wanted company, all she had to do was reach up and pull on a rein, to bring down his cold friendly nose against her cheek.

She was never lonely again. She never rode on Prince – she felt that would be almost an impertinence with someone who was so much a friend, and who moreover looked so weary and battered. But she would set him off rocking while she skipped, so that they seemed to be keeping each other company, and she talked to him all the time, while he nodded intelligently in reply. And every night she crept down with her two blankets and slept curled up between his feet.

One day Mrs Mitching decided to give a whist-drive in her house for the wives of chimney sweeps, and it occurred to her that the basement play-room would be just the right size for the purpose. She went along to inspect it, and found Esmeralda having her weekly clean-out with brush and dustpan.

'That's right, that's right,' she said absently, glancing about. 'But what is this? A rocking horse?' Esmeralda stood mute.

'Do you not think you are a little old for such toys? Yes, yes, I think it had better be given away to some poor child. It is the duty of children who live in rich houses, such as you, Esmeralda, to give away your old toys to the little slum children who have nothing. It can be taken away when the van for the Bombed Families calls here tomorrow morning. But you must certainly clean it up a little first. You should be quite ashamed to pass on such a shabby old toy without doing your best to improve its appearance. After all, you know, it may gladden some poor little life in Stepney or Bethnal Green. So give it a good scrub this evening. Now what was I doing? Ah yes, seventeen feet by sixteen, ten tables – let me see—'

Esmeralda passed the rest of the day in a sort of numbness. After tea she took some sugar-soap and a scrubbing brush from the housemaid's cupboard and started to scrub Prince.

'Well,' she thought, 'perhaps I didn't *deserve* to be so happy. I never thought of scrubbing him. Perhaps someone else will take better care of him. But oh, what shall I do, what shall I do?'

She scrubbed and scrubbed, and as the shabby grey peeled away, a silvery gleam began to show along Prince's back and sides, and his mane and tail shone like floss. By the time she had finished it was quite dark, and a long ray of moonlight, striking across the floor, caught his head and for a moment dazzled her eyes.

For the last time she went up, fetched her blankets, and settled herself beside him. Just before she fell asleep it seemed to her that his nose came down and lightly touched her wet cheek.

Next day Esmeralda hid herself. She did not want to see Prince taken away. Mrs Mitching superintended his removal.

'Good gracious,' she said, when she saw him shining in the sun. 'That is far too valuable to be taken to Stepney. I shall give it to the museum.' So the Bombed Families van dropped Prince off at the museum before going on to Stepney.

All day Esmeralda avoided the basement play-room. She felt that she could not bear to look at the empty patch in the middle of the floor.

In the evening Hooper felt sorry for her, she seemed so

restless and moping, and took her out for a stroll. They went to the museum, where Hooper liked to look at the models of fashions through the ages. While she was studying crinolines and bustles Esmeralda wandered off, and soon, round a corner she came on Prince, railed off from the public with a red cord, and a notice beside him which read: 'Donated by the Hon. Mrs Mitching, November 19—.'

Esmeralda stretched out her hand, but she could not quite touch him over the cord.

'Now, Miss,' said an attendant. 'No touching the exhibits, please.' So she looked and looked at him until Hooper said it was time to go home.

Every day after that she went to the museum and looked at Prince, and Hooper said to Cook, 'That child doesn't look well.' Mrs Mitching was away from home a good deal, organizing the grand opening of a new welfare centre and clinic, so she did not notice Esmeralda's paleness, or her constant visits to the museum.

One night something woke Esmeralda. It was a long finger of moonlight which lay lightly across her closed lids. She got up quietly and put on her old brown dress and thin shoes. It was easy to steal out of that large house without anyone hearing, and once outside she slipped along the empty streets like a shadow. When she reached the museum she went at once, as if someone had called her, to a little door at one side. Someone had left it unlocked, and she opened it softly and went into the thick dark.

The museum was a familiar place by now, and she went confidently forward along a passage, and presently came out into the main hall. It did not take her long to find Prince, for there he was, shining like silver in the moonlight. She walked forward, stepped over the rope, and put her hand on his neck.

'Esmeralda,' he said. His voice was like a faint, silvery wind.

'You never spoke to me before.'

'How could I? I was choked with grey paint.'

'Oh,' she cried, 'I'm so terribly lonely without you. What shall I do?'

'You never rode on me,' he said.

'I didn't like to. You were so old and tired, it would have seemed like taking a liberty.'

'Ride on me now.'

Timidly she put her foot into the stirrup and swung herself on to his back.

'Settle yourself in the saddle and hold tight. Are you all right?'

'Yes,' she said.

Like a feather in the wind they went rocking up the ray of moonlight and passed through the high window as if it had been mist. Neither of them was ever seen again.

More Than You Bargained For

Once there was a little girl called Ermine Miggs, who lived with her mother in a flat in Southampton Row. Her real name was Erminetrude, but that was too long for anyone to pronounce. Her mother went out to work every day except Sundays, but Ermine was not strong, so she did not go to school. In the winter she sat in the big front room by the warm, popping gas fire and read and read and read. In the summer she used to wander along Theobalds Road, Lambs Conduit Street, Great Ormond Street and the Gray's Inn Road, or sit in Russell Square or Lincoln's Inn Fields.

They were very poor – the furniture in the flat consisted of a tin box, a home-made table, a stool and a bed, and they had painted the floor green to do for a carpet, but they were happy; they had enough to eat, the gas fire to sit by, hot water for baths, and the sun shone into their window; moreover there was a fig tree across the street in a bit of garden behind a wall, and in the summer Ermine used to drag the bed up to the window and lie there looking at it. Their greatest treasure was an old gramophone and half a dozen records which they played again and again; Mrs Miggs when she was ironing or mending and Ermine when she was by herself in the flat and feeling lonely. The only thing she did long for was a cat to keep her company, but Mrs Miggs said that it was unkind to keep a cat where there was no grass for it, so Ermine had to do without. She always stopped to stroke the black cat in the ABC, the tortoise-shell in the grocery, the kitten in the laundry and the putty-coloured cat in the bicycle shop.

It was a hot, dusty May. Everything seemed very grimy. Layers of soot settled more quickly on the window ledges because of the lack of wind, and the pavements looked dirty because it had not rained for weeks. People went about saying how they longed to get away from London into the country. Ermine and her mother did not wish it. They liked London in the summer, and Ermine, in any case, had never been in the country and did not know what it was like at all.

They kept the flat cool and clean with the floor scrubbed and the curtains drawn, and a bunch of radishes soaking in a blue bowl of water, ready for anyone who came in to take a cool peppery bite. Ermine used to take an apple and some cheese, and twopence to buy ice-cream, and go out for the whole day into one or another of the squares or the cool galleries of the British Museum.

One evening as she was coming home under the dusty blue dome of sky she found a dirty-looking shilling lying on a path in Bloomsbury Square. She took it home and left it to soak in the radish-bowl (when they had eaten all the radishes).

'You'd better keep it,' said her mother. 'It's your birthday in a few days and I'm afraid you won't be getting any present except a new shirt, and that you need anyway.'

Ermine polished the shilling with the dishcloth, wondering what she should do with it – there were so many different possibilities. A shilling would buy quite a few books off a twopenny or threepenny stall in the Charing Cross Road – but in a way it was wasteful to buy books when she could get them at the Public Library for nothing. Or she could go on a river trip or a long bus ride, or wander round Woolworth's and find half a dozen pretty trifles.

On her birthday she put on the new blue shirt, polished her sandals, took her apple and the special birthday cream cheese which her mother had left for her and went out into the hot May day. She ate her lunch in Russell Square and then strolled down to the little streets south of the British Museum where there are all sorts of odd small shops selling secondhand books and antiques. She spent an hour or so browsing through dirty old books and looking at twisted Persian slippers, little brass figures from Burma, Italian powder horns, Egyptian wall hangings and many other things, without finding anything that she wanted.

She was delving in a box of articles marked 'Ninepence' outside a shop in Museum Street when she felt a pain in her finger as if something had jabbed it. She withdrew her hand hurriedly – it must have been pricked by an old brooch or pin – and stood sucking it. Then she noticed something covered with bright beads underneath the heap of bric-a-brac. She pulled it out. It was a little snake, about a foot long, worked all over with tiny glass beads – red, blue and black. On its stomach the black beads were formed into letters which read: 'Turkish Prisoners, 1917.'

'What a queer creature,' thought Ermine, dangling it between her hands. She did not quite like it, but somehow it interested her.

'Do you want the snake, dear?' said a brisk little sandy-haired woman, coming to the door of the shop.

'I don't think so, thank you,' Ermine answered.

'It's a real bargain – you won't often find a thing like that for ninepence.'

'No, I think I won't, just the same, thank you.'

'Well put it back in the box then,' the woman snapped angrily, and went inside. Ermine could see her looking through the window, and hurriedly moved on to the next shop which sold secondhand gramophone records.

'Of course,' she thought, 'I'll get a record – something we've never heard before. Then it will be a surprise for Mother as well.'

She stooped over the box marked 1/- and started looking slowly through the records, twisting her head about to read the titles which always seemed to be upside down. Most of the records looked rather battered, and some were bent or cracked, but one seemed to be brand-new – it was clean and glossy and its paper case was uncrumpled. Ermine studied the title. It was a concerto grosso for oboe and orchestra by Mr Handel. The name was unfamiliar to her, but she preferred that – it would be more of a surprise, and it would take them longer to learn it. She was standing half-decided, holding her shilling, when a man came out from inside the shop with a huge stack of records in his arms. All of a sudden they began to slip different ways, and the whole pile would have crashed on to the pavement had not Ermine jumped forward and steadied them with both hands.

'Thank you, duck,' said the man. 'That wouldn't have done, would it? They're a lot of junk but still, no one wants broken records all over the street. Just help me tip them into the two-and-sixpenny box would you? That's the stuff.'

'May I have this one, please?' Ermine said, going back to the shilling box and pulling out her concerto grosso.

'Ah, you've found yourself something nice there,' said the man cheerfully. 'I guess that one slipped in out of the five bob box by mistake – however, that's my lookout. But you can reckon you've got quite a bargain.'

'I'm glad of that,' said Ermine, following him in to the shop. 'It's my birthday present.'

'Is it then? Well, you treat it carefully and it'll last you for plenty of birthdays. I'll tell you what – seeing you've saved me the trouble of sweeping fifty records off the pavement, I'll give you some fibre needles. And a sharpener, as it's your birthday.'

'Oh, thank you *very* much,' said Ermine, overwhelmed, as he handed her the two parcels.

'Now don't run home with it – walk.'

'I shouldn't dream of playing it until Mother gets home anyway,' she replied with dignity. He laughed. 'Goodbye, and thank you – it *was* kind of you to give me these.'

Towards tea-time she walked slowly and happily home, hugging her presents. The sun was still very hot, and it was pleasant to go into the cool, curtained flat and wash her dusty hands and feet. She cut some bread and butter, made lemonade in a jug, and then carefully undid the record and put it on the turntable, wound the gramophone and put in one of the new needles, all ready for her mother's arrival.

Soon she heard a quick footstep on the stairs, and Mrs Miggs came in saying: 'Ouf, isn't it hot. Had a nice birthday, lovey? What did you get yourself?'

'A new record – and the man gave me some needles and a sharpener because it's my birthday; wasn't it nice of him? And it was really a five-shilling one anyway, got into the shilling box. It's all ready to play while we're having tea.'

'Shan't be a second then – I must just wash and I'll be with you. Oh, lovely, you've made cress sandwiches.'

She was back in a moment with a tiny birthday cake decorated with pink candles and silver balls.

'There you are, dearie – I made it last night when you were asleep.'

'Oh, *Mother*—'

'Come on, goose – let's hear this record.'

As soon as Ermine put the needle down and the disc began to revolve, a strange thing happened.

Ermine found herself walking down a steep, narrow lane, in between two high walls. At the bottom of the lane she crossed a cobbled road and came to another wall in which there was a door. She opened the door, and passing through found herself in a garden. There were tall trees close at hand, interspersed with holly bushes. A little path led among them, and following it she came to a wide lawn, with a stone terrace at one end and a pool at the other. Beyond the pool was a hedge and an arched gateway with a glimpse of bright flowers through it. Ermine went this way and found a little formal garden with brick paths and all sorts of sweet-smelling flowers whose names she did not know, besides roses and wallflowers and others which she remembered seeing in flower shops. Another archway led from the paved garden to a smaller lawn, in the centre of which grew a huge tree, all covered with blossom. Ermine thought that it was an apple tree, but she had never seen one so large. She started to cross the grass to it, but at that moment the music slowed down and came to an end.

Ermine rubbed her eyes in bewilderment, and looked at the record, lying quietly on its turntable.

'Goodness,' said her mother. 'That music made me think of all sorts of things I haven't remembered for years. I was in such a dream I never even noticed you turn over.'

'I didn't turn over.' But when Ermine looked at the record the uppermost side was numbered '2'. 'It must have turned itself – we certainly started it on the right side.'

'What a curious record,' said her mother. 'And only a shilling – there's a bargain for you. Come on now – cut your cake.'

Ermine wondered if her mother had seen the garden too, but did not quite like to ask her.

Later on in the evening when Mrs Miggs was having a bath Ermine played the record again, and exactly the same thing happened. She walked down the alley between the walls, went across the road and through the door, under the trees, and then wandered about in the garden. She went a different way this time, past a lily pond and a little brick-paved stream with forget-me-nots trailing on its banks, but as before, finally came to the lawn with the great apple tree on it, and as before, was just starting to cross the grass when the music ceased. She looked at the record. It was on its second side.

Next day she went back to the shop and told the man how much they had enjoyed it.

'Glad you liked it,' he said. 'Come in and have a look round any time you like, and a chat. Always pleased to see friends in the shop.'

As Ermine left, her eye was caught again by the little bead-covered snake in the box next door. She glanced down at it, and then looked up to see the woman staring at her in an unfriendly manner through the window. She went hastily on.

That evening she told her mother about the woman and the snake.

'Funny to be so cross just because you didn't buy it,' commented Mrs Miggs. 'Ninepence wouldn't make much difference to her, you'd think. But I expect the people who keep those curio shops do get rather odd – it's only natural when you think that they spend their lives among stuffed crocodiles and the like. Let's play your record again – I've taken a great fancy to it.'

Goodness knows how many times Ermine played her record over during the next month or two. She never tired of it, and every time she played it, it performed its trick of turning over in the middle without any help – only Ermine never saw this happen because by that time she was in the garden, finding some new path to walk down, or some new flower to examine. On the hottest days she had only to wind the gramophone, place the needle on the disc, and at once be transported to the shade of those trees and the spreading green of the great lawn. The apple tree gradually shed its blossom in a pale carpet on the grass and small green apples formed. More roses came out, and the narcissi withered.

In London it grew hotter. Ermine became disinclined to go out, and spent more and more time indoors listening to the record. One afternoon she had only been as far as the bottom of Southampton Row to buy a lettuce, but when she came home her head ached and she could hardly drag herself up the stairs.

'You look feverish, dearie,' said her mother. 'Better go to bed. Goodness, your head is as hot as fire.'

Ermine gratefully climbed in between the cool sheets, but she could not get comfortable. She seemed to ache all over, and the bed soon became hot and tangled. She moved about miserably, listening to the lorries rattling past outside; it seemed to become dark all of a sudden, though of course the street lamps were shining on the ceiling.

'Try to keep still,' her mother's voice said. 'Would you like some music? Do you think that would help you to sleep?'

'Oh yes,' Ermine answered eagerly. Now she was going down the walled lane. It was dark, and a single lamp threw leaf-shadows across the road at the bottom.

When she reached the garden she saw bright moonlight falling across the lawns. She wandered for some time in and out of the shadows and at length came to the apple tree. She could dimly distinguish green apples the size of plums hanging among the leaves. Below them something glittered. She crossed the grass (which she had never been able to do before) and then stood drenched with icy fear. A great serpent was twined round the trunk of the tree, gazing at her with ruby-coloured eyes. The moonlight struck on it here and there, and she could see that it was striped and barred, red, black and blue. She opened her mouth to shriek but no sound came out; it was like a nightmare. And then, thank heaven, the music stopped and she was back in her hot bed, tossing and turning. 'The snake, the snake!' she said desperately, but her mouth seemed to be clogged with fur, and her tongue was as large as a football.

'What snake, lovey?' she heard her mother say, and then she was swept off into red-hot darkness. People came and went, her mother and a doctor; drinks and medicine were trickled between her lips, darkness alternated with light. Sometimes she was tormented by a glimpse of apples, hanging in cool clusters among leaves, sometimes she saw a huge snake spiralling round and round like a Catherine wheel on the gramophone and playing a jangling tinny tune. Sometimes everything vanished altogether and she was only conscious of her aching self.

One day she began to get better and sat propped up on pillows sipping chicken broth.

'Well, you gave us a fright,' said her mother, who looked pale and thin, but cheerful.

'I had a fright too,' Ermine answered slowly, thinking of the snake. Speech was tiring, and she lay silent, staring about the room at the dusty golden sunlight. Presently her eyes dropped to the little home-made table by her bed and she gave a faint cry.

'What is it, ducky?' said Mrs Miggs coming anxiously.

'That snake. How did it get here?'

'Well, when you were feverish – you know you've been ill for three weeks, darling – you kept calling out, "The snake, the snake!" and I thought perhaps you were thinking of the one in the shop that you'd told me about. So I went along and bought it in case you were fretting for it.'

Fretting for it! Ermine eyed the snake with revulsion. She wanted to cry 'Take it away!' but that would have seemed rude and heartless. Suddenly a thought struck her. 'Mother!'

'Yes, ducky?'

'You've been here all day?'

'Yes, what about it?'

'But what about your job?'

'Oh, I had to give that up,' said Mrs Miggs lightly. 'Never mind, I'll soon get another one when you're better. Don't you fret your head about that.'

'But how have you been managing?' Ermine asked mistily, and then another thing about the room struck her. 'The gramophone?'

'Yes, I had to sell it. I'd much rather have you than a gramophone, after all. We'll get another one by and by. Now come along – drink up the last of that soup and off to sleep with you.'

It took Ermine a long time to recover. She sat about the flat, thin and weak, looking wearily at her books. Sometimes she took the record out of its paper case and rubbed her finger round it curiously, wondering if she could hear a faint sound of the wind in those trees. She could not help longing to hear it again, though at the same time she dreaded it. Was the snake still twined in the apple tree? Had it been there all the time?

She always put the record back hurriedly if she heard her mother coming.

One day she announced that she was perfectly able to look after herself and was going out to sit in the square.

Mrs Miggs looked at her searchingly, gave her a quick pat, and said:

'Take care of yourself then. I'll go off and do a bit of job-hunting if you're sure you're all right.'

'Quite sure.'

The leaves were beginning to hang heavily on the trees, and the grass was yellow and parched. Ermine walked very slowly to a seat in Bloomsbury Square and sank on to it. Her legs felt like skeins of wool.

Everything round her was dead and quiet. People were away on holiday, she supposed, and London was empty. It smelt of tar and dust. She thought of early morning in her garden, the dew thick on uncut grass and apples hanging among the leaves.

Suddenly behind her she heard a faint mew, a tiny note of distress. Turning her head she saw a strange little animal with a head like a cat, but a long thin body and a rusty-coloured coat. When she put out her hand he ran up eagerly and rubbed against it, purring.

'Well, you funny puss,' she said, stroking it. 'Where do you come from?'

Her finger found a collar, and running it round she came to a little engraved nameplate which said 'Adamson' and gave a number in Museum Street.

'I'd better take you home,' she said, and picked it up. It seemed quite willing to be carried and sat with its forepaws dangling over her arm, looking alertly round as she walked along Great Russell Street and turned into Museum Street.

When she came to the number on the collar she found to her surprise that it was the record shop.

'Mr Adamson?' she said.

'Hullo, it's the birthday girl. What's happened to you, though? You've grown, or got thinner or something. And you've brought back Ticky for me – I was beginning to worry about him. You're a fine one, you are,' he scolded the cat. 'Giving me heart failure like that. I suppose you want some milk. Now *you* sit down *there* –' he moved an armful of sheet music off a backless chair and pushed Ermine gently on to it – 'while I give Ticky his milk. Where did you find him?'

'Only in Bloomsbury Square, but he seemed very miserable.'

'He's partly mongoose, you see – his granny was one.

He's not used to city life and he goes out and gets scared. He's taken a fancy to you, though, I can see. Now, what shall I give you for bringing him back? Like another record? You're fond of Handel, I seem to remember.'

'It wouldn't be much use to me now, I'm afraid,' she said, laughing a little. 'I got ill, and Mother lost her job and had to sell our gramophone.'

'A lady selling a gramophone, eh? Rather thin, young-ish, dark hair? An old model in a walnut box with a detachable handle?'

He went to the back of the shop and pulled it out from under a typing desk.

'Haven't got rid of it yet, you see. To tell you the truth, never thought I would. People won't go for this sort of thing now, all for these automatic pickups with short and long-playing, though mark you, this has a beautiful tone, one of the best I've heard for a long time. But I could see she wanted to sell it pretty badly, so I thought, Well, why not let it lodge here for a bit. So you've been ill, eh? And your ma's out of a job? That won't do. Well now, I'll tell you what. I'll put on my jacket and shut up, because it's closing time anyway, and we'll take this gramophone, which is your reward for bringing back Ticky, and we'll go and call on your ma and have a chat with her.'

He began putting up the shutters, slamming them into their grooves.

'Oh, you are kind,' said Ermine, her eyes full of tears.

'Nonsense, nonsense. One good turn deserves another. Are we ready now? Yes, you take Ticky, he won't be left behind. Southampton Row? Blimey, did your ma come all that way with this?'

It only took them five minutes, though. It was dusk by now, and Ermine saw a crack of light under the flat door which showed that her mother was back. Her footsteps sounded discouraged, though she put on a cheerful smile for Ermine as she said:

'No luck yet, ducky—' Then she saw Mr Adamson behind, and her expression became inquiring.

'I expect you remember me, ma'am,' he said. 'Your daughter did me a good turn this afternoon – brought back my cat that had been missing for two days. So I'm just carrying home her reward, a gramophone I happened to have by me.'

Mrs Miggs's jaw dropped.

'I— I don't know what to say,' she began. 'You must let me—'

'No, I certainly will not let you.'

Ermine noticed that Ticky, whom she still held in her arms, was beginning to get very restless and anxious. She let him jump down, and he raced across to the little bedside table and pounced upon something that lay on it.

'What's he got there?' asked Mr Adamson anxiously, turning from Mrs Miggs. 'You don't keep pet mice, do you?'

'No, it's the snake,' said Ermine, fascinated. 'He's

tearing it to bits.' Tiny beads and bits of stuffing were flying about as Ticky, growling tremendously, worried and gnawed at it.

'Oh, I say, what a shame. I *am* sorry. Here, Ticky, you bad—'

'No, no, don't stop him. It doesn't matter.'

The elders fell into talk again. Ermine heard Mr Adamson say:

'I'm opening another branch in St Martin's Lane – think you could look after this one for me?' and her mother answered:

'Well it's very kind of you and I'd jump at the chance—'

'Kind? Nonsense. Then that's settled. Here, you, bright-eyes, put that Handel record on the gramophone and let's make sure it's still working.'

Ermine was half afraid as she put on the record and wound the handle, but she could not have disobeyed. With the first notes she forgot her fear, for she was walking down the alley and a few red leaves were drifting ahead of her. Smoke from a bonfire hung cloudily among the trees in front. She went through the door in the wall, down the path among the hollies, along beside the lawn and through the paved garden. Then she came to the apple-tree lawn. The tree was weighed down by its heavy golden fruit, but today there was no serpent – not so much as a blue or red glass bead in the grass.

She ran to the tree, and reaching up, felt one of the apples come away, heavy and round, into her hand. Then the music stopped and she came back to herself, blinking, in the familiar room.

'That child's been asleep, I do believe,' remarked her mother. 'Look how pink her cheeks are.'

'If I was asleep,' said Ermine, 'where did I find this?'

She held out her hand. In it, heavy and round, lay a golden apple.

The Third Wish

Once there was a man who was driving in his car at dusk on a spring evening through part of the forest of Savernake. His name was Mr Peters. The primroses were just beginning but the trees were still bare, and it was cold; the birds had stopped singing an hour ago.

As Mr Peters entered a straight, empty stretch of road he seemed to hear a faint crying, and a struggling and thrashing, as if somebody was in trouble far away in the trees. He left his car and climbed the mossy bank beside the road. Beyond the bank was an open slope of beech trees leading down to thorn bushes through which he saw the gleam of water. He stood a moment waiting to try and discover where the noise was coming from, and presently heard a rustling and some strange cries in a voice which was almost human – and yet there was something too hoarse about it at one time and too clear and sweet at another. Mr Peters ran down the hill and as he neared the bushes he saw something white among them which was trying to extricate itself; coming closer he found that it was a swan that had become entangled in the thorns growing on the bank of the canal.

The bird struggled all the more frantically as he approached, looking at him with hate in its yellow eyes, and when he took hold of it to free it, hissed at him, pecked him, and thrashed dangerously with its wings which were powerful enough to break his arm. Nevertheless he managed to release it from the thorns, and carrying it tightly with one arm, holding the snaky head well away with the other hand (for he did not wish his eyes pecked out), he took it to the verge of the canal and dropped it in.

The swan instantly assumed great dignity and sailed out to the middle of the water, where it put itself to rights with much dabbling and preening, smoothing its feathers with little showers of drops. Mr Peters waited, to make sure that it was all right and had suffered no damage in its struggles. Presently the swan, when it was satisfied with its appearance, floated in to the bank once more, and in a moment, instead of the great white bird, there was a little man all in green with a golden crown and long beard, standing by the water. He had fierce glittering eyes and looked by no means friendly.

'Well, sir,' he said threateningly, 'I see you are

presumptuous enough to know some of the laws of magic. You think that because you have rescued – by pure good fortune – the King of the Forest from a difficulty, you should have some fabulous reward.'

'I expect three wishes, no more and no less,' answered Mr Peters, looking at him steadily and with composure.

'Three wishes, he wants, the clever man! Well, I have yet to hear of the human being who made any good use of his three wishes – they mostly end up worse off than they started. Take your three wishes then – ' he flung three dead leaves in the air ' – don't blame me if you spend the last wish in undoing the work of the other two.'

Mr Peters caught the leaves and put two of them carefully in his notecase. When he looked up the swan was sailing about in the middle of the water again, flicking the drops angrily down its long neck.

Mr Peters stood for some minutes reflecting on how he should use his reward. He knew very well that the gift of three magic wishes was one which brought trouble more often than not, and he had no intention of being like the forester who first wished by mistake for a sausage, and then in a rage wished it on the end of his wife's nose, and then had to use his last wish in getting it off again. Mr Peters had most of the things which he wanted and was very content with his life. The only thing that troubled him was that he was a little lonely, and had no companion for his old age. He decided to use his first wish and to keep the other two in case of an emergency. Taking a thorn he pricked his tongue with it, to remind himself not to utter rash wishes aloud. Then holding the third leaf and gazing round him at the dusky undergrowth, the primroses, great beeches and the blue-green water of the canal, he said:

'I wish I had a wife as beautiful as the forest.'

A tremendous quacking and splashing broke out on the surface of the water. He thought that it was the swan laughing at him. Taking no notice he made his way through the darkening woods to his car, wrapped himself up in the rug and went to sleep.

When he awoke it was morning and the birds were beginning to call. Coming along the track towards him was the most beautiful creature he had ever seen, with eyes as blue-green as the canal, hair as dusky as the bushes, and skin as white as the feathers of swans.

'Are you the wife that I wished for?' asked Mr Peters.

'Yes I am,' she replied. 'My name is Leita.'

She stepped into the car beside him and they drove off to the church on the outskirts of the forest, where they were married. Then he took her to his house in a remote and lovely valley and showed her all his treasures – the bees in their white hives, the Jersey cows, the hyacinths, the silver candlesticks, the blue cups and the lustre bowl for putting primroses in. She admired everything, but what pleased her most was the river which ran by the foot of his garden.

'Do swans come up here?' she asked.

'Yes, I have often seen swans there on the river,' he told her, and she smiled.

Leita made him a good wife. She was gentle and friendly, busied herself about the house and garden, polished the bowls, milked the cows and mended his socks. But as time went by Mr Peters began to feel that she was not happy. She seemed restless, wandered much in the garden, and sometimes when he came back from the fields he would find the house empty and she would only return after half an hour or so with no explanation of where she had been. On these occasions she was especially tender and would put out his slippers to warm and cook his favourite dish – Welsh rarebit with wild strawberries – for supper.

One evening he was returning home along the river path when he saw Leita in front of him, down by the water. A swan had sailed up to the verge and she had her arms round its neck and the swan's head rested against her cheek. She was weeping, and as he came nearer he saw that tears were rolling, too, from the swan's eyes.

'Leita, what is it?' he asked, very troubled.

'This is my sister,' she answered. 'I can't bear being separated from her.'

Now he understood that Leita was really a swan from the forest, and this made him very sad because when a human being marries a bird it always leads to sorrow.

'I could use my second wish to give your sister human shape, so that she could be a companion to you,' he suggested.

'No, no,' she cried. 'I couldn't ask that of her.'

'Is it so very hard to be a human being?' asked Mr Peters sadly.

'Very, very hard,' she answered.

'Don't you love me at all, Leita?'

'Yes, I do, I do love you,' she said, and there were tears in her eyes again. 'But I miss the old life in the forest, the cool grass and the mist rising off the river at sunrise and the feel of the water sliding over my feathers as my sister and I drifted along the stream.'

'Then shall I use my second wish to turn you back into a swan again?' he asked, and his tongue pricked to remind him of the old King's words, and his heart swelled with grief inside him.

'Who would darn your socks and cook your meals and see to the hens?'

'I'd do it myself as I did before I married you,' he said, trying to sound cheerful.

She shook her head. 'No, I could not be as unkind to you as that. I am partly a swan, but I am also partly a human being now. I will stay with you.'

Poor Mr Peters was very distressed on his wife's account and did his best to make her life happier, taking her for drives in the car, finding beautiful music for her to listen to on the radio, buying clothes for her and even suggesting a trip round the world. But she said no to that; she would prefer to stay in their own house near the river.

He noticed that she spent more and more time baking wonderful cakes – jam puffs, petits fours, eclairs and meringues. One day he saw her take a basketful down to the river and he guessed that she was giving them to her sister.

He built a seat for her by the river, and the two sisters spent hours together there, communicating in some wordless manner. For a time he thought that all would be well, but then he saw how thin and pale she was growing.

One night when he had been late doing the accounts he came up to bed and found her weeping in her sleep and calling:

'Rhea! Rhea! I can't understand what you say! Oh, wait for me, take me with you!'

Then he knew that it was hopeless and she would never be happy as a human. He stooped down and kissed her goodbye, then took another leaf from his notecase, blew it out of the window, and used up his second wish.

Next moment instead of Leita there was a sleeping swan lying across the bed with its head under its wing. He carried it out of the house and down to the brink of the river, and then he said 'Leita! Leita!' to waken her, and gently put her into the water. She gazed round her in astonishment for a moment and then came up to him and rested her head lightly against his hand; next instant she was flying away over the trees towards the heart of the forest.

He heard a harsh laugh behind him, and turning round saw the old King looking at him with a malicious expression.

'Well, my friend! You don't seem to have managed so wonderfully with your first two wishes, do you? What will you do with the last? Turn yourself into a swan? Or turn Leita back into a girl?'

'I shall do neither,' said Mr Peters calmly. 'Human beings and swans are better in their own shapes.'

But for all that he looked sadly over towards the forest

where Leita had flown, and walked slowly back to his empty house.

Next day he saw two swans swimming at the bottom of the garden, and one of them wore the gold chain he had given Leita after their marriage; she came up and rubbed her head against his hand.

Mr Peters and his two swans came to be well known in that part of the country; people used to say that he talked to the swans and they understood him as well as his neighbours. Many people were a little frightened of him. There was a story that once when thieves tried to break into his house they were set upon by two huge white birds which carried them off bodily and dropped them in the river.

As Mr Peters grew old everyone wondered at his contentment. Even when he was bent with rheumatism he would not think of moving to a drier spot, but went slowly about his work, milking the cows and collecting the honey and eggs, with the two swans always somewhere close at hand.

Sometimes people who knew his story would say to him:

'Mr Peters, why don't you wish for another wife?'

'Not likely,' he would answer serenely. 'Two wishes were enough for me, I reckon. I've learned that even if your wishes are granted they don't always better you. I'll stay faithful to Leita.'

One autumn night, passers-by along the road heard

the mournful sound of two swans singing. All night the song went on, sweet and harsh, sharp and clear. In the morning Mr Peters was found peacefully dead in his bed with a smile of great happiness on his face. In between his hands, which lay clasped on his breast, were a withered leaf and a white feather.

The Boy Who Read Aloud

Once there was a boy called Seb who was unfortunate. His dear mother had died, his father had married again, and the new wife brought in three daughters of her own. Their names were Minna, Hanna and Morwenna, and they were all larger and older than Seb – big, fat, red-haired hateful girls. Minna pinched, Hanna tweaked hair and kicked shins, while Morwenna could pull such terrible faces that she put even the birds in a fright and her mother had forbidden her to do it indoors in case she cracked the cups and plates on the kitchen dresser. The mother was just as bad as her daughters, greedy, unkind, and such a terrible cook that nine months after they were married Seb's father wasted away and died from the food she fed him on. As for Seb, he had to manage on crusts, for that was all he got.

Now Seb had three treasures which his true mother had left him when she died. These were a little silver mug, a little silver spoon, and a book of stories. The book of stories was what he prized most, for when she was alive his true mother had read them aloud to him every day and as soon as he grew old enough to learn his letters he read them back to her while she did the ironing or peeled the potatoes or rolled out the pastry. So, now, when he opened the book, it was as if his true mother were back with him, telling him a story, and for a little he could forget how things had changed with him.

You can guess how hard Seb tried to keep these treasures hidden from his step-sisters. But they were prying, peering, poking girls, and presently Minna came across the silver cup hidden under Seb's mattress.

'You mean little sniveller, keeping this pretty cup hidden away!' she cried. 'I am the eldest, it should be mine, and I'll pinch and pinch you till you give it to me!'

'For shame, Seb!' said his step-mother when she heard him crying out at the pinches. 'Give the cup to your sister at once!'

So poor little Seb had to give it up.

Then Hanna found the silver spoon hidden under Seb's pillow.

'Let me have it, let me have it, you little spalpeen!' she screeched, when he tried to keep it from her. 'Or I'll drag out every hair in your head.'

And her mother made Seb give her the little spoon.

Now Seb took particular pains to keep his precious book out of view, hiding it first in one place and then in another, between the bins of corn, under a sitting hen, inside a hollow tree, beneath a loose floorboard. But one evening Morwenna found it tucked up on a rafter, as they were going to bed. Quickly Seb snatched the book from her and darted off to his attic room where he shut himself in, pushing the bed against the door. Morwenna was after him in a flash – though, mind you, it was only pure spite that made her want the book for, big as she was, she could read no more than a gatepost can.

'You'd better give it to me, you little mizzler!' she bawled through the door. 'Or I shall make such a fearsome face at you that you'll very likely die of fright.'

Seb trembled in his shoes at this threat, but he knew that Morwenna could do nothing till morning, since she was not allowed to pull faces indoors.

Huddling in bed, clutching the book to him, he decided that the only thing for him to do was to run away. He would get up very early, climb out of the window, and slide down the roof.

But where should he go and how should he live?

For a long time, no plan came to him. But at last, remembering the book in his hands, he thought, 'Well, there is one thing I can do. I can read. Perhaps somebody in the world would like me to read stories to them.'

'In the village,' he thought, 'by the inn door, there is a board with cards stuck up on it, showing what work is to be had. I will go that way in the morning and see if anybody wants a reader.'

So at last he went to sleep, holding the little book tight against his chest.

In the morning he woke and tiptoed out of the house long before anyone else was stirring. (Minna, Morwenna and Hanna were all lazy, heavy sleepers who never clambered from their beds till the sun was half across the sky.)

Seb went quietly through the garden and quietly down the village until he came to the notice-board. On it there were cards telling of jobs for gardeners, jobs for cooks, jobs for postmen, ploughmen and painters. Looking at them all he had begun to think there was nothing for him when up in the top corner he noticed a very old, dog-eared card with a bit torn off. It said:

ELDERLY BLIND RETIRED SEA
WOULD LIKE BOY TO READ
ALOUD DAILY

What a strange thing, thought Seb. Fancy reading aloud to the sea! Fancy the sea going blind at all!

But still, he supposed, thinking it over, the sea could get old like anybody else, old and blind and bored. Didn't the emperor Caligula have chats with the sea, and who takes the trouble nowadays even to pass the time of day with his neighbour, let alone have a conversation with the ocean?

There would be no harm, anyway, in going to find out whether the job had been taken already. Seb knew the way to the sea because when his true mother had been alive they had sometimes spent days at the shore. It was about twenty miles but he thought he could walk it in a couple of days. So he started at once.

Now, had Seb but known it, the truth of the matter was this: that card had been up on the board such a long time that it had been torn, and some of the words were missing. It should have read:

ELDERLY BLIND RETIRED SEA CAPTAIN
WOULD LIKE BOY TO READ NEWSPAPER
ALOUD DAILY. APPLY WITHIN

Nobody ever had applied for the job, and in the end the sea captain had grown tired of waiting and had gone off to another town.

But Seb knew nothing of all this, so he started off to walk to the sea, with his treasured book of stories in his pocket.

It was still very early and few folk were about.

As he walked along Seb began to worry in case he had forgotten how to read aloud, because it was now a long time since his true mother had died. 'I had better practise a bit,' he thought.

When he had gone about five miles and felt in need of a rest he came to a gate leading into a deserted barnyard.

'I'll go in here,' he thought, 'and practise my reading. Because there's no doubt about it at all, it's going to seem very queer reading to the sea till I've grown accustomed to it.'

There was an old rusty Rolls-Royce car in the yard, which looked as if it had not been driven since the days when ladies wore long trailing skirts and you could get four ounces of bull's-eyes for a halfpenny. Seb felt rather sorry for the poor thing, so broken-down, forlorn and battered did it seem, and he decided to read to it.

He sat down cross-legged in front of the radiator, took out his book and read a story about the sun-god's flaming chariot, and how once it was borrowed by a boy who had not passed his driving-test, and how he drove the chariot, horses and all, into the side of a hill.

All the time Seb was reading there came no sound or movement from the car. But when he had finished and stood up to go, he was astonished to hear a toot from behind him. He turned himself about fast, wondering if somebody had been hiding in the car all the time. But it was empty, sure enough.

Then he heard a voice, which said,

'Was that a true tale, boy?'

'As to that,' said Seb, 'I can't tell you.'

'Well, true or not,' said the voice (it came from the radiator and had a sort of purring rumble to it, like the sound of a very large cat), 'true or not, it was the most interesting tale I have ever heard. In fact it was the *only* tale I have heard, and I am greatly obliged to you, boy, for reading it to me. No one else ever thought of doing such a thing. In return I will tell you something. In a well in the corner of the yard hangs a barrel of stolen money; five days ago I saw two thieves come here and lower it down. Wind the handle and you will be able to draw it up.'

'Did you ever!' said Seb, and he went to the well in the corner and turned the handle which pulled the rope. Up came a barrel filled to the top with silver coins.

'There's too much here for me,' Seb said. 'I could never carry it all.' So he took enough to fill one pocket (the book was in the other), wound the barrel down into the well again, and went on his way, waving goodbye to the Rolls-Royce car as long as he could see it.

He bought some bread with his money at the next village, and a bottle of milk.

After another five miles' walking he began to feel tired again, so he stepped aside from the road into the garden of an old empty house.

'This would be a good place to read another of my stories,' he thought.

So he read aloud a tale of two friends who arranged to meet one night near a hole in a wall. But they were frightened away by a lion and so they missed seeing one another.

When Seb had finished he heard a harsh voice behind him (he was sitting with his back to the house) which said,

'Was that a true tale, boy?'

'As to that,' said Seb, 'I can't tell you.'

'True or not,' said the voice, 'it has given me something to think about in the long, empty days and nights. I never heard a tale before. So in return I will tell you something useful. Growing in my garden you will find a red flower which, if you pick and eat it, will cure any illness.'

'But I haven't got any illness,' Seb said. 'I am quite well.'

'If you eat this flower you will never fall ill, in the whole of your life. But take care not to pick the yellow flower which grows next to it, for that is poisonous and would kill you at once.'

Seb wandered through the garden until he found the red and yellow flowers growing side by side.

"Twould be a pity to pick the red one,' he thought, 'so pretty it looks growing there. Anyway I daresay somebody will come along who needs it more than I do.'

So he thanked the house kindly and went on his way, waving until he was out of sight.

Presently it grew dark, so he ate some more of his bread, drank the milk, and went to sleep under an old thorn tree. Next morning, to thank the tree for watching over him all night, he read aloud a story about a girl who ran away from a suitor and turned herself into a laurel bush.

'Boy,' said a rough, prickly voice when he had finished, 'is that a true tale?'

'As to that,' said Seb, 'I don't know.'

'True or not,' said the voice, 'I enjoyed it and it sounds true, so I will tell you something in return. Lodged in my topmost fork is the blue stone of eternal life, which a swallow dropped there a hundred years ago. If you care to climb up you may have it. Carry it in your pocket and you will live for ever.'

Seb thanked the tree and climbed up. The stone was very beautiful, dark blue, with gold marks on it and white lines. But, he said to himself, do I really want to live for ever? Why should *I* do so out of all the people in the world?

So he put the stone back in the crotch of the tree. But, unknown to him, as he turned to climb down, he dislodged the stone again and it fell into his pocket.

He went on, waving goodbye to the tree as long as it was in sight, and now he came to the sea itself, with its green waves rolling up on to the sand, each one breaking with a roar.

'Will the sea be able to hear me if I read aloud?' Seb wondered.

Feeling rather foolish, because the sea was so very large and made so much noise, he sat down on the sand. Taking out his book he read first one story and then another. At first it seemed as if nobody heard him, but then he began to hear voices, many voices, saying,

'Hush! Hush!'

And looking up he noticed that all the waves had started to smooth out as if a giant palm had flattened them, so that hardly a ripple stirred as far as he could see. The water creamed and lapped at his feet, like a dog that wants to be patted, and as he waited, not knowing whether to go on or not, a long, thin white hand came out of the green water and turned over the page.

So Seb read another story and then another.

Meanwhile what had happened at home?

When they found Seb had run away the three sisters were very angry, but specially Morwenna.

'Just let him wait till I catch him!' she said. 'I'll make such a face at him that his hair turns to knitting needles.'

'Oh let him go,' said the mother. 'What use was he at all, but only a mouth to feed?'

None the less Morwenna and her sisters went off looking for Seb. They asked of this one and that one in the village, who had seen him, and learned that he had taken the road to the sea. So they followed after until they came to the barn-yard, and there they heard a plaintive voice wailing and sighing.

'Oh, won't some kind soul tell me a story?' it sighed. 'Alack and mercy and curse it. I have such a terrible craving to hear another tale! Oh, won't somebody take pity on me?'

'Who's been telling you tales?' said Morwenna, seeing it was the old Rolls-Royce car that spoke. 'Was it a little runt of a boy with a book he'd no right to sticking out of his breeches pocket? Speak the truth now, and I'll tell you another story.'

'Yes, 'twas a boy,' the old car said. 'He read me from a wondrous book and in return I told him about the silver in the well.'

'Silver in the well? Where?' screeched Minna and Hanna. Colliding together in their greed they made a rush for the well-head and wound up the handle. But Minna was so eager to get at the silver and keep her sisters from it that she jumped right on to the barrel when it came up, the rope broke, and down she went. So that was the end of Minna.

'Oh, well, never mind her,' said Morwenna. 'Come on, let you, for it's plain 'twas this way he went.' And she hurried on, taking no notice at all of the poor old car crying out, 'My story, my story!'

'Bother your story, you miserable old heap of tin!' she shouted back.

So they came to the empty house, and here again they heard a voice moaning and lamenting.

'Ochone, ochone, why did I ever listen to that boy's tale? Now I've nothing in me but an insatiable thirst to hear another.'

'Was it a bit of a young boy with a little black book?' Morwenna said. 'Answer me that and I'll tell you a story.'

'Ah, it was, and in return for the tale he told me I showed him where to find the red flower that cures you of any sickness.'

'Where is it? Where?' And the sisters went ramping through the garden till they found it. But in her haste to snatch it before her sister, Hanna grabbed the yellow flower as well, ate it, and dropped down dead on the very spot.

'Oh, well, she's done for,' said Morwenna, and she hurried on, taking no notice of the old house which wailed, 'My story, my story!' behind her.

'Plague take your story, you mouldy old heap of brick,' she called back.

So she came to the thorn tree.

'Have you seen a boy?' she asked it. 'Did he tell you a story?'

'Indeed he did, and in return I was telling him about the stone of eternal life in my topmost fork.'

'Let me lay my hands on that same stone!' said Morwenna, and she made haste to scramble up the tree. But because she was such an awkward, clumsy girl she fell from the top fork in her greedy hurry, and hung head down among the thorns.

'If you'd waited a moment longer,' said the tree, 'I could have told you that the boy took the stone with him.'

'Oh, you villainous old tree!' cried Morwenna, kicking and twisting, and making such faces as turned the birds pale in their tracks. But she was stuck fast, and hangs there to this day.

Meanwhile Seb's step-mother had married again, a man as mean-natured as she was herself. By and by they began to hear tales of a marvellous boy, who sat on the shore and read tales to the sea.

'And the sea's given him great gifts!' said one. 'They say he's been shown where the lost treasure of the Spanish galleon lies, with cups of gold and plates of pearl and wine-glasses all carved out of great rubies, and a hundred chests of silver ingots!'

'They say he's been told where every storm is, all over the world, and which way it's heading!' said another.

'They say he can listen to the voice of the sea as if it were an old friend talking to him!' said a third. 'And devil a bit of a tide has there been since he began reading aloud, and a great inconvenience it is to the navigation in all realms of the world!'

'Can that boy be Seb?' wondered the step-mother and her husband. They resolved to go and see for themselves. So they harnessed up the pony-cart and made their way to the sea.

Sure enough, there on the sand was Seb, reading away from his little book. So many times he'd been through it now, he and the sea just about knew it by heart, between them.

'Why, Seb!' says his step-mother, sugar-sweet. 'We've been in such anxiety about you, child, wondering where you'd got to. Sure you'll be catching your mortal end of cold, sitting out on this great wet beach. Come home, come home, dear, for there's a grand cup of cocoa waiting for you, and a loaf with honey.'

'That's very kind of you ma'am,' Seb says back, all polite. 'But if my sisters are there I'd just as lief not, if it's all the same to you.'

'Oh, they've left,' she says quickly. 'So come along, dear, because the pony's beginning to fidget.'

And without waiting for yea or nay she and her husband hustled Seb into the pony-cart and drove quickly home. Didn't they give him a time, then, as soon as they got in, pinching, poking and slapping one minute, buttering him up with sweet talk the next, as they tried to find out his secrets.

'Where's the sunken Spanish galleon? Where's the plates of pearl and glasses of ruby and the hundred chests of silver ingots?'

'I'm not remembering,' says Seb.

'Didn't the sea tell you?'

'Sure the sea told me one thing and another, but I was paying no heed to tales of ruby glasses and silver ingots. What do I care about silver ingots?'

'You little wretch!' she screamed. 'You'd better remember, before I shake the eyes out of your head!'

'But I do remember one thing the sea told me,' he says.

'What was that?'

He'd got his head turned, listening, towards the window, and he said, 'The sea promised to come and help me if ever I was in trouble. And it's coming now.'

Sure enough, the very next minute, every single wall of the house burst in, and the roof collapsed like an eggshell when you hit it with a spoon. There was enough sea in the garden to fill the whole Atlantic and have enough left over for the Pacific too. A great green wave lifted Seb on its shoulder and carried him out, through the garden and away, away, over the fields and hills, back to his new home among the conches and coral of the ocean bed.

As for the step-mother and her husband, they were never seen again.

But Seb is seen, it's said; sometimes at one great library, sometimes at another, you'll catch a glimpse of him, taking out longer and longer books to read aloud to his friend the sea. And so long as he keeps the blue stone in his pocket, so long he'll go on reading, and hearing wonderful secrets in return, and so long the tides will go on standing still while they listen.

Is this a true tale, you ask?

As to that, I can't tell ...

Nutshells, Seashells

It was customary in the summer time for Miss Solliver's academy of dancing to remove itself to her farmhouse by the sea.

'Because,' said Miss Solliver, 'how can a lot of little cockneys express trees and grass and water in their dancing if they have never seen such things?' It was hardly true to say that her pupils were a lot of little cockneys – the members of her famous Ballets Doux had in their veins some of the bluest blood in Europe, but it was true that they were mostly city-bred and knew little about the country. Even the elegant Natasha Borodinova, whose father had once owned thousands upon thousands of acres, had never set foot in a real wood until she came to Miss Solliver's. The problem was soon solved, however, by hiring a large coach and taking them about on appropriate excursions – to a moonlit glade when they were doing *Sylphides*, a lake before a performance of *Swan Lake*, and so on.

This year there would be no need for the coach. The new ballet they were going to start rehearsing was called *Neptune*. It dealt with the sea, and there the sea was, ready to be studied, just at the foot of the cliffs. Several members of the corps de ballet looked at it carefully out of their bedroom windows as they unpacked; Natasha herself did so, and then glancing the other way into her mirror, performed some flowing, arching movements like those of a wave which at the last moment decides not to turn over.

Little Liz Miller, the youngest and smallest pupil, could not see the sea from her window. Her room, which she shared with two other girls, was downstairs and looked out into the garden, which was surrounded by a thick, high hazel hedge. Nothing could be seen of the sea from the garden; it was warm and sheltered even on the windiest days, and had a wide, flat lawn, admirable for practice.

After tea they all went out and limbered up. Presently Miss Solliver appeared and told them her plans, allotting the parts of Neptune, Alcestis, Tritons, Nereids, Dolphins and the rest. The part of Neptune was being taken by Boris Grigorieff and that of Alcestis by Natasha. Already they were in a far corner of the lawn practising a *pas de deux* which Miss Solliver was describing to them, and looking more like two swallows than two dancers as they curvetted about. The rest of the cast flitted and bounded in the wildest confusion enjoying themselves in the evening sun. Serious work would begin tomorrow.

Little Liz Miller escaped from it all and ran down the

lane which she had been told led to the sea. In a moment she could hear nothing of the laughter and voices – the road was deep sunk between banks, and shared its course with a stream which poured out of a hole in the bank and then cataracted down among tall grasses towards the sea.

Liz was so happy that she thought she would burst. For one thing it was her birthday, and her mother had given her a box to open on the train which proved to contain a large cake iced with pink icing and covered with silver balls. And then it was so wonderful to have come here. Liz had never been away from home before; never imagined places like this, like the sprawling whitewashed farmhouse all tangled round with fuchsia, or the strange bumpy up and down hills surrounding it, or the sudden swoop of cliff to the sea, or the sea itself, as blue as a street light and going in every direction at once.

Liz was the only real cockney in the school; she had been born within the sound of Bow Bells and her mother, Mrs Miller, was the charwoman who polished the long, long expanses of glassy floor in the London classrooms. Miss Solliver had taken in little Liz out of kindness to Mrs Miller, who had difficulties with a sick father and no husband and very little money.

'Mrs Miller is convinced that the child is an infant genius,' said Miss Solliver, smiling indulgently, to the Assistant Principal, Madame Legume, 'because she can skip and roller-skate. I am afraid it goes no further than that. But she will get good food with us and come to no harm, and be out of her mother's way. Poor little thing! She moves like a milkman's pony, all legs and joints. We shall never be able to make anything of her.'

'It is very charitable of you to take her in, *chérie*,' replied the ponderous Madame Legume.

Little Liz was not aware of this. She knew that her skipping and roller-skating were considered vulgar accomplishments, so she did not talk about them, but she had the purest and most loving admiration for all the other members of the school from Natasha downwards, and her only desire was to emulate them. She fully expected that in due time, if she worked hard, she would become a ballerina. She did not know that they were laughing at her and treating her like a mongrel puppy that had bounced in among a collection of aristocratic greyhounds.

She had to stop halfway down the lane and sit on the bank for a moment, hugging herself with happiness. Her birthday; and the cake; and having the privilege of sharing it with all these godlike creatures; it was almost too much. Even Natasha had eaten a piece, after delicately removing the silver balls and dropping them back into the little girl's hand.

'You eat them for me, Baby. They will break my teeth.'

The balls were in her pocket now, with some old hazelnuts found under the garden hedge as she came through.

But the last and almost unbearable happiness was that Miss Solliver had told her she could be a baby dolphin in the ballet. 'If you are good and do as you are told and don't get in the way.' To dance in a real ballet! She rolled round on to her stomach and lay kicking her legs. She did not know exactly what a dolphin was – some kind of a bird, perhaps.

There were harebells growing in the grass; she picked some and stuck them in her buttonhole, and then jumped up and ran on down the hill. Here was the sea, round this next corner, and a wonderful flat expanse of sand, just right for skipping on. Rather guiltily looking round to see that no one else from the school was about – but no, they were all up dancing in the garden – she pulled her skipping rope out of her pocket. When Liz was happy she had to skip. But first she must pick up those long pink shells and add them to the collection that was beginning to weigh down her pocket.

'Nutshells, seashells –' she sang, for she always made up her own skipping rhymes.

'Nutshells, seashells,
Silver balls, harebells,
River lanes, waterfalls,
Harebells, silver balls.'

And she began to skip.

When Liz skipped it was something quite special. Perhaps Miss Solliver had never seen her do it? The rope that she held seemed to become alive and partner her in a whirling dance, thinking up things to do for itself. Other children, back in the alley where Liz had learned to skip, could twirl the rope under them twice while they were in the air. Liz could do it seven times; and while she was in the air she moved from side to side like a gull glancing about over the water. Other children could skip a hundred times running, or a thousand times, but Liz could probably have gone on for ever if she had wanted to. She could toss the rope from her, catch it in mid-air, cross it into a figure eight and skip forward through the top loop and back through the bottom one; she could dance a mazurka or a reel while the rope flashed round her like a sword, she could dance a waltz or a minuet while it wove a web round her as shining and insubstantial as the web of ribbons round a maypole. She could swing the rope round underneath her by one handle until it made a spinning circular platform, while she spun round in the other direction above it; sometimes the rope was a planet and she was the sun, or the rope was Niagara and she was M. Blondin whirling down it in a barrel with her legs hooked over her ears; sometimes it was a tight-rope with its ends attached to nothing in particular and she was skipping along it; sometimes it was a cradle and she was rocking herself off to sleep in it.

As she skipped she sang her skipping rhyme, and at the end, when she had done all the different sorts of skipping that she could think of, she flipped out all the contents of her pockets and began to juggle with them. Pink shells, harebells, hazel-nuts and silver balls tossed up and down over the rope, and Liz skipped underneath them, keeping them all in the air and herself as well. At last she flopped down on a rock, letting them scatter round her. To her surprise there was a loud burst of applause from the sea.

She looked round, rather pink and embarrassed, to see who had surprised her at her forbidden pastime. The whole sea appeared to be crammed with people.

In the midst of them all was a huge man, very like Mr Sammons who kept the whelk stall in Vauxhall Bridge Road. He was sitting on something that might have been a whelk stall, trimmed up a bit; it rose up and down on the waves and was pulled by two great fish like the stone ones on either side of the Mercantile Insurance Building doorway, only these were very much alive, plunging and bouncing, and the man had to keep pulling on the reins. All around the stall, which was encrusted with lobsters and crabs, cockles and mussels, was swimming every sort of fish that Liz had ever seen on a barrow – cod, skate, halibut, herring, mackerel, sole, plaice and rock salmon – and many that she hadn't; not to mentions sea lions and walruses which she had once seen at the zoo. But in among these were much odder creatures: girls with tails playing on combs wrapped in paper, men with faces of fish, playing on mouth-organs; fish with wings, blowing trumpets; young ladies coming out of large whelk shells; birds with fins riding on oysters; lobsters blowing out long paper snakes that rolled up again with a click; fish with the faces of men, carrying shrimping nets; and so forth.

'Coo,' said Liz, shaken out of herself by this extraordinary scene. 'It's like Hampstead Heath on Bank Holiday.'

'Hello there, Liz,' shouted Neptune, waving a three-pronged toasting fork with an ice-cream cone on each prong. 'What can we do for you, dearie?'

'For *me*? Why?'

'You called us, didn't you? With your song about nut-shells and seashells.'

'But that was just a skipping song I made up.'

'Any little song will do for an incantation,' said Neptune, 'if you're doing something important.'

'But I wasn't doing anything important.'

'Your skipping is important, my girl. It's Art, that's what it is.'

'Miss Solliver says it's vulgar.'

'Well, nuts to Miss Solliver, whoever she may be. But that isn't the point. The point is, you called for us, whether you meant to or not, and here we are, so what would you like? Anything you've a fancy for? Free cruise to Madeira? Streamlined modern kitchen installed in your home? Winning ticket for the pools? Pearl necklace? Strawberry or vanilla? Whelks in vinegar?'

'No, there's nothing at all, really, thank you,' said Liz, beaming all over again at the thought of her happiness, 'I've got all I want already.'

A long sigh, of admiration, envy and amazement went up from the sea.

'Still,' said Neptune rallying, 'we could give her a good time, couldn't we, boys and girls? How about a bit of deep-sea rock, eh? Or a mug with a Present from Neptune on it? You come for a ride in my chariot and look at the sights before you go back.'

So she skipped out over the heaving backs of dolphins into the chariot and they went careering off, everyone singing Cockles and Mussels and offering her ice-cream, potato crisps and prawns in jellyfish.

'There you are,' said Neptune, when at last they put her down again after she had seen the sights. 'Now don't forget, if there's ever anything you need, or if you're in any sort of trouble – I don't say it's likely, mind, but you never know your luck – don't forget your old pal. Ta, ta, now, don't lose the skipping rope.'

Liz had thought she was happy when she went down the lane, but she was ten times happier when she ran up it. She was longing to confide in someone: perhaps she could tell one of the girls she slept with, but not tonight, it was far too late; the moon was up, and the lane was in deep shadow between its banks. It was strictly forbidden to be out after dark and Liz wondered if she could crawl through the hazel hedge and climb in her window without being caught. She resolved to try.

But as she stole along behind the hedge she was alarmed to hear the voices of Miss Solliver and Madame Legume who were, apparently, strolling in the moonlight on the other side.

'Yes, the casting is none of it bad except for the dolphins.

It is a pity that we have to have the little Miller girl in the show – it will give people a wrong idea of our standards. But it would look so invidious if she were the only one left out and her mother would be upset.'

'Yes! That child!' sighed Madame. 'No one could ever teach her to dance gracefully; too much vulgar bounce. I wonder if it would not be kinder to tell her and let her leave.'

'No, we'll keep her a bit longer, till things are easier for her mother. Everyone in the school quite understands the position. It's a nuisance about *Neptune* though – we'll have to keep her well at the back of the stage—'

The voices moved away again.

Liz stood where she was, almost turned to stone. Her face, which had been flushed, became very white. After a little while she turned and walked slowly back into the lane. She was stiff, as if her arms and legs ached all over, there was no vulgar bounce about her now. Then she sat down and looked at the little stream which came pouring out of its hole in the bank, as if she could not understand what she had heard and needed time to take it in. The water tumbled down, making its gentle noise in the quiet night, and still she looked and looked, until presently tears began to run down her face and she stood up because she was too wretched to stay sitting still.

'I can't go back there,' she thought, 'they all laugh at me and know I'm no good. How silly I must have been not to see that before.'

She did not blame them; in fact she felt sorry for them because it must have been so tiresome. It was not their laughter that ached in her bones; it was that dreadful sentence: 'No one could ever teach her to dance gracefully.'

Where was she to go? Then she saw a couple of harebells nodding in the moonlight and remembered her skipping rhyme:

Nutshells, seashells,
Silver balls, harebells –

It was easy to find a couple of nutshells in the hedge.
She ran down to the beach and picked up a handful of
shells. But what about the silver balls? Then she remembered that her skipping rope had silver ball-bearings in
the handles. She would have to break it to get them out.
What did that matter when she was never going to skip or
dance again – unless Neptune could help her? But suppose
the song didn't work? She gave a little sob as she knelt
down and cracked the handles on a rock.

Miss Solliver was very worried to hear next morning
that Liz Miller was missing.

'It has occurred to me that we were rather near her
window when we were talking last night,' she said to
Madame Legume. 'Do you suppose she could have heard
us? I don't know what I shall say to her mother if anything
has happened to her.'

Later on a pair of sandshoes and a broken skipping
rope, identified as belonging to Liz, were found at the
foot of the cliff. As nothing more was seen of her she was
presumed to have been drowned; the whole school was
much upset, the plans for the Neptune ballet were laid
aside and they all went back to London earlier than usual.
Miss Solliver wrote a polite note to Mrs Miller regretting
that her daughter had been drowned and suggesting that
it would be best if she did not continue her employment as

cleaner in the London school because the place would no doubt be painful to her; Miss Solliver enclosed a cheque in lieu of notice.

Seven years later a new ballerina took London by storm. Miss Solliver, full of curiosity, went to see her in the ballet *Atlantis* produced by a Mr Thalassoglu whom no one had ever heard of.

'She really is most strange,' said Miss Solliver to Madame Legume, in between two scenes. 'I suppose it's a trick of the lighting, but sometimes it's hard to decide whether she's swimming or flying. Do you suppose she's really hanging on wires?'

She leaned forward and stared intently at the silvery figure darting about the streets of the drowned city.

'It's odd, she reminds me of someone a little – who can it be?'

After the performance a journalist friend of Miss Solliver's offered to introduce her to the ballerina. They went round to her dressing-room.

In the far corner was old Grandfather Miller in a bathchair; knitting beside the fire was Mrs Miller; on the dressing-table lay a skipping rope. The ball-bearings were made from pearls, and round the coral handles was inscribed: 'A Present from Neptune'.

A Harp of Fishbones

Little Nerryn lived in the half-ruined mill at the upper end of the village, where the stream ran out of the forest. The old miller's name was Timorash, but she called him uncle. Her own father and mother were dead, long before she could remember. Timorash was no real kin, nor was he particularly kind to her; he was a lazy old man. He never troubled to grow corn as the other people in the village did, little patches in the clearing below the village before the forest began again. When people brought him corn to grind he took one-fifth of it as his fee and this, with wild plums which Nerryn gathered and dried, and carp from the deep millpool, kept him and the child fed through the short bright summers and the long silent winters.

Nerryn learned to do the cooking when she was seven or eight; she toasted fish on sticks over the fire and baked cakes of bread on a flat stone; Timorash beat her if the food was burnt, but it mostly was, just the same, because so often half her mind would be elsewhere, listening to the bell-like call of a bird or pondering about what made the difference between the stream's voice in winter and in summer. When she was a little older Timorash taught her how to work the mill, opening the sluice-gate so that the green, clear mountain water could hurl down against the great wooden paddle-wheel. Nerryn liked this much better, since she already spent hours watching the stream endlessly pouring and plaiting down its narrow passage. Old Timorash had hoped that now he would be able to give up work altogether and lie in the sun all day, or crouch by the fire, slowly adding one stick after another and dreaming about barley wine. But Nerryn forgot to take flour in payment from the villagers, who were in no hurry to remind her, so the old man angrily decided that this plan would not answer, and sent her out to work.

First she worked for one household, then for another.

The people of the village had come from the plains; they were surly, big-boned, and lank, with tow-coloured hair and pale eyes; even the children seldom spoke. Little Nerryn sometimes wondered, looking at her reflection in the millpool, how it was that she should be so different from them, small and brown-skinned, with dark hair like a bird's feathers and hazelnut eyes. But it was no use asking questions of old Timorash, who never answered except by grunting or throwing a clod of earth at her. Another difference was that she loved to chatter, and this was perhaps the main reason why the people she worked for soon sent her packing.

There were other reasons too, for, though Nerryn was willing enough to work, things often distracted her.

'She let the bread burn while she ran outside to listen to a curlew,' said one.

'When she was helping me cut the hay she asked so many questions that my ears have ached for three days,' complained another.

'Instead of scaring off the birds from my corn-patch she sat with her chin on her fists, watching them gobble down half a winter's supply and whistling to them!' grumbled a third.

Nobody would keep her more than a few days, and she had plenty of beatings, especially from Timorash, who had hoped that her earnings would pay for a keg of barley wine. Once in his life he had had a whole keg, and he still felt angry when he remembered that it was finished.

At last Nerryn went to work for an old woman who lived in a tumbledown hut at the bottom of the street. Her name was Saroon and she was by far the oldest in the village, so withered and wrinkled that most people thought she was a witch; besides, she knew when it was going to rain and was the only person in the place who did not fear to venture a little way into the forest. But she was growing weak now, and stiff, and wanted somebody to help dig her corn-patch and cut wood. Nevertheless she hardly seemed to welcome help when it came. As Nerryn moved about at the tasks she was set, the old woman's little red-rimmed eyes followed her suspiciously; she hobbled round the hut watching through cracks, grumbling and chuntering to herself, never losing sight of the girl for a moment, like some cross-grained old animal that sees a stranger near its burrow.

On the fourth day she said,

'You're singing, girl.'

'I – I'm sorry,' Nerryn stammered. 'I didn't mean to – I wasn't thinking. Don't beat me, please.'

'Humph,' said the old woman, but she did not beat Nerryn that time. And next day, watching through the window-hole while Nerryn chopped wood, she said,

'You're not singing.'

Nerryn jumped. She had not known the old woman was so near.

'I thought you didn't like me to,' she faltered.

'I didn't say so, did I?'

Muttering, the old woman stumped off to the back of the hut and began to sort through a box of mildewy nuts. 'As if I should care,' Nerryn heard her grumble, 'whether the girl sings or not!' But next day she put her head out of the door, while Nerryn hoed the corn-patch, and said,

'Sing, child!'

Nerryn looked at her, doubtful and timid, to see if she really meant it, but she nodded her head energetically, till the tangled grey locks jounced on her shoulders, and repeated, 'Sing!'

So presently the clear, tiny thread of Nerryn's song began again as she sliced off the weeds; and old Saroon came out and sat on an upturned log beside the door, pounding roots for soup and mumbling to herself in time to the sound. And at the end of the week she did not dismiss the girl, as everyone else had done, though what she paid was so little that Timorash grumbled every time Nerryn brought it home. At this rate twenty years would go by before he had saved enough for a keg of barley wine.

One day Saroon said,

'Your father used to sing.'

This was the first time anyone had spoken of him.

'Oh,' Nerryn cried, forgetting her fear of the old woman. 'Tell me about him.'

'Why should I?' old Saroon said sourly. 'He never did anything for *me*.' And she hobbled off to fetch a pot of water. But later she relented and said,

'His hair was the colour of ash buds, like yours. And he carried a harp.'

'A harp, what is a harp?'

'Oh, don't pester, child. I'm busy.'

But another day she said, 'A harp is a thing to make music. His was a gold one, but it was broken.'

'Gold, what is gold?'

'This,' said the old woman, and she pulled out a small, thin disc which she wore on a cord of plaited grass round her neck.

'Why!' Nerryn exclaimed. 'Everybody in the village has one of those except Timorash and me. I've often asked what they were but no one would answer.'

'They are gold. When your father went off and left you and the harp with Timorash, the old man ground up the harp between the millstones. And he melted down the gold powder and made it into these little circles and sold them to everybody in the village, and bought a keg of barley wine. He told us they would bring good luck. But I have never had any good luck and that was a long time ago. And Timorash has long since drunk all his barley wine.'

'Where did my father go?' asked Nerryn.

'Into the forest,' the old woman snapped. 'I could have told him he was in for trouble. I could have warned him. But he never asked *my* advice.'

She sniffed, and set a pot of herbs boiling on the fire. And Nerryn could get no more out of her that day.

But little by little, as time passed, more came out.

'Your father came from over the mountains. High up yonder, he said, there was a great city, with houses and palaces and temples, and as many rich people as there are fish in the millpool. Best of all, there was always music playing in the streets and houses and in the temples. But then the goddess of the mountain became angry, and fire burst out of a crack in the hillside. And then a great cold came, so that people froze where they stood. Your father said he only just managed to escape with you by running very fast. Your mother had died in the fire.'

'Where was he going?'

'The king of the city had ordered him to go for help.'

'What sort of help?'

'Don't ask *me*,' the old woman grumbled. 'You'd think he'd have settled down here like a person of sense, and mended his harp. But no, on he must go, leaving you behind so that he could travel faster. He said he'd fetch you again on his way back. But of course he never did come back – one day I found his bones in the forest. The birds must have killed him.'

'How do you *know* they were my father's bones?'

'Because of the tablet he carried. See, here it is, with his name on it, Heramon the harper.'

'Tell me more about the harp!'

'It was shaped like this,' the old woman said. They were washing clothes by the stream, and she drew with her finger in the mud. 'Like this, and it had golden strings across, so. All but one of the strings had melted in the fire from the mountain. Even on just one string he could make very beautiful music, that would force you to stop whatever you were doing and listen. It is a pity he had to leave the harp behind. Timorash wanted it as payment for looking after you. If your father had taken the harp with him, perhaps he would have been able to reach the other side of the forest.'

Nerryn thought about this story a great deal. For the next few weeks she did even less work than usual and was mostly to be found squatting with her chin on her fists by the side of the stream. Saroon beat her, but not very hard. Then one day Nerryn said,

'I shall make a harp.'

'Hah!' sniffed the old woman. 'You! What do you know of such things?'

After a few minutes she asked,

'What will you make it from?'

Nerryn said, 'I shall make it of fishbones. Some of the biggest carp in the millpool have bones as thick as my wrist, and they are very strong.'

'Timorash will never allow it.'

'I shall wait till he is asleep, then.'

So Nerryn waited till night, and then she took a chunk of rotten wood, which glows in the dark, and dived into the deep millpool, swimming down and down to the depths where the biggest carp lurk, among the mud and weeds and old sunken logs.

When they saw the glimmer of the wood through the water, all the fish came nosing and nibbling and swimming round Nerryn, curious to find if this thing which shone so strangely was good to eat. She waited as long as she could bear it, holding her breath, till a great barrel-shaped monster slid nudging right up against her; then, quick as a flash, she wrapped her arms round his slippery sides and fled up with a bursting heart to the surface.

Much to her surprise, old Saroon was there, waiting in the dark on the bank. But the old woman only said,

'You had better bring the carp to my hut. After all, you want no more than the bones, and it would be a pity to waste all that good meat. I can live on it for a week.' So she cut the meat off the bones, which were coal-black but had a sheen on them like mother-of-pearl. Nerryn dried them by the fire, and then she joined together the three biggest, notching them to fit, and cementing them with a glue she made by boiling some of the smaller bones together. She used long, thin, strong bones for strings, joining them to the frame in the same manner. All the time old Saroon watched closely. Sometimes she would say,

'That was not the way of it. Heramon's harp was wider,' or 'You are putting the strings too far apart. There should be more of them, and they should be tighter.'

When at last it was done, she said,

'Now you must hang it in the sun to dry.'

So for three days the harp hung drying in the sun and wind. At night Saroon took it into her hut and covered it with a cloth. On the fourth day she said,

'Now, play!'

Nerryn rubbed her finger across the strings, and they gave out a liquid murmur, like that of a stream running over pebbles, under a bridge. She plucked a string, and the noise was like that a drop of water makes, falling in a hollow place.

'That will be music,' old Saroon said, nodding her head, satisfied. 'It is not quite the same as the sound from your father's harp, but it is music. Now you shall play me tunes every day, and I shall sit in the sun and listen.'

'No,' said Nerryn, 'for if Timorash hears me playing he will take the harp away and break it or sell it. I shall go to my father's city and see if I can find any of his kin there.'

At this old Saroon was very angry. 'Here have I taken all these pains to help you, and what reward do I get for it? How much pleasure do you think I have, living among dolts in this dismal place? I was not born here, any more than you were. You could at least play to me at night, when Timorash is asleep.'

'Well, I will play to you for seven nights,' Nerryn said.

Each night old Saroon tried to persuade her not to go, and she tried harder as Nerryn became more skilful in playing, and drew from the fishbone harp a curious watery music, like the songs that birds sing when it is raining. But Nerryn would not be persuaded to stay, and when she saw this, on the seventh night, Saroon said,

'I suppose I shall have to tell you how to go through the forest. Otherwise you will certainly die, as your father did. When you go among the trees you will find that the grass underfoot is thick and strong and hairy, and the farther you go, the higher it grows, as high as your waist. And it is sticky and clings to you, so that you can only go forward slowly, one step at a time. Then, in the middle of the forest, perched in the branches, are vultures who will drop on you and peck you to death if you stand still for more than a minute.'

'How do you know all this?' Nerryn said.

'I have tried many times to go through the forest, but it is too far for me; I grow tired and have to turn back. The vultures take no notice of me, I am too old and withered, but a tender young piece like you would be just what they fancy.'

'Then what must I do?' Nerryn asked.

'You must play music on your harp till they fall asleep; then, while they sleep, cut the grass with your knife and go forward as fast as you can.'

Nerryn said, 'If I cut you enough fuel for a month, and catch you another carp, and gather you a bushel of nuts, will you give me your little gold circle, or my father's tablet?'

But this Saroon would not do. She did, though, break off the corner of the tablet which had Heramon the harper's name on it, and give that to Nerryn.

'But don't blame me,' she said sourly, 'if you find the city all burnt and frozen, with not a living soul to walk its streets.'

'Oh, it will all have been rebuilt by this time,' Nerryn said. 'I shall find my father's people, or my mother's, and I shall come back for you, riding a white mule and leading another.'

'Fairy tales!' old Saroon said angrily. 'Be off with you, then. If you don't wish to stay I'm sure *I* don't want you idling about the place. All the work you've done this last week I could have done better myself in half an hour. Drat the woodsmoke! It gets in a body's eyes till they can't see a thing.' And she hobbled into the hut, working her mouth sourly and rubbing her eyes with the back of her hand.

Nerryn ran into the forest, going cornerways up the mountain, so as not to pass too close to the mill where old Timorash lay sleeping in the sun.

Soon she had to slow down because the way was so steep. And the grass grew thicker and thicker, hairy, sticky, all twined and matted together, as high as her waist. Presently, as she hacked and cut at it with her bone knife, she heard a harsh croaking and flapping above her. She looked up, and saw two grey vultures perched on a branch, leaning forward to peer down at her. Their wings were twice the length of a man's arm and they had long, wrinkled, black, leathery necks and little fierce yellow eyes. As she stood, two more, then five, ten, twenty others came rousting through the branches, and all perched round about, craning down their long black necks, swaying back and forth, keeping balanced by the way they opened and shut their wings.

Nerryn felt very much afraid of them, but she unslung the harp from her back and began to play a soft, trickling tune, like rain falling on a deep pool. Very soon the vultures sank their necks down between their shoulders and closed their eyes. They sat perfectly still.

When she was certain they were asleep, Nerryn made haste to cut and slash at the grass. She was several hundred yards on her way before the vultures woke and came cawing and jostling through the branches to cluster again just overhead. Quickly she pulled the harp round and strummed on its fishbone strings until once again, lulled by the music, the vultures sank their heads between their grey wings and slept. Then she went back to cutting the grass, as fast as she could.

It was a long, tiring way. Soon she grew so weary that she could hardly push one foot ahead of the other, and it was hard to keep awake; once she only just roused in time when a vulture, swooping down, missed her with his beak and instead struck the harp on her back with a loud strange twang that set echoes scampering through the trees.

At last the forest began to thin and dwindle; here the tree-trunks and branches were all draped about with grey-green moss, like long dangling hanks of sheepswool. Moss grew on the rocky ground, too, in a thick carpet. When she reached this part, Nerryn could go on safely; the vultures rose in an angry flock and flew back with harsh croaks of disappointment, for they feared the trailing moss would wind round their wings and trap them.

As soon as she reached the edge of the trees Nerryn lay down in a deep tussock of moss and fell fast asleep.

She was so tired that she slept almost till nightfall, but then the cold woke her. It was bitter on the bare mountainside; the ground was all crisp with white frost, and when Nerryn started walking uphill she crunched through it, leaving deep black footprints. Unless she kept moving she knew that she would probably die of cold, so she climbed on, higher and higher; the stars came out, showing more frost-covered slopes ahead and all around, while the forest far below curled round the flank of the mountain like black fur.

Through the night she went on climbing and by sunrise she had reached the foot of a steep slope of ice-covered boulders. When she tried to climb over these she only slipped back again.

What shall I do now? Nerryn wondered. She stood blowing on her frozen fingers and thought, 'I must go on or I shall die here of cold. I will play a tune on the harp to warm my fingers and my wits.'

She unslung the harp. It was hard to play, for her fingers were almost numb and at first refused to obey but, while she had climbed the hill, a very sweet, lively tune had come into her head, and she struggled and struggled until her stubborn fingers found the right notes to play it. Once she played the tune – twice – and the stones on the slope above began to roll and shift. She played a third time and, with a thunderous roar, the whole pile broke loose and went sliding down the mountainside. Nerryn was only just able to dart aside out of the way before the frozen mass careered past, sending up a smoking dust of ice.

Trembling a little, she went on up the hill, and now she came to a gate in a great wall, set about with towers. The gate stood open, and so she walked through.

'Surely this must be my father's city,' she thought.

But when she stood inside the gate, her heart sank, and she remembered old Saroon's words. For the city that must once have been bright with gold and coloured stone and gay with music was all silent; not a soul walked the streets and the houses, under their thick covering of frost, were burnt and blackened by fire.

And, what was still more frightening, when Nerryn looked through the doorways into the houses, she could see people standing or sitting or lying, frozen still like statues, as the cold had caught them while they worked, or slept, or sat at dinner.

'Where shall I go now?' she thought. 'It would have been better to stay with Saroon in the forest. When night comes I shall only freeze to death in this place.'

But still she went on, almost tiptoeing in the frosty silence of the city, looking into doorways and through gates, until she came to a building that was larger than any other, built with a high roof and many pillars of white marble. The fire had not touched it.

'This must be the temple,' she thought, remembering the tale Saroon had told, and she walked between the pillars, which glittered like white candles in the light from the rising sun. Inside there was a vast hall, and many people standing frozen, just as they had been when they came to pray for deliverance from their trouble. They had offerings with them, honey and cakes and white doves and lambs and precious ointment. At the back of the hall the people wore rough clothes of homespun cloth, but farther forward Nerryn saw wonderful robes, embroidered with gold and copper thread, made of rich materials, trimmed with fur and sparkling stones. And up in the very front, kneeling on the steps of the altar, was a man who was finer than all the rest and Nerryn thought he must have been the king himself. His hair and long beard were white, his cloak was purple, and on his head were three crowns, one gold, one copper, and one of ivory. Nerryn stole up to him and touched the fingers that held a gold staff, but they were ice-cold and still as marble, like all the rest.

A sadness came over her as she looked at the people and she thought, 'What use to them are their fine robes now? Why did the goddess punish them? What did they do wrong?'

But there was no answer to her question.

'I had better leave this place before I am frozen as well,' she thought. 'The goddess may be angry with me too, for coming here. But first I will play for her on my harp, as I have not brought any offering.'

So she took her harp and began to play. She played all the tunes she could remember, and last of all she played the one that had come into her head as she climbed the mountain.

At the noise of her playing, frost began to fall in white showers from the roof of the temple, and from the rafters and pillars and the clothes of the motionless people. Then the king sneezed. Then there was a stirring noise, like the sound of a winter stream when the ice begins to melt. Then someone laughed – a loud, clear laugh. And, just as, outside the town, the pile of frozen rocks had started to move and topple when Nerryn played, so now the whole gathering of people began to stretch themselves, and turn round, and look at one another, and smile. And as she went on playing they began to dance.

The dancing spread, out of the temple and down the streets. People in the houses stood up and danced. Still dancing, they fetched brooms and swept away the heaps of frost that kept falling from the rooftops with the sound of the music. They fetched old wooden pipes and tabors out of cellars that had escaped the fire, so that when Nerryn stopped playing at last, quite tired out, the music still went on. All day and all night, for thirty days, the music lasted, until the houses were rebuilt, the streets clean, and not a speck of frost remained in the city.

But the king beckoned Nerryn aside when she stopped playing and they sat down on the steps of the temple.

'My child,' he said, 'where did you get that harp?'

'Sir, I made it out of fishbones after a picture of my father's harp that an old woman made for me.'

'And what was your father's name, child, and where is he now?'

'Sir, he is dead in the forest, but here is a piece of a tablet with his name on it.'

And Nerryn held out the little fragment with Heramon the harper's name written. When he saw it, great tears formed in the king's eyes and began to roll down his cheeks.

'Sir,' Nerryn said, 'what is the matter? Why do you weep?'

'I weep for my son Heramon, who is lost, and I weep for joy because my grandchild has returned to me.'

Then the king embraced Nerryn and took her to his palace and had robes of fur and velvet put on her, and there was great happiness and much feasting. And the king told Nerryn how, many years ago, the goddess was angered because the people had grown so greedy for gold from her mountain that they spent their lives in digging and mining, day and night, and forgot to honour her with music, in her temple and in the streets, as they had been used to do. They made tools of gold, and plates and dishes and musical instruments; everything that could be was made of gold. So at last the goddess appeared among them, terrible with rage, and put a curse on them, of burning and freezing.

'Since you prefer gold, got by burrowing in the earth, to the music that should honour me,' she said, 'you may keep your golden toys and little good may they do you! Let your golden harps and trumpets be silent, your flutes and pipes be dumb! I shall not come among you again until I am summoned by notes from a harp that is not made of gold, nor of silver, nor any precious metal, a harp that has never touched the earth but came from deep water, a harp that no man has ever played.'

Then fire burst out of the mountain, destroying houses and killing many people. The king ordered his son Heramon, who was the bravest man in the city, to cross the dangerous forest and seek far and wide until he should find the harp of which the goddess spoke. Before Heramon could depart a great cold had struck, freezing people where they stood; only just in time he caught up his little daughter from her cradle and carried her away with him.

'But now you are come back,' the old king said, 'you shall be queen after me, and we shall take care that the goddess is honoured with music every day, in the temple and in the streets. And we will order everything that is made of gold to be thrown into the mountain torrent, so that nobody ever again shall be tempted to worship gold before the goddess.'

So this was done, the king himself being the first to throw away his golden crown and staff. The river carried all the golden things down through the forest until they came to rest in Timorash's millpool, and one day, when he was fishing for carp, he pulled out the crown. Overjoyed, he ground it to powder and sold it to his neighbours for barley wine. Then he returned to the pool, hoping for more gold, but by now he was so drunk that he fell in and was drowned among a clutter of golden spades and trumpets and goblets and pickaxes.

But long before this Nerryn, with her harp on her back and astride of a white mule with knives bound to its hoofs, had ridden down the mountain to fetch Saroon as she had promised. She passed the forest safely, playing music for the vultures while the mule cut its way through the long grass. Nobody in the village recognized her, so splendidly was she dressed in fur and scarlet.

But when she came to where Saroon's hut had stood, the ground was bare, nor was there any trace that a dwelling had ever been there. And when she asked for Saroon, nobody knew the name, and the whole village declared that such a person had never been there.

Amazed and sorrowful, Nerryn returned to her grandfather. But one day, not long after, when she was alone, praying in the temple of the goddess, she heard a voice that said,

'Sing, child!'

And Nerryn was greatly astonished, for she felt she had heard the voice before, though she could not think where.

While she looked about her, wondering, the voice said again,

'Sing!'

And then Nerryn understood, and she laughed, and, taking her harp, sang a song about chopping wood, and about digging, and fishing, and the birds of the forest, and how the stream's voice changes in summer and in winter. For now she knew who had helped her to make her harp of fishbones.

The Boy with a Wolf's Foot

Once when I was travelling on a train from Waterloo to Guildford I looked out of the window and saw a boy and a great Alsatian dog running through the fields. Just for a few moments they seemed to be able to run faster than the train.

This is that boy's story.

The night of Will Wilder's birth was one of rain and gale; the wind went hunting along the railway embankment between Worplesdon and Woking like something that has been shut in a cave for twenty years.

Have you ever noticed what a lot of place names begin with a W in that part of the world? There's Wandsworth and Wimbledon, Walton and Weybridge and Worcester Park; there's Witley and Wanborough and West Byfleet; then, farther east, Waddon and Wallington, Woodmansterne, Woodside, Westerham, Warlingham, and Woldingham; it's as if ancient Surrey and Kent had been full of the wailing of wild things in the woods.

Maybe it was the wind that caused the train derailment; anyway, whatever the cause, young Doctor Talisman, who, tired out, had fallen asleep in his non-smoking carriage after coming off duty at the Waterloo Hospital, was woken by a violent grinding jerk and at the same moment found himself flung clean through the train window to land, unhurt but somewhat dazed, in a clump of brambles that luckily broke his fall.

He scrambled through the prickles, trying to rub rain and darkness from his eyes, and discovered that he was standing, as it were, in a loop of train. The middle section had been derailed and sagged down the embankment, almost upside down; the two ends were still on the track. People were running and shouting; lights flared; the rain splashed and hissed on hot metal; the wind howled over all.

Pulling himself together the doctor made his way to the nearest group.

'I'm a medical man,' he said. 'Is anybody in need of help?'

People were glad to turn to him; there were plenty of cuts and bruises and he was kept busy till the ambulances managed to make their way to the spot – which took time, for the crash had happened quite a long way from the nearest road, and they had to come bumping over grass and round bushes and past stacks of timber and bricks, through a bit of dark countryside that was half heath, half waste-land, with the River Wey running through it.

'Any seriously hurt?' an ambulance attendant asked, finding the young doctor working among the injured.

'One broken leg; several concussions; and there's one man killed outright,' said the doctor sadly. 'What makes it worse is that he had a young baby with him – born today I'd guess. The child's all right – was thrown clear in his carry-cot. Hasn't even woken.'

At that moment the baby did wake and begin to cry – a faint thread of sound in the roaring of the wind.

'He'd best come along with us,' said the ambulance man, ''till we find someone to claim him. Hear the wind – hark to it blow! You'd think there was a pack of wolves chasing along the embankment.'

Police and firemen arrived on the scene; the doctor was given a lift back to his home in Worplesdon. Next day he went along to the hospital where the injured people had been taken, and inquired after the baby.

'It's a sad thing,' the matron said. 'We've found out his father had just fetched him from the London hospital where he was born; his mother died there yesterday. Now the father's dead too the child has no relations at all; seems to be alone in the world. They'd just come from Canada, but had no family there. So the baby will have to go to the orphanage. And there's another queer thing: one of his feet is an odd shape, and has fur growing on it; as if the poor child hadn't enough bad luck already.'

Young Doctor Talisman sighed, looking at the dark-haired baby sleeping so peacefully in his hospital cot, still unaware of the troubles he had inherited.

'I'll call in at the orphanage from time to time and see how he goes on,' he promised. 'What's his name?'

'Wilder. Will Wilder. Luckily we found his birth certificate in the father's suitcase. What are you looking for, doctor?'

'I was just wondering what I had done with my watch,' Dr Talisman said. 'But I remember now; I took it off when I was helping to pull hurt people out of the wreckage last night and buckled it on to the branch of a tree growing on the embankment; I'll go back and find it sometime.'

True to his word, the doctor called at Worplesdon Orphanage to see young Will Wilder and, having formed the habit, he went on doing it year after year; became a kind of adopted uncle and, as there was nobody else to do it, took Will for trips to the zoo and the pantomime, days at the beach, and weekends canoeing on the river. No real relatives ever turned up to claim the boy. Nor did the doctor ever marry and have children of his own; somehow he was always too busy looking after his patients to have time for courtship; so a closeness grew between the two of them as year followed year.

Young Will never made friends at school. He was a

silent, inturned boy, and kept himself to himself. For one thing his odd foot made him lame, so he could not run fast; he was no good at football or sports, which helped separate him from the others. But though he could not run he loved speed, and went for long rides on a bicycle the doctor gave him; also he loved books and would sit reading for hours on end while everyone else was running and fighting in the playground. And, from being a silent, solitary boy he became a thoughtful, solitary young man. He did well at his exams, but seemed to find it hard to decide on a career. While he was thinking, he took a job in the public library, and lived on his own in a bedsitter. But he still called in on the doctor once or twice a week.

One time when he called in he said, 'I've been reading up the old history of this neighbourhood. And I found that way back, centuries back, there was a whole tribe of Wilders living in these parts.'

'Is that so?' said the doctor with interest. 'Maybe they were your ancestors. Maybe that was why your parents were travelling here, from Canada, to find the place their forefathers had come from. What did they do, those Wilders? Where did they live?'

'They were gypsies and tinkers and charcoal burners,' Will said. 'They lived in tents and carts on a piece of land known as Worplesdon Wilderness. I haven't been able to discover exactly where it was. It seems the Wilders had lived there so long – since Saxon times or before – that they had a sort of squatters' right to the land, although they never built houses on it.'

'You ought to try and find an ancient map of the neighbourhood,' the doctor said, 'and discover where it could have been.' He glanced at his watch – not the watch he had buckled on a tree on the railway embankment, for somehow he had never found time to go back and reclaim that one, but another, given him by a grateful patient. Patients were always giving him presents, because he was a good doctor, and kind as well. 'Dear me, how late it's getting. I must be off to the hospital; I promised to look in on old Mrs Jones.'

They walked to the gate together, Will limping; then Will mounted the bike and pedalled swiftly away. 'I wish something could be done about that foot of his,' the doctor thought, sighing over the contrast between Will's slow, limping walk and his speedy skilful progress on the bike. During the years since Will's babyhood the doctor had read up all the cases of foot troubles he could find, from fallen arches to ingrowing toenails, but he had never come across any case exactly like Will's. 'But there's that new bone specialist just come to the Wimbledon hospital; I'll ask his opinion about it.'

'I've found out a bit more about those Wilders,' Will said, next time he called on the doctor. 'They had a kind of a spooky reputation in the villages round about.'

'Gypsies and people living rough often did in the old days,' said the doctor. 'What were they supposed to do?'

'Anything from stealing chickens to hobnobbing with the devil! People were scared to go past Worplesdon Wilderness at night.'

'I wish we knew where it had been exactly,' said the doctor. 'Maybe where the football fields are now. Oh, by the way, there's a new consultant, Dr Moberley, at the Wimbledon hospital, who'd very much like to have a look at your foot, if you'd agree to go along there some time.'

Will's face closed up, as it always did when his foot was mentioned.

'What's the good?' he said. 'No one can do anything about it. Oh, very well –' as the doctor began to protest. 'To please you I'll go. But it won't be any use.'

'That certainly is a most unusual case,' the consultant said to Dr Talisman when they met at the hospital the following week. 'The only thing at all similar that I've ever come across was a case in India, years ago.'

'Could you do anything for him?'

'I'm not sure. I'll have to consider, and read up some old histories. I'll talk to you again about him.'

But in the meantime Will came to the doctor one evening and said,

'I've decided to go to Canada.'

'Why go there?' Dr Talisman was astonished. For, privately, he thought that in such an outdoor kind of place the boy with his lame foot would be at even more of a disadvantage. But Will surprised him still further by saying,

'The museum has given me a small grant to do some research into legends about wolves.'

'Wolves? I didn't know you were interested in wolves.'

'Oh yes, I am,' said Will. 'I've been interested in wolves for a long time. Ever since I was a child and you used to take me to the zoo, remember?'

Dr Talisman did remember then that Will always stopped for a long time by the wolves' enclosure and seemed as if he would rather stay watching them than look at anything else in the zoo; as if he felt he could learn something important from them.

'You won't be going to Canada for good?' he said. 'I shall miss you, Will.'

'Oh no, I'll be back. I just want to go to a place where there are still wolves wild in the woods. And while I'm over there I'll see if I can find out anything about my parents. Do you remember, among my father's things there was a little book with a couple of addresses in a town called Wilderness, Manitoba? A Mrs Smith and a man called Barney Davies. Of course they may be dead by now but I shall go there and see.'

'When are you off?'

'Tomorrow.'

'But what about Dr Moberley? He was going to think about your case.'

'He wouldn't have been able to do anything,' said Will, and limped down the garden to where his bike leaned against the fence.

'What about the Worplesdon Wilders? Did you find out any more about them?'

Will paused, his foot on the pedal.

'Yes,' he said, 'there was a tale in the Middle Ages that some of them practised something called lycanthropy.'

'Lycanthropy? But that's—'

'And there was one who lived in Saxon times – he was known as Wandering Will. He was supposed to come back every twenty years – to see how his descendants were getting on. And when he came back—'

'Oh dear, there's my phone,' said the doctor. 'Just a minute. Don't go yet, Will.'

But when the doctor returned from answering the phone, Will had cycled away.

'I wonder if he'll take his bike to Canada?' the doctor thought, looking after him.

Will did; the great plains of northern Canada are wide and flat, endless pine forest and corn prairie, corn prairie and pine forest, through which the roads, straight as knives, run on seemingly for ever; wonderful roads they are for cycling, though you seldom see a cyclist on them. People stared in amazement to see the little dot that was Will come pedalling over the horizon, on and on across that huge flatness, sometimes under the broiling sun, sometimes in a fierce wind that had swept straight down from the North Pole. Will was so quiet and serious, so straightforward and eager after knowledge, that people everywhere were ready to answer his questions. Yes, there were still wolves in the woods; yes, the Indians still believed that if you trod on a wolf's footprint you were drawn after him and must follow him helplessly day and night through the forest. And there were wolves in the prairie too, the Indians thought; when a wave of wind passed over those great inland seas of maize or wheat they would say, 'Look, a wolf is running through the corn!' and they believed that when the last sheaf was harvested, the wolf who was hiding in it must be caught, or there would be no grain harvest next year.

Did the wolves ever attack people? Will asked. Opinions were divided on that; some said yes, wolves would follow a sleigh all day, and pounce on the travellers when dark came; others said no, wolves seldom or never harmed a man but preyed only on small game, rabbits, chipmunks, or woodmice.

So Will went on, and at last he came to the town of Wilderness, which stood beyond the forest, on the edge of a great frozen swamp. Its wooden frame houses were so old, so grey, that they looked more like piles of lichen than human dwellings; not many people lived here now, and all the ones who did were old; they sat on their weathered porches in the sun all summer long, and in rocking-chairs by large log fires through the winter.

Will asked if Mrs Smith lived here still. No, somebody said, she died last winter. But, yes, old Barney Davies was still alive; he lived in the last house on the left, before the forest began.

So Will went to call on old Barney Davies; a little shrunken wisp of a man, as weathered and grey as his house. He sat by a pine-knot fire, over which Will heated a can of beans that he took from his pack.

'Yes,' said old Barney, eating his share of the beans, 'your grandfather used to live here. A quiet fellow he was, come from farther east. And his son, your father, yes, he lived here too, married Mary Smith and they went off saying they'd be back. But they never came back. Your grandfather died a couple of years after they left. Friend of mine, he was. I've a few of his things still, if you'd like to see them.'

'I'd like to very much,' said Will, making coffee in an old kerosene tin. So Barney Davies rummaged in a wooden chest and presently brought out a rope of Indian beads and a tobacco pouch and a mildewed leather belt and a small oilskin bag which held a wad of old, yellowed linen folded so damp and flat that Will had trouble prising it apart.

'Did my grandfather come from England?' he asked, holding the wad near the fire to dry it.

'Never said. Maybe he did. Never let on. Used to talk about England some. Made a living mending folks' pots and pans. A rare clever hand he was at that.'

'What else did he do?'

'Used to spend a lot of time in the woods. Whole days,

weeks together he'd be away. Not hunting or trapping. Never brought anything back. Seemed as if he was searching for something he never found.'

By now Will had got the linen a bit dried and, very slowly, with infinite care, he unfolded it.

'Kind of an old map?' said Barney Davies, taking the pipe from his mouth. 'Nowhere round here, though, I reckon.'

'No,' Will said, 'it's an English map.'

Ye Wildernesse of Whorplesdene, said the aged script across the top of the mildewed sheet. A river ran across the middle, the River Wey. Pine forests were drawn in one corner, ash forests in another. Camp, it said, between the pine forest and the ash. Norman Village, in another corner. Pitch kettles, charcoal fire. And, crossways, a path seemed to be marked. By straining his eyes, Will thought he could just make out the inscription along the path – which seemed, as far as he could judge, to follow the track now taken by the main line from Woking to Guildford: he read the name aloud.

'Wandering Will's Way.'

'Wandering Will,' said old Barney. 'I mind your grandfather talking about him.'

'What did he say?'

'The Indians believe in something called the Wendigo,' old Davies said. 'Half man, half wolf. Runs through the forest. When you hear him, you have to follow. Or if you tread on his footprint, or if he crosses your track.

Wandering Will was the same sort of critter, I reckon, only back in England. When he takes hold of you, he gives you a kind of longing for places where folk have never been, for things nobody knows.'

'Yes I see.'

'Want to keep the map?'

'May I?'

'Sure. It's properly yours. Well,' said old Barney, 'guess it's time for me to have my nap. Nice meeting you. So long, young fellow. Be going back to England now, I reckon?'

'Quite soon,' said Will. He put the map carefully in his pocket, mounted his bike, and rode away along the road that skirted between forest and swamp.

He reckoned that before nightfall he ought to be able to reach the next town, Moose Neck, forty miles farther on.

But he reckoned without the weather.

In mid afternoon a few flakes of snow began to fall, and by dusk they had increased to a blizzard. Will did not dare continue cycling, he could not see ahead; there was nothing to prevent his going straight into the swamp, or into the river that crossed it.

He dismounted, tightened the strings of his Parka, wrapped his waterproof cape round him, and huddled under the shelter of a spruce tree. Colder and colder it grew, darker and darker. The wind wailed through the forest like a banshee, like a mourning dragon, like a pack of starved dinosaurs. But in spite of the wind's roar, Will found it hard to keep his eyes open.

'I mustn't go to sleep,' he thought. 'To sleep in this would be certain death. But I'm so tired – so tired ... I shall have to go to sleep ...'

His eyes closed ...

It seemed to him that he was not alone. All about him he could feel the nearness of live creatures, feel movement and stirring and warm breath. It seemed to him that he opened his eyes and saw many pairs of green lights, shining luminous in the dark; he knew they were the eyes of wolves. He could feel fur, and the warmth of bodies pressed tight against him.

'Don't be afraid,' their voices were telling him. 'Don't be afraid, we are your friends.'

'I'm not afraid,' Will said truly. 'But why are you my friends? Most men are afraid of you.'

'We are your friends because you are part of our family. You are the boy with a wolf's foot.'

'Yes, that is true,' said Will in his dream.

'You do not belong here, though. You must go back to the place you came from; you will not get what you are seeking here.'

'What am I seeking?' Will asked.

'You will know when you find it.'

'Where shall I find it?'

'In your own place, where the wolves hunt no longer, save in dreams, or in memory, or in thought, or in fear. In your own corner of your own land, where your forefathers were friends to wolves, where your cradle lay across the wolf's path. You must go back. You must go back.'

'Yes,' said Will in his sleep. 'I must go back.'

He sank deeper into warmth and darkness.

When he next opened his eyes, a dazzling sun was rising over the swamp. No wolves were to be seen; but all round the spruce tree were the prints of paws like dogs' paws, only bigger; a tuft of grey fur had lodged under a flap of Will's Parka. He tucked it between the folds of his map of Worplesdon Wilderness.

Then, through the loose, soft new snow he bicycled on to Moose Neck.

When Will returned to England, he caught the 18.06 stopping train from Waterloo to Guildford. He got out at Worplesdon, left the station, climbed over a fence, and limped back along beside the track until he came to a piece of waste-land, dotted all over with clumps of bramble, and with piles of bricks and stacks of old timber.

Then he sat himself down on the embankment beside a clump of willow, and waited.

It was dark. The wind was rising.

Presently he felt a puff of cold air on his cheek, and heard a voice in his ear.

'Well, my child? Finding me took you long enough, and far enough! Now you have found me at last, what do you want?'

'I'm not certain,' said Will. 'When I was younger I always wanted one thing – to be able to run faster than a train. But now – I'm not sure. I seem to want so many different things.'

'Well, think carefully! If you wanted it, I could take away your wolf's foot; I could help you run faster than a train. Do you want to try?'

It seemed to Will that the cold wind caught him by the arms; he was running along the grassy embankment – fast, faster – black air and signal lights streamed past him, there was a black-and-gold ribbon ahead of him; he caught up and overtook the 22.50 from Waterloo and raced into Guildford ahead of it. Then the wind swung him round and took him back to where he had been before.

'That was wonderful!' Will gasped, grabbing the old willow to steady himself. 'But I know now that it's not what I want. I want to learn, I want to find out hundreds of things. Can you help me do that?'

'Yes, I can help you! Goodbye then, my child. You won't see me again, but I shall be with you very often.'

'Goodbye, great-grandfather,' said Will.

Dr Talisman was sitting late in his study, writing up his notes on the day's cases, when he heard his bell ring. He went to the door.

'Will! So you're back from Canada! It's good to see you – come and have some coffee.'

'It's good to be back.' Will limped into the doctor's study.

'So – did you hear many legends about wolves?'

'Yes, I did,' said Will. 'And some true tales too.'

'And did you find the town where your father had lived?'

'Yes, I found it.'

'By the way,' Dr Talisman said, 'Moberley thinks he can operate on that foot of yours and cure your lameness; make you the same as everybody else.'

'That's kind of him,' said Will, 'but I've decided I don't want an operation. I'd rather keep my foot the way it is.'

'Are you quite sure?' said the doctor, somewhat astonished. 'Well – you know your own mind, I can see. And have you decided on a career?'

'Yes,' Will said. 'I'm going to be a doctor, like you – Oh, I think this is yours: I found it tonight.'

And he handed the doctor a tarnished old watch that looked as if it had been buckled round the branch of a tree for twenty years.

Humblepuppy

Our house was furnished mainly from auction sales. When you buy furniture that way you get a lot of extra things besides the particular piece that you were after, since the stuff is sold in lots: Lot 13, two Persian rugs, a set of golf-clubs, a sewing-machine, a walnut radio-cabinet, and a plinth.

It was in this way that I acquired a tin deedbox, which came with two coal-scuttles and a broom cupboard. The deedbox is solid metal, painted black, big as a medium-sized suitcase. When I first brought it home I put it in my study, planning to use it as a kind of filing-cabinet for old typescripts. I had gone into the kitchen, and was busy arranging the brooms in their new home, when I heard a loud thumping coming from the direction of the study.

I went back, thinking that a bird must have flown through the window; no bird, but the banging seemed to be inside the deedbox. I had already opened it as soon as it was in my possession, to see if there were any diamonds or bearer bonds worth thousands of pounds inside (there weren't), but I opened it again. The key was attached to the handle by a thin chain. There was nothing inside. I shut it. The banging started again. I opened it.

Still nothing inside.

Well, this was broad daylight, two o'clock on Thursday afternoon, people going past in the road outside and a radio schools programme chatting away to itself in the next room. It was not a ghostly kind of time, so I put my hand into the empty box and moved it about.

Something shrank away from my hand. I heard a faint, scared whimper. It could almost have been my own, but wasn't. Knowing that someone – something? – else was afraid too put heart into me. Exploring carefully and gently around the interior of the box I felt the contour of a small, bony, warm, trembling body with big awkward feet, and silky dangling ears, and a cold nose that, when I found it, nudged for a moment anxiously but trustingly into the palm of my hand. So I knelt down, put the other hand into the box as well, cupped them under a thin little ribby chest, and lifted out Humblepuppy.

He was quite light.

I couldn't see him, but I could hear his faint inquiring whimper, and I could hear his toenails scratch on the floorboards.

Just at that moment the cat, Taffy, came in.

Taffy has a lot of character. Every cat has a lot

of character, but Taffy has more than most, all of it inconvenient. For instance, although he is very sociable, and longs for company, he just despises company in the form of dogs. The mere sound of a dog barking two streets away is enough to make his fur stand up like a porcupine's quills and his tail swell like a mushroom cloud.

Which it did the instant he saw Humblepuppy.

Now here is the interesting thing. I could feel and hear Humblepuppy, but couldn't see him; Taffy, apparently, could see and smell him, but couldn't feel him. We soon discovered this. For Taffy, sinking into a low, gladiator's crouch, letting out all the time a fearsome throaty wauling like a bagpipe revving up its drone, inched his way along to where Humblepuppy huddled trembling by my left foot, and then dealt him what ought to have been a swinging right-handed clip on the ear. 'Get out of my house, you filthy little canine scum!' was what he was plainly intending to convey.

But the swipe failed to connect; instead it landed on my shin. I've never seen a cat so astonished. It was like watching a kitten meet itself for the first time in a looking-glass. Taffy ran round to the back of where Humblepuppy was sitting; felt; smelt; poked gingerly with a paw; leapt back nervously; crept forward again. All the time Humblepuppy just sat, trembling a little, giving out this faint beseeching sound that meant: 'I'm only a poor little mongrel without a smidgeon of harm in me. *Please* don't do anything nasty! I don't even know how I came here.'

It certainly was a puzzle how he had come. I rang the

auctioneers (after shutting Taffy *out* and Humblepuppy *in* to the study with a bowl of water and a handful of Boniebisk, Taffy's favourite breakfast food).

The auctioneers told me that Lot 12, Deedbox, coal-scuttles and broom cupboard, had come from Riverland Rectory, where Mr Smythe, the old rector, had lately died aged ninety. Had he ever possessed a dog, or a puppy? They couldn't say; they had merely received instructions from a firm of lawyers to sell the furniture.

I never did discover how poor little Humblepuppy's ghost got into that deedbox. Maybe he was shut in by mistake, long ago, and suffocated; maybe some callous Victorian gardener dropped him, box and all, into a river, and the box was later found and fished out.

Anyway, and whatever had happened in the past, now that Humblepuppy had come out of his box, he was very pleased with the turn his affairs had taken, ready to be grateful and affectionate. As I sat typing I'd often hear a patter-patter, and feel his small chin fit itself comfortably over my foot, ears dangling. Goodness knows what kind of a mixture he was; something between a spaniel and a terrier, I'd guess. In the evening, watching television or sitting by the fire, one would suddenly find his warm weight leaning against one's leg. (He didn't put on a lot of weight while he was with us, but his bony little ribs filled out a bit.)

For the first few weeks we had a lot of trouble with Taffy, who was very surly over the whole business and blamed me bitterly for not getting rid of this low-class intruder. But Humblepuppy was extremely placating, got back into his deedbox whenever the atmosphere became too volcanic, and did his very best not to be a nuisance.

By and by Taffy thawed. As I've said, he is really a very sociable cat. Although quite old, seventy cat years, he dearly likes cheerful company, and generally has some young cat friend who comes to play with him, either in the house or the garden. In the last few years we've had Whisky, the black-and-white pub cat, who used to sit washing the smell of fish-and-chips off his fur under the dripping tap in our kitchen sink; Tetanus, the hairdresser's thickset black, who took a fancy to sleep on top of our china-cupboard every night all one winter, and used to startle me very much by jumping down heavily on to my shoulder as I made the breakfast coffee; Sweet Charity, a little grey Persian who came to a sad end under the wheels of a police-car; Charity's grey-and-white stripey cousin Fred, whose owners presently moved from next door to another part of the town.

It was soon after Fred's departure that Humblepuppy arrived, and from my point of view he couldn't have been more welcome. Taffy missed Fred badly, and expected *me* to play with him instead; it was sad to see this large elderly tabby rushing hopefully up and down the stairs after breakfast, or hiding behind the armchair and jumping out on to nobody; or howling, howling, howling at me until I escorted him out into the garden, where he'd rush to the lavender-bush which had been the traditional hiding-place of Whisky, Tetanus, Charity, and Fred in succession. Cats have their habits and histories, just the same as humans.

So sometimes, on a working morning, I'd be at my wits' end, almost on the point of going across the town to our ex-neighbours, ringing their bell, and saying, 'Please can Fred come and play?' Specially on a rainy, uninviting day when Taffy was pacing gloomily about the house with drooping head and switching tail, grumbling about the weather and the lack of company, and blaming me for both.

Humblepuppy's arrival changed all that.

At first Taffy considered it necessary to police him, and that kept him fully occupied for hours. He'd sit on guard by the deedbox till Humblepuppy woke up in the morning, and then he'd follow officiously all over the house, wherever the visitor went. Humblepuppy was slow and cautious in his explorations, but by degrees he picked up courage and found his way into every corner. He never once made a puddle; he learned to use Taffy's cat-flap and go out into the garden, though he was always more timid outside and would scamper for home at any loud noise. Planes and cars terrified him, he never became used to them; which made me still more certain that he had been in that deedbox for a long, long time, since before such things were invented.

Presently he learned, or Taffy taught him, to hide in

the lavender-bush like Whisky, Charity, Tetanus, and Fred; and the two of them used to play their own ghostly version of touch-last for hours on end while I got on with my typing.

When visitors came, Humblepuppy always retired to his deedbox; he was decidedly scared of strangers; which made his behaviour with Mr Manningham, the new rector of Riverland, all the more surprising.

I was dying to learn anything I could of the old rectory's history, so I'd invited Mr Manningham to tea.

He was a thin, gentle, quiet man, who had done missionary work in the Far East and fell ill and had to come back to England. He seemed a little sad and lonely; said he still missed his Far East friends and work. I liked him. He told me that for a large part of the nineteenth century the Riverland living had belonged to a parson called Swannett, the Reverend Timothy Swannett, who lived to a great age and had ten children.

'He was a great-uncle of mine, as a matter of fact. But why do you want to know all this?' Mr Manningham asked. His long thin arm hung over the side of his chair; absently he moved his hand sideways and remarked, 'I didn't notice that you had a puppy.' Then he looked down and said, 'Oh!'

'He's never come out for a stranger before,' I said.

Taffy, who maintains a civil reserve with visitors, sat motionless on the nightstore heater, eyes slitted, sphinx-like.

Humblepuppy climbed invisibly on to Mr Manningham's lap.

We agreed that the new rector probably carried a familiar smell of his rectory with him; or possibly he reminded Humblepuppy of his great-uncle, the Rev. Swannett.

Anyway, after that, Humblepuppy always came scampering joyfully out if Mr Manningham dropped in to tea, so of course I thought of the rector when summer holiday time came round.

During the summer holidays we lend our house and cat to a lady publisher and her mother who are devoted to cats and think it a privilege to look after Taffy and spoil him. He is always amazingly overweight when we get back. But the old lady has an allergy to dogs, and is frightened of them too; it was plainly out of the question that she should be expected to share her summer holiday with the ghost of a puppy.

So I asked Mr Manningham if he'd be prepared to take Humblepuppy as a boarder, since it didn't seem a case for the usual kind of boarding-kennels; he said he'd be delighted.

I drove Humblepuppy out to Riverland in his deed-box; he was rather miserable on the drive, but luckily it is not far. Mr Manningham came out into the garden to meet us. We put the box down on the lawn and opened it.

I've never heard a puppy so wildly excited. Often I'd been sorry that I couldn't see Humblepuppy, but I was never sorrier than on that afternoon, as we heard him rushing from tree to familiar tree, barking joyously, dashing through the orchard grass – you could see it divide as he whizzed along – coming back to bounce up against us, all damp and earthy and smelling of leaves.

'He's going to be happy with you, all right,' I said, and Mr Manningham's grey, lined face crinkled into its thoughtful smile as he said, 'It's the place more than me, I think.'

Well, it was both of them, really.

After the holiday, I went to collect Humblepuppy, leaving Taffy haughty and standoffish, sniffing our cases. It always takes him a long time to forgive us for going away.

Mr Manningham had a bit of a cold and was sitting by the fire in his study, wrapped in a Shetland rug. Humblepuppy was on his knee. I could hear the little dog's tail thump against the arm of the chair when I walked in, but he didn't get down to greet me. He stayed in Mr Manningham's lap.

'So you've come to take back my boarder,' Mr Manningham said.

There was nothing in the least strained about his voice or smile but – I just hadn't the heart to take back Humblepuppy. I put my hand down, found his soft wrinkly forehead, rumpled it a bit, and said,

'Well – I was sort of wondering: our spoilt old cat seems to have got used to being on his own again; I was wondering whether – by any chance – you'd feel like keeping him?'

Mr Manningham's face lit up. He didn't speak for a minute; then he put a gentle hand down to find the small head, and rubbed a finger along Humblepuppy's chin.

'Well,' he said. He cleared his throat. 'Of course, if you're *quite* sure—'

'Quite sure.' My throat needed clearing too.

'I hope you won't catch my cold,' Mr Manningham said. I shook my head and said, 'I'll drop in to see if you're better in a day or two,' and went off and left them together.

Poor Taffy was pretty glum over the loss of his playmate for several weeks; we had two hours' purgatory every morning after breakfast while he hunted for Humblepuppy high and low. But gradually the memory faded and, thank goodness, now he has found a new friend, Little Grey Furry, a nephew, cousin or other relative of Charity and Fred. Little Grey Furry has learned to play hide-and-seek in the lavender-bush, and to use our cat-flap, and clean up whatever's in Taffy's food bowl, so all is well in that department.

But I still miss Humblepuppy. I miss his cold nose exploring the palm of my hand, as I sit thinking, in the middle of a page, and his warm weight leaning against my knee as he watches the commercials. And the scritch-scratch of his toenails on the dining-room floor and the flump, flump, as he comes downstairs, and the small hollow in a cushion as he settles down with a sigh.

Oh well. I'll get over it, just as Taffy has. But I was wondering about putting an ad into *Our Dogs* or *Pets' Monthly*: Wanted, ghost of mongrel puppy. Warm welcome, loving home. Any reasonable price paid.

It might be worth a try.

The Lost Five Minutes

There was once a dragon who kept a museum and did quite well from it. He had become (at some point during the several thousand years of his life) rather bored with just eating people, and the museum made a nice change and a new interest. He charged ten-pence entry fee and instead of requests to the public not to smoke and climb over the guard ropes and touch the exhibits, there were simply signs saying, *If you do not behave yourself properly the dragon will eat you.*

You'd think such signs might have stopped people from being very keen to visit the museum. Not a bit of it; there was a kind of daredevil fascination about going there. People simply flocked. Maybe it was from the excitement of not knowing quite what the dragon would consider proper behaviour, maybe – human nature being what it is – because everyone had a sneaking hope of seeing somebody else misbehave and get swallowed. But quite apart from these reasons, the museum was a particularly nice and unusual one, everything in it being made of glass. In the main hall stood Cinderella's glass coach and slippers, on the first floor was a glass doll's house all complete with furniture, lovely music was played all day long on a glass harmonica, and in smaller rooms there were collections of glass fruit from Venice (every colour of the rainbow), glass animals, and a whole aviary full of birds with spun-glass tails.

For that matter the dragon himself was made of glass: stretched out in the sun or coiled round the great ilex tree in front of his museum he made a stunning spectacle, each feather and scale flashing like a frozen waterfall, his three heads keeping a sharp lookout for customers in every direction. It was due to his three heads, in fact, that the dragon had given up his regular habit of eating people, since, either because of old age or greed or just general cantankerousness, the heads could never come to an agreement over whose turn it was to swallow the next victim. And all this fuss before meals gave the dragon indigestion and hiccups, so, on the whole, he had found it simpler not to swallow anybody. Of course the public did not know this.

In every museum there has to be somebody to dust the exhibits and take the entry money, unlock the doors in the morning, and tell people where to find the ladies' room. The dragon had occasionally encountered difficulty in hiring assistants, but at present he was very well suited: the post was filled by a blind girl called Anthea, who was extremely careful and conscientious, besides being very pretty; she never broke anything when she dusted, having that extra sixth radar-sense of where objects are that blind people often possess; she wasn't a bit frightened of the dragon, since she had never seen how huge and dazzling he was; and because she was blind, people never tried to cheat her out of the ten-pence entry fees. And in the evenings she told fairy tales to the dragon, which also made a pleasant change for him. Nobody had ever done such a thing before.

One day, however, Anthea came to grief.

The dragon had recently come by a new treasure for his museum: a very beautiful clock, every single part made of glass, hands, face, chimes, pendulum, mainspring, and all. It stood under a glass dome and when you looked at it you felt that you could see time itself in motion. The clock was more than five hundred years old and had neither lost nor gained a minute, nor stopped, since the day it was first wound up.

Well! Anthea had been showing the clock to the editor of the local paper, the *Wormley Observer*. He was a fat little fellow, all smiles, called Sam Inkfellow. She was just replacing the glass dome when somebody jogged her elbow. Instinctively Anthea clasped both hands round the dome to steady it, and set it carefully down, but as she did so she tipped it – *very* slightly – against the works of the clock, shaking loose five minutes from the mainspring. And before she could push the dome straight, the five minutes had slipped out from underneath and darted away through the museum window, like a handful of bees escaped from the hive.

The museum had a very efficient alarm system. Bells began to clang, doors automatically slammed, two carloads of police came whizzing round from headquarters, and the dragon cascaded off his ilex tree like a glacier from an erupting volcano. But the mischief was done: the five minutes could not be recovered.

'It was my fault,' poor Anthea said to the police. 'Please let everyone go, nobody has stolen anything. It was entirely my fault.'

The police could only agree. All the members of the public who had been shut in by the automatic doors were allowed to go.

'You realize this means I shall have to swallow you?' the dragon said very crossly to Anthea.

'Yes, I know; I really am sorry; please go ahead and get it over with.'

'Certainly not; things must be done in due order,' the dragon said hurriedly. 'I shall swallow you a week today, next Thursday, at eight a.m.' For he was not at all pleased at the troublesome prospect of having to find a new assistant, nor at the likelihood of hiccups and indigestion. 'After all, somebody may return the five minutes before then.'

He stuck up a sign saying LOST: FIVE MINUTES. FINDER PLEASE RETURN TO WORMLEY MUSEUM. REWARD.

Meantime the *Wormley Observer* came out with huge headlines: DRAGON TO SWALLOW ANTHEA NEXT THURSDAY A.M.

Special excursion buses were to be run to the town from as far away as Brighton, the *Observer* published a timetable of events, and wooden seats were hastily erected in the main square facing the museum. Extra police were fetched in and a one-way traffic system organized; the shops sold little dragon flags, a commemorative stamp was issued, and a public holiday was proclaimed.

'All this publicity is very distasteful,' said the dragon.

'I really am sorry,' said Anthea.

But Sam Inkfellow, editor of the *Wormley Observer*, was rubbing his hands. He had a guaranteed sale of eighty thousand copies for next week's issue (in full colour), the Press Association had paid him large sums for the story with pictures, and he was charging ten guineas a head standing room in the *Observer* offices, which overlooked the square.

Anthea's family were very upset. Her brother Bill came and tried to reason with the dragon.

'Can't you substitute some other penalty?' he asked.

'Sorry,' said the dragon, 'I regret the necessity quite as much as you. But rules are rules. You produce the lost five minutes, I'll cancel the swallowing.'

'Would any five minutes do?'

'Oh, certainly, just so long as they are a *spare* five minutes.'

When he heard this, Bill became slightly more cheerful. Surely, he thought, someone about the town must have five minutes to spare. Or even three, or two; it shouldn't be impossible to collect a few minutes together.

Elderly people seemed likelier to have time to spare, so he called on the old lady who lived next door to his mother. She was working in her garden, picking up scattered rose petals and brushing all the grass blades straight, so that they pointed in one direction.

'Mrs Pentecost, could you possibly spare five minutes for my sister Anthea? Or even two, or one?'

'Oh, good gracious, no, my dear boy! Why, when you get to my age, there's so little time left that you have to hoard every minute like gold. Sorry, but no, no indeed!'

Perhaps it would be better to try somebody young, Bill thought, so he went to a schoolmate of Anthea's.

'Sally, could you possibly spare me a minute or two for Anthea?'

'Oh, honestly, Bill darling, I'm so rushed I haven't a *second* to spare, let alone a minute, what with getting my hairpiece set, and my false lashes stuck on, and my nail varnish dried, and reading my horoscope in *Seventeen*, and looking for a new leather jacket—'

Bill saw that he would get no help there.

Nobody, anywhere, had any time to spare, not just at that moment.

'If you were to come back next week—' they said. 'Now next week I'll have *plenty* of spare time. Or next month, even better. But just *now*, I do seem to be so terribly short of time—'

So it went on, all week. On Wednesday evening Bill went to see the dragon.

'Can't you suggest anybody, sir?'

The dragon scratched one of his glass chins, with a sound like icicles tinkling together.

'What about the town genius?' he suggested after a while.

'That's a good idea!' said Bill. 'Why didn't I think of it? I'll go directly.'

And he got on his bicycle and set out.

The town genius, whose name was Marcantonio Smith-to-the-power-Nine, did not live in the town nowadays; he had done so, but found he got little work done because people constantly came to him asking him to solve their problems. So now he lived in a tower with a studio in the nearby forest, where he painted, and sculpted, and wrote poetry, and conceived new kinds of mathematics, and invented perpetual motion, and did everything a genius ought.

Bill found him in the studio, standing in front of a huge slab of marble. On the marble he had a football-sized lump of colourless, shining material, like nothing so much in the world as a good big bit of glass putty, and he was squeezing it, and kneading it, and thumping it, and palming it into a ball, and then flattening it out, and then rolling it into a sausage, and then tearing it into thin strips, and those into small nuggets, shaping them all into different things, animals, stars, flowers, figures, faces, and then flinging the whole mass together and beginning again.

He smiled kindly at Bill, who came hesitating over and stood by the slab.

'Well, my boy? What can I do for you?'

All this time Smith never stopped playing with his lump of stuff.

Bill told the sad tale of Anthea and the lost five minutes.

'I was wondering if you could possibly help us,' he said. 'The dragon's due to swallow her tomorrow at eight sharp unless I can find somebody to give me five minutes.'

'Five minutes? Is that all?' said Marcantonio Smith-to-the-power-Nine, and he pinched off a bit of his glass putty. 'Do you want them marked out?' He flattened the small lump he had pinched off, shaped it into an oblong, and marked five divisions on it as if he were scoring fudge.

Bill gaped, watching him, and he laughed.

'No need to look so astonished, my boy!'

'It seems so easy for you!'

'It's always easy to be kind.'

'It didn't seem so for the other people in the town,' Bill said. 'How is it you have so much time when nobody else has any at all?'

'That's because I only do the things that interest me. Do you want your five minutes in a bag?'

'Oh, please don't trouble, sir. I wish I could do something for you!'

'Bring your sister to visit me some time. I like fairy tales too.'

Bill promised he would, and hurried off with his precious little slab of minutes.

But on the way home he met a man mending a puncture in his motor bike tyre.

'Oh, my dear boy! Is that five minutes you have there?

Do, do give me just a couple of them – *please*! I'm on my way with a pardon for my son, who is to be shot for a crime he didn't commit, and I got this puncture – I shall be too late – do, please help me!'

Bill was very upset. I can't let the poor man's son be shot for a crime he didn't commit, though, he thought; maybe the dragon will let me off two of the minutes.

Very carefully he broke two off his little cake of five. 'Heaven bless you, my boy. You're a real friend in need!'

Bill went on his way. Near the town harbour he met a man running downhill, hell-for-leather.

'Help!' he called. 'Is that three minutes you've got there? Give me two of them, like a good lad! Do you see that ship, that's just casting off anchor? If only I can get to her before she sails, I've got a bit of paper to deliver on board that will stop two great countries going to war against each other, but I'm going to be too late – for heaven's sake, help me!'

Very unwillingly, Bill gave him a couple of minutes – maybe, after all, the dragon will be satisfied with just one, he thought – and the man rushed away down the hill.

Now there was only one minute left. And as Bill was passing the school, a teacher put his head out of the window and said,

'Please, my dear boy! I see that is a spare minute you have in your hand. Be a good lad and give it here – if I had just *one* minute more, before the end-of-period bell went, I could teach this class of thickheads how to save the world!'

Well, you can't refuse a request like that, can you? So Bill handed over his last minute. By now it was seven o'clock Thursday morning.

So Bill went along to the dragon and explained that, although Mr Smith had given him five minutes, due to one reason or another he had been obliged to part with them.

'Since it's now my fault the five minutes are lost,' he said, 'will you please swallow me instead of Anthea?'

The dragon considered. He saw the benefits of this arrangement, because at least Anthea would then still be available to dust the exhibits and tell him fairy tales at night.

'Very well,' he said at length grudgingly. 'But you are both putting me to a lot of trouble.'

By now huge crowds of people were gathered in Wormley Square, all anxious to watch the swallowing.

'Ma,' said a child to his mother, 'shall we be able to see the young lady go all the way down inside the dragon?'

'D'you think he'll chew her?' said a man to his wife.

'I am excited, Henry!' said a girl to her boyfriend. 'Which head will he swallow with, d'you think?'

This remark was overheard by the dragon's heads, who instantly began arguing.

'Belial had the last swallow, it's my turn!'

'No it isn't, Thammuz, it's mine!'

'Shut up, Dagon and Thammuz, it's neither of you, it's my turn!'

The dragon retired behind his ilex to sort the matter out. Eight o'clock struck and people began to grumble because nothing had happened.

'What's the crowd waiting for?' asked a traveller in false teeth who happened to be passing through the town.

'Don't you know? Our dragon's going to swallow the young lady because she let five minutes escape from the clock last Thursday.'

'No, she didn't, it was five hours!'

'Anyway it isn't her, it's the young gentleman he's going to swallow.'

'It wasn't from the clock they escaped.'

'They didn't escape, he ran over them on his motor bike and squashed them flat.'

'No he didn't, they rolled down the hill and fell on to a ship!'

'That's a lie! My hubby told me the teacher at the school gave them to his physics class and they dissolved them in sulphuric acid!'

Everybody began arguing. People came to blows.

But the traveller pushed his way to the ilex tree and said to the dragon,

'If you are really about to swallow that young lady for losing five minutes, you are being unfair! I happened to be in your museum last Thursday and I saw that man there jog her elbow. He did it on purpose. *He's* the one you ought to swallow!'

'Really?' said the dragon, and he turned to the man the traveller had indicated and swallowed him down without more ado (Belial happened to be the nearest head and did the job). Everybody saw fat little Sam Inkfellow travel slowly and spirally down through all the glass coils. It took a long time, gave the dragon frightful indigestion and hiccups, and he was sorry for himself for three days after, but all the townspeople were delighted, as Inkfellow had published unpleasant, and mostly untrue, stories about them all in his paper at one time or another.

'No hard feelings, I hope?' said the dragon to Anthea when his hiccups had died down and he was feeling better. 'You'll come back and start helping in the museum again, won't you?'

'I'm afraid not,' said Anthea. 'No hard feelings, but Bill and I are going to go and work for the town genius. So goodbye.'

And that is what they did. The dragon had terrible trouble finding another assistant. And in the end, Anthea married Marcantonio Smith-to-the-power-Nine.

Moonshine in the Mustard Pot

Deborah had been anxious about what she would find to do while staying with Granny. 'Shall I take toys?' she asked, and her father said, 'It's a very small house. Better not take much, there'd be nowhere to put them.'

At home, in spite of having her own room crammed with toys, Deborah was bored as often as not, and would trail in search of her mother, yawning. 'What shall I do, Mum?' And her mother, quick as lightning, always found her a job: tidy the spoon-and-fork drawer, polish the silver teapot, weed the moss out of the front steps. Not bad things in themselves, but jobs done to fill a gap are like going on your favourite walk with somebody who walks at the wrong pace; there's no satisfaction in them. Deborah never seemed to learn this, though; sooner or later she would be wandering back again saying, 'I'm bored; what shall I do?'

Granny's house, in a little street in York, certainly was tiny. The first thing Deborah noticed about it was that it sat flat on the ground: no front steps to climb (or weed). Somehow, inside, you could feel the earth, right there under the floor; it was a bit like going out in very thin-soled slippers. Her father said, 'I hope I've brought enough warm clothes for her; I wasn't sure what to pack.' Deborah's mother was sick; that was why she was here. 'Well, if the weather gets cold, the child can wear my woollies,' Granny said. 'She's almost as big as I am.'

It was true, Granny was small, suited to her house, thin and straight as a candle in her cotton-print pinafore over two layers of jerseys. Her hair, fine and soft and white as smoke, she wore pinned back in a bun; and her face was white as well, so pale that Deborah feared at first she must be ill too, but no ill person could possibly be as energetic as Granny. 'It's just old age,' she explained about the paleness later. But the black eyes in this white face sparkled like two live coals; they were never still for a single second.

The minute Deborah's father had gone, Granny showed her over the house. There were four rooms and a pantry. The doors were so narrow that you could only just carry a chair through them. The stairs, equally narrow, led straight out of the kitchen, through another tiny door. 'Suppose you wanted to get a big piece of furniture up?' said Deborah. 'Wouldn't have room to put it anywhere if I did,' said Granny. 'Besides, I don't like big furniture, I like things I can move myself. The biggest load isn't the best.'

Indeed, all her things were small and light – stools, low narrow beds, tiny velvet nursing chairs. 'Bought at auctions,' said Granny with satisfaction. 'Never paid more than a pound for anything yet. And I make sure I can lift it before I bid.' She had painted and upholstered every-thing herself: clear soft blues, apple-green, warm brick-red, white, rose-pink, purple, indigo, chocolate-brown. The whole house sang and flashed with colour. 'How did you paint the ceilings, Granny?' 'With a brush tied to a mop handle, of course. Never believe in getting in a man for jobs you can do yourself. Take days and make the fiend's own mess and charge double, the robbers. Now: I've just bought this little chest for the bathroom, I thought you might like to help me paint it.'

'Oh, yes!' said Deborah. 'What colour?'

The bathroom was brand-new, Granny's pride. 'Your Uncle Chris made it for me when he was home from India for a month. Didn't tell the Council. What the eye doesn't see, the heart doesn't grieve over. Oh, he's a clever one, that Chris.' About the size of a kitchen table, the bathroom was tucked in a corner of Granny's bedroom. 'Before, I had to go all the way to the wash-house.' The wash-house was in the tiny garden, out at the back, across a brick-paved yard and also a narrow lane, which was a public right-of-way. 'Not very convenient when you want to brush your teeth,' said Deborah. 'Oh, I did *that* in the kitchen sink.' 'But what about in the winter when it snows?' 'Well, you get used to anything.' But Deborah was glad Uncle Chris had made the bathroom. It was lined with dark-blue tiles and had a white basin and toilet seat, so they decided to paint the chest scarlet, and it took them till lunch-time. 'And after lunch, while it dries,' said Granny, 'I'll show you my allotment, where I grow my vegetables.'

'Not your back garden?'

'No, that's for sitting in.'

The back garden, past the wash-house, and about the same size as the kitchen, had grass and four apple trees, covered with young uncurling leaves and coral buds. 'Apples off them lasted me all winter,' said Granny. 'Coxes, Laxtons, Bramleys, and Beauty of Bath.' Deborah had never heard these names and now learned them in a jingle, 'Cox and Laxton, left of the path, on the right Bramley and Beauty of Bath.'

Granny fetched her bicycle out of the wash-house. It was painted apple-green (the same paint as the kitchen dresser) and was so ancient that the back wheel was protected by a skirt-guard of strings threaded from holes in the rear mudguard to the hub. A square hamper was strapped on the carrier. 'For vegetables,' explained Granny. She added a cushion on top of this and sat Deborah on top of the cushion; so they rode through the city of York to Granny's allotment, which lay out on the far side. Granny pedalled along at a spanking pace and the traffic kept respectfully out of her way.

'Granny,' yelled Deborah through the mixed sun and wind and shadow of their headlong course, 'can you explain something Dad said?'

'What was that, child?'

'He said, "I hope Deb will be all right with her. Mother takes her life in her hands twenty times a day."'

Granny swept the bike up to a hawthorn hedge covered with white blossom and a gate which led to the allotments.

'That's the way life ought to be taken,' she said. 'If you have your life in your hands, then you can steer it, can't you? I wouldn't give a brass button for the sort of life that's just left lying around, like wet washing. Now, we'll do the hoeing and weeding first, then I'll introduce you to the bees.' Hoeing and weeding was not at all dull, as Deborah had expected it would be, because in among her vegetables Granny had scarlet anemones and dark-blue grape hyacinths and dark velvet-brown wallflowers and clumps of primroses; there was always something beautiful to look at and smell. 'I like them and the bees like them,' said Granny. 'Nothing but vegetables makes a dull garden.'

Also, while they hoed, Granny taught Deborah some of what she called her gardenwork poems: Bonnie Kilmeny gaed up the glen, Where the pools are bright and deep, Loveliest of trees the cherry now, No man knows Through what wild centuries Roves back the rose. 'I have different ones for doing housework, of course, and different again for sewing and going to sleep. Everybody ought to have plenty of different sets of poems stowed away.'

Deborah had never thought of poems as something you could *have*, like flowers or stamps or coloured stones. 'Of course you can,' said Granny. 'And the best of it is, that everybody can have them at the same time. And they cost no more than moonshine in the mustard pot.'

'Moonshine in the mustard pot – what's that, Granny?'

'Why, nothing at all.'

Granny was full of interesting proverbs. 'If that was a bear, it would have bit you,' she said when you were looking for something and it was right under your nose. 'I'd rather have stags led by a lion than lions led by a stag. He that would live for ever must eat sage in May. Ask a kite for a feather, she'll tell you she has only enough to fly with.'

'Now you can come and meet the bees, but you must put on a hat first.'

Secretly, Deborah was rather nervous of the bees, who lived in three square white hives by the hedge, but they seemed to be wholly busy helping themselves to nectar from the hawthorn blossoms. 'This is their hard-work time,' said Granny. 'Well, all times are busy for bees, once the daffodils begin. Of *course* they must get to know you. Don't you know that you have to tell bees everything?'

'What happens if you don't?'

'They pine and grieve and sing a sad song. And the honey tastes bitter. Or there is none. Besides,' said Granny as they put on old panama hats draped with white veiling that made them look like Tibetan monks from Mount Everest, 'your name, Deborah, *means* a bee, didn't you know? So that's a special reason for saying good afternoon to them.'

She lifted off the tops of the hives like box-lids and Deborah, peering down through the drifts of her veil, saw the black and gold bees, more than any multiplication table could calculate, in their tireless to-and-fro. The combs, pale caskets of wax, were built between glass panels so that Granny could see how the honey was getting on. It glowed light and dark gold through the rind of wax, and the bees made a continuous murmur, a blend of all their different humming notes, with one steady note in the centre.

'Perhaps that's the Queen Bee's note?' said Deborah.

On the bike ride home (they kept on their hats and veils for the ride and were the wonder of York) Granny taught Deborah a bees' poem – 'Heavy with blozzomz be The Rozes that growzez In the thickets of Zee.'

After tea Deborah helped Granny water and feed all her plants, of which she had about fifty, ten to each windowsill. She talked to them all the time she was attending to them, scolding and praising, telling them news of the plants in the other rooms and the garden. 'They grow better if you do that,' she explained.

'Do you say poetry to them too?'

'You can do,' said Granny, 'but plants seem to like real news best. Sometimes I read the paper aloud to them. They do like music, it's true. And of course you have to listen to them as well.'

'Listen?'

'In case they've got any grievances. Terrible ones for sulking, some plants can be.'

When the plants were done, there was the starling to be given his lesson.

'When he first came to live here I could hardly abide him,' said Granny. 'Squawk, squawk. Not one decent sensible thing to say for himself. But Mr Jones (who's the music teacher at the Comprehensive and plays the piano in Chapel on Sundays), he lent me a book of tunes you can teach birds. Hundred years ago, everybody was doing it. Now it's all television, nobody has time.'

The starling, Jack, who had a lame leg, had been rescued by Granny from a cat and had decided to take up residence in her house. He came and went as he chose, through a hinged pane in the kitchen window, but spent most of his time sitting among the willow-pattern china on the green dresser. He was as glossy himself as a lustre mug. 'I will say for him, he's clean as a Quaker,' said Granny. 'I've never known him clarty the place but once, and then the curtains were drawn and he couldn't find his way out. Here's the book, do you want to teach him a tune?'

The book, which looked quite old, was called *100 Prettie Tunes to teach Canarays or Other Cage Birdes*. But Deborah was obliged to confess that she could not read music.

'Can you not, child? Oh well, I'll soon teach you that.' And in half an hour she had. 'See, it goes up and down along the stave – that one is *God Save The Queen*, Queen Anne it would have been then I daresay – so you can see how it works – and this note here, like a ball of wool on a knitting-needle, that's C –' she sang it in her thin, clear old voice. 'But how do you know?' said Deborah. 'Well, if you don't know you can find out from the tuning-fork,' said Granny and took it out of a stone marmalade jar on the dresser, a thick Y of blue metal, 'but you'll soon find you remember the note.' Deborah found this was true. They began teaching Jack the first line of *Lillibullero* but quite soon he became tired and stuck his head under his wing. 'You'd better go off to bed too, child,' said Granny. 'Oh, but I don't go to bed nearly as early as this at home,' said Deborah. 'No, but at home I daresay you don't get up so early,' said Granny. 'I'm always up at six and through the housework before breakfast, so as to have it out of the way for the day.'

Deborah ate her supper in front of the kitchen fire: cup of cocoa, piece of dripping-toast, and the crusty end of the loaf spread thick with globby home-made yellow plum jam.

'Now,' said Granny, 'you must choose your bedroom.

The back one's bigger, and has the sun in the morning, and looks over the garden, but then you have to come through my room to get to the bathroom. Or, if you like, you can have my room, and then you're right beside the bathroom – but then *I* shall have to come past *you* – and I warn you, old people are always getting up in the night. After seventy you sleep with one eye open.'

Deborah thought she would have the back room; she didn't want to turn Granny out of her bed. Granny gave her a small torch in case she needed to find her way to the bathroom in the dark. Also an apple.

'Eat an apple going to bed, make the doctor beg his bread.'

Perhaps because of the apple, or the cocoa, or the strange bed, or because she had learned so many new things during the previous day that her mind was buzzing with them, like all three bee-hives put together – Deborah woke after she had been asleep about four hours, and sat straight up in bed. Perhaps, after all, it was the moon that had woken her – a bent square of light lay, half on the white wall, half on the blue-painted floor. There seemed no need for her torch, after all, but Deborah took it just in case Granny's room was darker. She slipped out of bed on to her little braided rag rug (made long ago by Granny who had promised to show Deborah how) and tiptoed across the shiny blue floor into the other room. That was quite light too, with reflected moonlight from the windows of the houses across the street. There lay

Granny, a small breathing shape, flat in her bed. But the minute Deborah set foot in her room she sat bolt upright, throwing off the covers. Her straight white hair, free from its knot, hung round her face like a child's. Her eyes were fast shut.

'Who are you? And where are you from?' she said sharply. Her voice was different from her daytime voice – higher and clearer too; a younger person's voice.

Deborah's heart battered against her ribs, like Jack the starling looking for his way out through the curtains.

'It's Deborah, G-Granny,' she stammered. 'I'm Deborah!'

Granny turned her impatient, sightless face towards the door. 'No, who *are* you?' she snapped. 'Who *are* you, I said – and where are you *from?*'

'But I'm Deb – your grand-daughter Deborah. From – from home. From London.'

'Who *are* you?' Granny repeated for the third time. 'Where are you *from?*'

Deborah was so terribly daunted and abashed by this that she retreated on tiptoe from the doorway, back across her moonlit floor, and then jumped into bed and pulled the bedclothes tight round her chin. She was half afraid that Granny would come after her. Nothing of the kind had ever happened to her before. She felt terribly queer – as if she had found herself, by mistake, inside the egg of some strange bird who was shouting Trespassers will be Prosecuted in her ear. Or a mermaid's egg – do mermaids have eggs?

Luckily she had not wanted to go to the bathroom too desperately; before she knew it, she had slipped back into sleep.

In the morning, Granny was so exactly the way she had been yesterday – which seemed so just and precisely Granny-ish that Deborah could not imagine her ever having been different – she was so neat and active, so brisk and talkative, nipping about with a mop and duster while the kettle sang, and the bacon frizzled – that Deborah plucked up courage, and while they were upstairs, making the beds, told what had happened in the night.

'You sat up in bed, Granny, as straight as a stick, and you said it in *such* a fierce tone that I was really frightened.'

Granny couldn't help laughing at the story – in fact she laughed so much that she had to sit down on Deborah's blue bedroom chair – but when she had recovered she said. '*That* won't do, will it now? We certainly can't have you frightened like that.'

'Why do you suppose you didn't believe me when I said I was Deborah?'

'I daresay because it seemed too simple.'

'How do you mean, Granny?'

'Well when you're asleep you're much more than just plain Deborah, aren't you? You might be a princess, or a fish, or a tree, or a horse, or the moon, or a whole lot of things one after the other – you're everything that you ever dreamed you were, all baked together in a pie of sleep.'

'But *you* were the one who was asleep, Granny – I was awake!'

'That's what I mean,' said Granny. 'If you're explaining to someone who's asleep, you've got to put it *all* in – not just the top layer. Do you see?'

'I'm not sure,' said Deborah.

'Well, of course, the first thing is not to be scared, if it should happen again. Just give me an answer. And if it isn't the right one, first time, go on trying till it is. Or walk past. After all, I'm only your old Granny!'

'But suppose *you're* a fish, or a tree, or the moon?'

'Sit down and eat your breakfast, child – the bacon's getting cold. Cold bacon hot again, that love I never.'

After breakfast they sides-to-middled some worn sheets – Granny let Deborah tear the old flimsy cotton which gave with a scrumptious purring rip, like wood splitting but softer. Then the torn edges had to be hemmed and the outer sides joined together; Deborah turned the handle of the sewing-machine while Granny guided the cotton under the bright foot and the rapid-thudding needle that flashed up and down. Then they changed over, Granny turned the wheel and Deborah learned to steer the material; it was more difficult than she had expected and she made some wild swerves before she mastered the knack, but, as Granny said, it all helped to strengthen the sheet and was good practice.

Then they added a bit more on to the patchwork quilt which was, Granny said, the ninth she had made; it was already single-bed size but needed to be double, since it was intended for a wedding present. The pieces were six-sided, the colours mostly dark reds and pale greens and cream colour, but each corner contained a circle made up of all kinds of patterned bits, and in these Deborah recognized pieces left over from several dresses that Granny had made and sent her in the past.

Then they white-washed the inside of the wash-house, using big brushes and buckets of distemper and getting so splashed that they had to have baths afterwards. Then they bicycled down to the shops, singing *Pop Goes the Weasel*, and bought half a pound of rice, which cost considerably more than twopence, and a tin of treacle, and Granny taught Deborah how to make a treacle tart. And then they ate it.

After lunch they went to the allotment and planted young leeks and sowed peas and two kinds of beans. 'You'll have to come back to help me eat them,' said Granny. 'I don't want to go away from here, ever,' said Deborah. On the ride back they went round by way of York Minster for Deborah to see it; the arched ceilings inside reminded her of Granny's patchwork quilt, except that they were creamy white, but they were covered with the same kind of patterns; and the windows were *exactly* like the inside of Granny's house; they gave just the same feeling of somebody's having thought very hard, deciding which were their favourite colours, and then put every single one of them in.

That night Deborah went to sleep almost before her head hit the pillow (Jack the starling had learned another six notes of *Lillibullero* but it had been hard work); then the moonlight woke her, four or five hours later, shining like a TV screen on the wall opposite her face. She crept across her room and was halfway to the bathroom door when, as before, Granny woke and sat bolt upright in bed.

'Who's that? Who are you?'

'I'm a bicycle,' Deborah said, guessing. Granny moved her head a little, frowning in her sleep, as if this *might* be the right answer, but not all of it. 'I'm the wind, I'm a streetlight, I'm a one-way street, I'm a zebra-crossing.'

At each of these things, Granny nodded. 'Where are you from?' she said.

'I'm – I'm from the other side of town,' said Deborah, and made her escape into the bathroom. When she came out again, Granny was lying down fast asleep, and never stirred.

'There you are, you see!' she said triumphantly next morning. 'I told you it was perfectly simple. All you have to do is say the right thing!'

That day they made new curtains for the kitchen (Granny had bought the material ten years ago at a jumble sale and had been saving it for just this use – it was plain black-and-white stripes with, just here and there, a bunch of green grapes printed on the cotton); they sponged the shiny indoor plants, sowed some broccoli and got ready a cold frame for vegetable marrows. They told each other stories. They bought a small, undressed doll at an auction (along with a stepladder, a jam cauldron, and five large earthenware crocks) and began planning its wardrobe. Deborah learned how to make shepherd's pie. They picked big bunches of grape hyacinths and narcissi, which smelt sweet as honey all over the house.

And that night, when Granny said, 'Who are you?' Deborah said, 'I'm a needle, I'm a spoon. I'm a length of cotton. I'm a ladder, I'm a bird, I'm a window.'

'Where are you from?'

'I'm from all around you, Granny.'

Instantly Granny lay down, perfectly satisfied, it seemed, with these answers.

During the next month of nights they played this game many times in Granny's sleep. It was like fishing, Deborah thought – except that she was not quite sure who was the fish and who the fisher. Granny asked the question and Deborah threw out her answer like a line; sometimes it was right, sometimes wrong. If it was wrong, Granny would not have it. 'I'm an apple, Granny.' 'No, you are *not*! *Who* are you, and where are you from?' Some nights Deborah got it right at once, sometimes she had to feel her way slowly, guess by guess, cold, warm, warmer, until she hit the right answer. 'I'm a line, a rope, a fish, a trout, an eel!' 'And where are you from?' 'From – from Newfoundland!' And where she got that answer from, goodness knows; but it seemed to satisfy Granny.

Of course, Deborah did not get up every night; some-times, tired from all they had done and said and learned and thought, she slept clean through the silent hours of dark. But she often had a curious feeling on those nights, even more than after the ones when she had woken, that Granny had been asking questions and she had been answering them, without the need for words.

At last a letter came. Deborah's mother was better. And then her father came to take her home.

Deborah did not want to go. She wanted to stay so badly that it seemed probable no one but Granny could have persuaded her to get into the car with her father. 'You'll be able to show your mother how well you can make a shepherd's pie and a treacle tart. And I'm going to give you these plants to look after for me, and you must write to me every single week and tell me how they are getting on.'

Loaded with all the things she had made – the pair of trousers, the doll with two sets of clothes, the pot of lemon curd, the cake, the Japanese garden made from stones and moss in a foil pie-pan, the pincushion stuffed with dried coffee-grounds, the clove orange – Deborah went home. 'Why can't everybody be like Granny?' she wept and her father, driving the car, said, 'It's just as well everybody isn't, or there wouldn't be room to move in the world with all the things that got made and everybody bustling about,' and he swerved his car to avoid an old lady who was bicycling along with a full basket.

In fact Deborah settled down at home again not too badly. She had all her new skills to practise, and she kept up the habit of learning a new poem every day, and she wrote to Granny, with pictures, about the growth of the plants and about her new baby brother, and sent patch-work pieces, and sometimes a poem that she had written herself. Granny always answered right away, on a post-card. 'Pieces v. useful. Glad to hear about the plants. Jack learned *Danny Boy*. Strawb. jam turned out well. Saving pot for you. Too busy to write more at present. G.'

The cards were always gorgeously coloured. Granny got them from a bookshop near the Minster, they were reproductions of pictures that had taken her fancy, and presently Deborah had half a wall full of them – battle-scenes, flowers, landscapes, ships, angels, breakfast tables.

And then one day Deborah's father had a telegram: YOUR MOTHER INJURED IN STREET ACCIDENT IN YORK HOSPITAL PLEASE COME.

'I always said she'd end up in trouble, riding that crazy old bicycle,' he said, distractedly throwing socks and razor and pyjamas into a bag.

Deborah got out her own bag and began packing it. 'No, no, dear, *you* can't go,' said her mother. 'It wouldn't be at all suitable. Children are only in the way when people are ill; it wouldn't do at all.'

But Deborah was so absolutely ferociously determined – 'Granny would *want* me. After all, I know how she does things – I'd know *everything* she wanted –' that in the end, somehow, without anyone actually having said yes, you can go, she was there in the car, driving to York with her father. 'We'll go straight to the hospital,' he said. 'But you won't be allowed in to see her, I'm sure, so don't expect it.'

'Why not?'

'Children never are allowed to visit sick people in hospitals.'

'Why not?'

He didn't really know. 'I suppose they'd bother the other patients.'

'I wouldn't!'

'Well, anyway ...'

At the hospital they talked to a matron. It seemed the accident hadn't been Granny's fault: two cars had collided and one had bounced back on to Granny who was coming up behind it on her bike. 'I'm afraid she's very ill indeed,' said the matron. 'She may not know you.' And there was absolutely no question of Deborah's being allowed in. She was told to wait in a dull empty room with nothing but a flat green bench and a smell of old flowers. Her father went with the matron and Deborah sat wretchedly, kicking her heels against the legs of the bench and trying to say over one of the poems she had learned. 'Where the bee sucks, there suck I, In a cowslip's bell I lie ...' But this seemed no place for poems.

The worst of it was, she began to be certain that she could hear Granny's voice. So sure was she that she moved out of the waiting-room and along a wide, huge, shiny corridor with doors all along each side. She listened, she walked a little farther, she listened again.

She came to a door that was not quite shut, and pushed it open a bit. And then she could definitely hear Granny's voice inside, with all its old impatience, saying,

'No – who are you? Who *are* you?'

She heard her father's voice. 'It's John, Mother. Don't you know me?' Granny's voice had been clear, but his sounded all choked up with worry and embarrassment.

Deborah put her head round the door. There were several people by a bed, doctors, she supposed, and nurses in white, and her father sitting on a chair. And Granny, trying to push herself up in the bed – at least it must be Granny because the white hair was certainly hers, but the face was mostly bandaged – and a nurse was trying to persuade her to lie down again.

'No, but who *are* you?' cried out Granny, as if she could hardly bear all this stupidity, and Deborah, running to the bedside, said, quickly, before anybody could stop her,

'Hullo, Granny! It's me – I'm a wing, I'm a flying leaf, no, I'm a bit of thistledown, I'm something high up and light, I'm a bird – *no* – I'm a *bee*, Granny! I'm Deborah! I'm a bee!'

Granny turned her head towards Deborah's voice and listened keenly. Then she slowly settled herself back into a curled-up lying position, facing Deborah. A nurse tucked the clothes round, but she pushed them sharply off again, as if they bothered her.

'Deborah,' she said. 'That's it! You're Deborah. And do you know what you must do?'

'What, Granny?'

'You have to go and tell the bees, child ... tell them ...'

'Yes, I'll tell them, Granny,' said Deborah. Tears were running down her cheeks, which was silly, because of *course* the bees must be told; anybody knew that was the first thing that must be done after an accident or any important happening.

A nurse led her out of the room – there was a lot going on – and she was put in a different place to wait: someone's office. But Deborah was thinking about the bees. Really they should be told at once; she slid down off her chair and walked to the end of the corridor, where she found a fire door and an outside flight of steps. She and Granny had passed the hospital once on one of their bicycle trips; she was pretty sure that she could find her way from there to the allotments.

The broad beans they had sown now dangled heavy pods, lumpy as Christmas stockings; some of the peas had pods, others were still in blossom. Marigolds and bachelors' buttons flashed among the rows of green. But the sun was gone by now; dew was falling. The sky was a pale oyster-green. All but the most far-wandering bees had returned to their hives for the night.

Deborah knelt in the cold, dewy grass by the middle hive. She said,

'It's about Granny. I think you ought to know—'

Inside the bees seemed to be listening. Their slumbrous murmur had dwindled to a sigh that was hardly louder than her own breathing. And then she heard – or did she imagine it? – a tiny voice that might have been from the hives or from somewhere deep inside her own head, a voice imperiously demanding,

'But who are *you*?'

'I'm Deborah,' she whispered. And then she lay face down on the wet grass and cried her heart out. It was there that her father, scolding, anxious, harassed, sad, finally found her.

'Did Granny die then?' said Deborah.

She was quiet now, calmer than her father, who could only nod.

'Well, I expect it was best,' Deborah said, after a minute. 'She would think it was better than not being able to ride her bike or dig in her garden or climb ladders, or any of the things she always did. Can you get someone to move her hives to Putney? Are there bee-movers?'

'Move them to *Putney*? Are you crazy? People don't keep bees in Putney!'

'Why not? Our garden's just as big as Granny's allotment. And there's all Putney Heath too. We've got to look after Granny's bees; besides, she left them to me; they're mine now. And you have to take care of bees; you can't just leave them to starve.'

'I don't know *what* your mother will say . . .'

But he knew she would get her way; as she had over the trip to York. On the way to London, while Deborah, curled in the back seat, taught lame Jack to whistle the first four bars of *Cherry Ripe*, her father, driving the car, thought to himself, We've got another of them in the family now. She's going to be exactly the same.

A Jar of Cobblestones

Some of you may know a town called Rye. In that town is a narrow, cobbled street, slicing up at an angle of thirty degrees from the dockside to the church. Mermaid Street, it's called, with the Mermaid Inn on the left near the top. And on the right, a little farther down, is this old haunted Jeake's House, built more than two hundred years ago by an astrologer. Well, one summer, exactly when I can't say, but not long ago, a young playwright called Julius Lapwing, who had been working in a sugar-beet factory all winter, found that he had earned enough money to rent a room in Jeake's House through the summer and write a play. So that is what he did.

The room he had was on the ground floor, looking out on to a little paved court with an old wooden swing in it. Ivy and jasmine swarmed over the windows, making the place rather dark. So the first thing Julius did was to paint the walls of his room white. No, first he had to scrub them with Swoosh; and in doing *that* he accidentally poked his scrubbing brush through a rotten board and found a little stone niche, like a fireplace without a chimney. And in the niche a big old green glass jar containing – would you believe it – six round flint cobblestones, each one the size of your fist. Rather nice and shiny they were, when Julius had washed the dust from them and put them, in their jar, on the window-sill, but he did wonder why somebody had taken the trouble to board them up in such a queer hideaway, what must have been many long years ago.

Well: at the end of a day's work the walls were white, and so was the high ceiling, and Julius was tired out But when he went to bed he found that his hands were sore and stinging, from the Swoosh detergent he had used to clean off the old paint. He tossed and fidgeted, he rubbed his hands with butter and then with calamine borrowed from his landlady. Still they burned and smarted. Then as he lay fretting his eye lit on the jar of big, smooth, cool cobblestones on the window-sill. Half asleep he staggered across the room, picked out a nice round stone, and tumbled himself back into bed, where he lay holding the beautiful heavy cold thing in both hands. And before he could count more than a sheep and a half, he had dropped asleep, straight into the middle of a dream.

It seemed to him that he was sitting out in the little paved court, with its smell of jasmine and ivy and snails. The moon was shining down, very bright. On the swing, basking in the moon's rays, idling herself to and fro by the tip of her tail, sat a mermaid. Julius was rather surprised to see her there, five miles and more from the sea, but being a polite young fellow he said Good evening and asked if she would fancy a cup of tea or a glass of cider. No thanks to that, Julius, she said, but I wouldn't refuse that cobblestone you're holding, it has old associations for me.

So Julius tossed her the stone, which she caught as if she had been wicket-keeping all her days, and, being a civil young chap, he asked her what the old associations were.

Two hundred years ago, said the mermaid, twiddling the swing back and forth with the tip of her tail, meanwhile tossing up the stone and catching it, very expert, two hundred years ago I had the misfortune to be netted by a family of mackerel fishers off Dungeness Point. And although I sobbed and pleaded, they wouldn't let me go, but fetched me into Rye on their donkey-cart and sold me to the inn across the street from this house, and the innkeeper hung me up for show, in a rope cradle that a sailor made for him.

That must have been uncomfortable, said Julius.

Painful, said the mermaid. Undignified too. And that wasn't the worst—

Julius was craning forward to hear what the worst was, but at that moment the church clock, a particularly loud one, struck seven and woke him; he was much surprised to find he had slept the whole night through. Even more surprised, hunting high and low among the blankets and bedding, to find never a trace of the sixth cobblestone!

Next night his hands were still giving trouble. And again, to cool them, he went to sleep clasping a round, cool cobble. And again he dreamed that he was out in his little court, chatting to the mermaid as she swung to and fro, playing toss-and-catch with the second stone.

The worst thing (she went on, as if there had been no interruption) was that just around that time there was an epidemic of pink-eye in the town. Somebody suggested it must be my fault. And in no time a mob was rushing up Mermaid Street shouting 'Get rid of the sea-witch! Take down the nasty magic thing and burn her!' Well! Just put yourself in my position. It had been vexatious enough to be strung up like a haddock in a rope cage, but the prospect of burning was a thousand times more disagreeable. And then they began pulling cobbles up out of the street and hurling them at me in a very rude way, bruising me all over my scales. However, just at that moment—

Just at that moment she broke off. The church clock was striking seven, and Julius woke up. Not a trace, anywhere, of the second cobble.

What happened just at that moment? Julius asked next night when, in his dream, he had tossed the third cobble to the mermaid and she had caught it.

—Just at that moment the astrologer who lived in this house then – Samuel Jeake, his name was and he looked rather like you – he came out into the street, very cross. 'What's the meaning of all this row?' he asked. '*Must* you make such a noise just when I'm trying to calculate the influence of Pluto in Libra?' Then he caught sight of me and said, 'What are you doing to that unfortunate young person?'

'We're going to burn her,' one of the men said. 'She's a witch, and in her wicked malice she's given pink-eye to half the people in the town. Lower away, boys!'

'Rubbish! Superstitious nonsense!' said the astrologer. 'The pink-eye, as any person of education could tell you, was caused by a conjunction of Saturn in Libra sextile. And furthermore I can tell you, without even consulting my astrolabe, that if you burn this young marine female it will lead to disastrous consequences for the town – I can't specify exactly what without going into the matter more carefully, but it will be something in the nature of a flood, or maybe an earthquake.'

Well, that made them stop and think, and while they were thinking—

While she was speaking the church clock struck seven and Julius woke up.

What happened while they were thinking? he asked, tossing the fourth cobble to the mermaid on the fourth night.

Why, she said, catching it deftly with her left hand and giving the swing a shove off with her tail, while they were thinking, Samuel Jeake put half a dozen cobbles in his pockets and picked me up under one arm. 'She ought to be put back in the sea,' he said, and he took me into his house, slamming the front door. Very decent treatment he gave me then – set me out here to soak in a tub of water, for besides being bruised I was dangerously dry. Furthermore he sent his housekeeper out for a gallon of oysters for my supper, and had her rub me with mint from his garden; most refreshing.

'I must just do a bit of calculation, my child,' says he, 'it should be reckoned out tonight while the moon's in the house of Aries – then tomorrow I'll hire a donkey-cart and return you to your native element.' A very pleasant-spoken gentleman he was, uncommonly like you now I come to look at you.

Splashing in my tub out here I was quite contented, but in the middle of the night—

In the middle of her sentence the church clock struck seven and Julius woke up.

So what happened in the middle of the night? he asked next evening when he had thrown her the fifth cobble.

In the middle of the night, the mermaid said, some men from the town who weren't at all satisfied that I should be put back in the sea, for they wanted a witch-burning, these men came sneaking up the hill to Samuel Jeake's house. He was working away at his astrological calculations in the front room, and he heard them muttering and whispering. One of them softly tried the door.

'It's locked, boys – we'll have to go round the back. Climb over the garden fence,' a voice said.

When they had gone the astrologer came out to me. 'Now this is a nuisance,' he said. 'I fear these rough fellows are not to be influenced by zodiacal arguments. I think I shall be obliged to take you to the sea tonight – though I would have preferred to finish my calculations first.'

Lifting me out of my tub, he carried me into the house, up two flights of stairs and a ladder, out through an attic window, and on to part of the roof that was like a narrow gully between two sand dunes on Camber Strand. Here there stood a strange-looking thing made from wood, and rope, and feathers, and metal that shone in the moonlight, and goodness knows what else.

'That's my flying machine,' said Samuel Jeake. 'I was

going to try it out tomorrow, when I had made certain the stars were favourable, but as your affairs are somewhat pressing, my dear young sea-child, I shall have the trial flight tonight instead; it was built to carry a passenger and I do not suppose you weigh a great deal.'

He put me into a basket underneath one wing, and then glanced over the edge of the roof. Down below I could hear noises and crashes in the garden.

'I hope they do not trample on my mint bed,' said Samuel Jeake. 'Well, well, here we go,' and he climbed into the basket under the other wing, tossing out some of the cobblestones he had been using as ballast, and winding very hard on a wooden windlass.

Up went the machine, over the peak of the roof, over the garden, over the town wall. The wall, as you know, runs down steep as a cliff, to the River Rother, which circles the town. Tide was high, and I could see the water shining bright as my scales.

'This is capital!' says Samuel Jeake, winding away at his handle. 'In fifteen minutes we shall be at Rye harbour.'

But at that moment his machine began to tilt sideways. 'Humph,' said he, scratching his head. 'I really ought to have finished those calculations, I fear.' In spite of all his winding, we lost way altogether; the machine fell down, down, and crashed on the river-bank. Luckily I was thrown into the water—

At that moment the church clock struck seven and Julius woke up.

He felt quite put out. He was impatient to hear the end of the story. It was plain that the mermaid must have escaped – presumably she had swum down the river to the sea. But what of the flying machine? And the astrologer? His speculations were interrupted by the arrival of a telegram. It said YOUR PLAY ACCEPTED COME TO MERMAID THEATRE THIS MORNING TO DISCUSS PRODUCTION.

Well! Julius was wild with excitement. He packed his toothbrush, his other pair of trousers, and the play he was working on, paid a month's rent to the landlady in lieu of notice, and rushed from the house. But he took the sixth cobblestone with him in his duffel-coat pocket. Some day, he thought, I'll come back and get her to tell me the end of that story. And he went running off to catch the London train, happy as a dog with a platinum tail.

It's not a common thing, after all, to hear that your play is being put on, *and* look forward to sharing a dream with a mermaid.

P.S. Samuel Jeake was a real astrologer, and he really did invent a flying machine and take off in it from the walls of Rye. The machine crashed but he escaped. Whether there was a mermaid on board I can't say, but he did live in the house halfway down Mermaid Street. I know because I was born in it.

Crusader's Toby

Sand was what the Knights came for, and sand there was, plenty of it. North of Swaycliffe the dunes stretched away, acres and acres of them, like the sandy breakers of an inland sea, crested with shaggy tufts of grass – long, swooping curves of sand, over which the gulls and curlews flew in parallel swoops as if they were playing on a switchback of air.

'There's enough sand here to bury the Pyramids,' Toby Knight said once, and his father said, 'You might as well throw in the Taj Mahal and the Empire State Building while you're at it.'

In between the dunes and the North Sea lay the beach itself, flat, white, empty sand, as empty and shining as the moon.

The curious thing was that neither of Toby's parents actually made much use of the sand.

To the right of the village – which was only eight houses,

a Post Office, and a pub – the little Sway river ran out, noiselessly fast, clear as pale brown ink in its sandy channel, pouring down past the huge width of the beach, into the waiting sea. And here, day-long every day, Mr Knight stood fishing on a comma-shaped spit of sand, around which the silent hurrying river had to curl its way. Sometimes he caught trout, sometimes he caught sea-fish, sometimes he caught nothing at all, but there he stayed, like a motionless speck in the vast bright emptiness of the beach.

And Toby's mother, meanwhile, was busy writing a book; she took her portable typewriter every day and climbed up to the little ruined church on the cliff, and wrote there.

The cliff was actually a grassy headland across on the other side of the Sway river; Mrs Knight had to walk a quarter of a mile inland up the river-bank and go over the bridge, and up a steep sandy path to reach it. Mostly Toby went with her and carried her typewriter. He liked to pay a daily visit to the crusader in the church. While his mother settled herself in the sun, leaning against a bit of flying-buttress, sitting on one chunk of Norman masonry and with her typewriter balanced on another, Toby went inside the airy roofless shell of sea-whitened stone to visit Sir Bertrand de Swaye, who lay gazing calmly towards the east, with his legs crossed and his hand on the hilt of his sword. He looked comfortable enough, except that his feet were tipped up higher than his head because the ground underneath his tomb had subsided. In fact the whole church was falling into the sea, piece by piece; Sir Bertrand's wife and five children had already disappeared into the sea several years before.

'Isn't the church rather a dangerous place for Mum to go and do her writing?' Toby asked his father once, but Mr Knight said no. 'It's only in the winter that the storms are bad enough to loosen the cliff and make bits of it slide into the sea. Anyway I did make her promise to sit at the landward end of the church. If she sits there I can see her when I'm fishing and we can wave to one another.'

The church certainly still looked solid enough, with its round arches all decorated in zigzag dogtooth, like the ends of crackers, and its eight massive circular pillars holding up nothing but sky.

The following spring, though, when they came back, two of the pillars had gone, fallen into the sea, and Sir Bertrand was tipped even more head-down, though he still appeared quite at ease, gazing towards Jerusalem, with his hand on his sword.

The best thing about Sir Bertrand, of course, was his dog, who, curiously enough, was also named Toby. This Toby was not at all like the usual crusaders' dogs who lie looking rather meek and suppressed under their masters' feet; he was too big for that, to start with. He lay on a kind of step at the end of Sir Bertrand's tomb, lower than his master, but with his head raised vigilantly high so that Sir Bertrand, looking past his own armoured toes, could probably just see Toby's upraised muzzle.

Old Mr Brooman, who lived in the village, said that Toby might be a kind of Afghan hound. 'Well, he could ha' been, stands to reason. Sir Bertrand got him when he was out in the Holy Land, they say. It's all overland from there to Afghanistan. The Arabs and Persians had Salukis; it's common sense that they must all ha' been related once.'

Mr Brooman lived in a little cobble-built cottage at the end of the short village street, right by the beach. He was retired, his wife dead, his children long since scattered about the world; one son was in South Africa, a daughter in New Zealand. He knew a lot about dogs; that was how Toby first met him, during their first summer at Swaycliffe, when Harriet, Toby's Jack Russell terrier, developed a bad limp and was very sorry for herself. There was no vet in the village but someone suggested that Mr Brooman might be able to help. And so he had: he was so very kind to Harriet, carefully examining her foot, finding the splinter that was the cause of the trouble, soaking it out, disinfecting the wound and putting on it some ointment of his own invention which healed it overnight, that Harriet instantly fell in love with him. After that, each time they came back to Swaycliffe, the very first thing she did was to gallop along to Mr Brooman's house, throw herself down in front of him and roll over and over, waving her paws in the air.

Mr Brooman had had various dogs in the past. His last one had been an Alsatian called Minnie. When Minnie died, he told Toby, he had resolved to have no more dogs. 'She was the finish. I knew I could never love any dog better than Minnie, so it was best not to have another. Besides, I'm getting on myself; I wouldn't like for to die and leave a dog lonely. No, that wouldn't do. A human being's got distractions; if someone dies, or goes off and leaves you lonely, there's things you can do to cheer yourself: you can read, you can study, you can do carpentry. But a dog can't do any of those things.'

Mr Brooman did a lot of carpentry; one summer he made a vaulting-horse for Toby so that he could practise athletics out on the empty beach; and he made a strong little table for Toby's mother and carried it up to the church for her, so that she could type more comfortably.

"Tis all made from bits of ship's teak, washed up on the sands, so that'll take no harm from the weather, ma'am; you can just leave it up there, rain or shine.'

Mr Brooman himself visited the church almost every evening; had done for years; it was he who had given the crusader's dog the name Toby.

'I always did think it suited him, some'ow. Funny you should have the same name, my boy. That's what's known as a coincidence. Yes, I've bin a-visiting this-ere old Toby for donkey's years; him an' me's had many a gossip. Wonderful bit of carving that is, when you think what a long time he's been here. Seven 'undred years old, that dog is.'

Crusader's Toby was a big dog, tall and rangy like a

greyhound, but stronger-looking. His coat was smooth but wavy, and his ears, cocked high and intelligently, were fringed inside like the petals of a chrysanthemum. As for his tail, one could see that it had been tremendously plumed, with long swags hanging below it all the way from tip to base, like the underside of an ostrich feather. Some of the plumes had broken off or worn away, unfortunately, but there were still enough left to show. He had a long, keen intelligent nose, big eyes well set in a broad forehead, and big strong feet.

'Good for running in all that sand,' Mr Brooman said. 'Wonderful clever those crusaders' dogs were – they could sniff out a Turk from a Christian, it's said.'

There were several legends about Crusader's Toby: he had saved his master's life three times over, once in battle against the Saracens, once from assassins sent by the Old Man of the Mountains to waylay him on the way back from the Holy Land, and once within sight of home when his ship was wrecked off the mouth of the Sway, and Toby had swum through the dangerous undertow, supporting his wounded master's head on his own powerful shoulders.

'That was why Sir Bertrand wanted his memorial carved separate, because he set such store by the dog, and he had it done while he was still alive, to make sure it was done proper. In fact there's some as say Sir Bertrand carved it hisself. He was a clever man. He writ a little book, too, all in Latin, about his adventures on the crusades, and it's still in the museum in York. That came out o' the castle that was here once; it was a Norman castle, up there on the headland by the church. But that fell into the sea two 'undred year back.'

Toby resolved to go and see Sir Bertrand's book in the museum one day, but York was a long way off. 'It's a pity it couldn't be kept here in the village,' he said.

'Ah, it is,' said old Mr Brooman. 'I don't hold wi' taking things away from where they belong. Things what comes from the village ought to stay in the village.'

Mr Brooman was a native of Swaycliffe, born and bred, though it was true he had travelled a long way from home in his time.

'In the army I was, see; had to go where I was sent. I been in India and in Australia too; and in the Mediterranean. Gibraltar, and then Malta; lots o' crusaders' stuff there. And in Hong Kong I was, for a while.'

Mr Brooman had also, when he was young, been a long-distance runner. It was hard to imagine this now; he was bent and red-faced, with broken veins in his cheeks, and a ragged white moustache; the front part of his head was bald, a thin fringe of white hair curved round the back. And he was very lame indeed with rheumatism and arthritis, never walked without the help of his thick stick. But while he was still in the army he had been an Olympic runner, had carried a blazing torch in the relay from Athens up across Europe in 1936, and had won a gold medal, which he kept on his mantelshelf alongside Minnie's photograph.

During the Easter holidays, when Toby was running and racing out on the sands with Harriet, who went wild with joy every time she saw the great shining bare flatness of the beach, Mr Brooman would often come limping out and sit on the cobbled sea-wall and shout advice.

'Don't clench your fists up so and tighten your chest, boy! You want to run easy, like as if your whole body was in one piece; you don't want to waste any little bit of energy on anything but the running itself, see? Mind you,' he added kindly, 'you shape well; you'll be a sprinter, I can see that; I'd fancy you at a hundred yards.'

And in the summer, when Toby came back and said that he had won the junior hundred yards at school, Mr Brooman said, 'Well there. What did I tell you?'

That was the summer Mr Brooman made the vaulting-horse, and spent long days out on the sand, teaching Toby to do long-fly and short-fly and something called High-and-Over.

In the evenings they went for walks along the beach, north or south; Mr Brooman limping lopsidedly but rapidly along, Toby hunting for shells and beach treasures, Harriet racing backwards and forwards across their track, now up on the dunes, now right down at the edge of the sea, which, when the tide was out, seemed about a mile away. The sun sinking behind the land dyed the crests of the dunes all red and ragged; and when it was down out of sight there would be a spreading luminous pink afterglow, turning the whole sky a brilliant peach-colour. It was

possible to walk north along the coast for five miles before
you came to the next town, Calnmouth, but Toby and Mr
Brooman didn't often get as far as that, because, after the
sun went down, dusk fell quickly, and then Mr Brooman
would say that his leg was getting tired.

At Easter, when they came back after a winter's absence,
Toby noticed that the familiar dunes had completely
changed their shape: mountains had piled up where he
remembered valleys; a favourite little hidden dell of his
where he had been accustomed to go and read on long,
hot peaceful afternoons, was now a wide-open shell-backed
plateau with a strange twisted tree, smooth and grey from
long soaking in the sea, half-buried in the middle of it.

'Ah, it was a terrible winter for storms,' said old Mr
Brooman – who had not changed at all since last year.
'Sometimes the wind blew for ten-fifteen days at a stretch;
all the coast's changed along here an' there's a great bit
out o' the beach up Calnmouth way and they've had to
build a plank bridge across. You'll find changes up at the
church, too.'

Toby saw what Mr Brooman meant as soon as he had
run across the bridge and up the cliff path: two more of
the round columns had fallen, and were to be seen, in bits,
down below on the beach, half-buried in sand. Sadder
still, Sir Bertrand de Swaye had disappeared too; only
Toby remained, still with his head raised, gazing alertly
towards the distant east, as if he wondered where his
master had gone.

Poor Toby, thought the human Toby, remembering what Mr Brooman had said: 'I wouldn't like for to die and leave a dog lonely.' It seemed hard that he should have lost his master after they had been so long together.

That evening, when they went for their first walk along the wet, shining beach, pink with sunset reflections, Mr Brooman told Toby a queer thing.

Harriet, mad with happiness at so much space after her confinement in London all winter long, was racing in crazy circles, down to the sea, up to the dunes, tearing back to Toby to spatter him with sand, then off again into the far distance to tease a feeding flock of gulls or sandpipers, dashing with a volley of barks among them to drive them into the air.

'Now, you watch, quiet-like,' said Mr Brooman. 'I don't *know* as it'll work, for I've never done it when there was someone else along, but watch and see.'

He pulled out his dog-whistle. This was a small silver gadget which he had often shown Toby. You could blow it like an ordinary whistle, but you could also twist the mouthpiece around, so that the sound it produced was too high for human ears, and could be heard by dogs alone.

They were walking on the beach south of the Sway river mouth, below the headland; one or two bits of broken Norman column lay near the cliff. Toby had already searched all over the sands for Sir Bertrand himself and had found no sign of him; the winter seas must have broken him up, or the undertow had dragged him out and buried him deep.

Above, on the grassy height, the frail bonelike ruins of the church were outlined in black against a pale-pink sky.

'Now then,' said Mr Brooman, and blew his silent whistle.

Harriet heard it at once.

She came racing towards them from far away on the sea's edge as if she had been pulled back on the end of a long elastic string.

But then, when she had nearly returned to Mr Brooman and Toby, she began behaving in an odd and unexpected manner. Instead of dashing up against them and covering them with sand in her usual way, she began barking and bouncing about, crouching right down on her elbows and then shooting up in the air, twisting sideways, sometimes rolling over and over, somersaulting and panting, with yards of her tongue out of her mouth as if she were laughing.

'How queer! She looks just as if she's playing with another dog – that's the way she carries on with some of her friends in London,' Toby said, puzzled.

'Ah. That's it,' said Mr Brooman. He put the whistle back in his pocket.

Now Harriet was off again, on a long slant back to the sea. But she ran with her head cocked to the left, taking sudden sideways swerves and snatches, as if another dog ran beside her and she was playfully bumping up against him, butting him with her head or shoulder, taking a teasing nip out of his ear.

'It's *crazy*,' said Toby. 'Mr Brooman – do you think—?'

What he wanted to suggest seemed so ridiculous that he hesitated, but Mr Brooman said it for him.

'Toby from up above's come down for a run and she's a-playing with him.'

'But—'

'He wakes up, now, you see, when I blows the old whistle. He'll be glad to have company. There's no dogs in the village since Mrs Grimes at the Post Office lost her Blackie. Old Toby likes a bit of company, you can see that.'

'But why,' said Toby the boy, watching Harriet, who looked as if she were being rolled over and over by a large invisible paw, 'why didn't he ever come down before?'

'Well, he didn't need to, did he? He had his master alongside. So long as they was together he was pleased to stay there. But now it's different. He's hunting for his master, see? Times I've been out with him, on the shore, I've felt him running along, close by the water's edge, a-looking and a-looking to see if he can't make out where has his master got to. Sometimes,' said Mr Brooman, looking around the huge empty beach to make sure no one could hear what he was going to say, 'sometimes I've almost been sure I could *see* his footprints by the edge of the water where the sand's all wet and soft – or the splashes he was a-throwing up when he went in the sea.

And then he'll come along close arter me, I can almost hear him, pad, pad, right be'ind, and I can hear him thinking, You're a yuman, why can't *you* tell me where he is?'

Toby looked at Mr Brooman with some doubt. Could the old man be getting a bit cracked from living alone?

But then Harriet came trotting up, tired for the moment, covered with sand, ready to fall in alongside the humans and go at their pace. She had no attention to spare for them, though; she was engrossed in conversation with someone bigger and taller and invisible who was lolloping at an easy pace beside her.

'*Do* dogs have ghosts?' Toby said.

Mr Brooman thought for a while.

'The way I figure it is this,' he said finally. 'What is there in you that lasts? It's your soul, ennit? call it that. The body part of you dries out and turns into earth, even the bones do that, give 'em long enough, arter you die. But there's some bit of you that's different, that makes you different from any other person, that sends invisible streamers out like a jellyfish, and they hooks on to things round about while you're still alive. Call that your soul. And that'll still be there after you've died, hooked on to all those things round about that you was fond of while you was alive. See what I mean?'

'You think dogs do that too?'

'Why not? Special if a dog gets to be very fond of his master. Then they hook together, like. I tell you what I think,' said Mr Brooman, glancing back at the black shell of the roofless church silhouetted against the pink sky on the headland behind them. 'I think that Sir Bertrand did carve that there statue of Toby hisself. It must ha' taken him a long, long time, it was done so faithful. And while he was a-doing it, a bit of Toby's soul must ha' got knitted into the stone, like, an' it's still there. Arter all, they say that painters put their soul into their pictures, don't they? You put your soul into anything you're really keen on.'

'Well then,' said Toby, 'is it Toby's soul, or Sir Bertrand's?'

'Now you foxed me there,' said Mr Brooman. 'Tell you the truth, I don't rightly know. Maybe it's both. Maybe when you get a friendship like that, they gets kind of woven together.'

Toby glanced again to his right, at Harriet so happy with her new friend. Having got her breath, she was beginning to bounce and gambol again, and next moment she set off on another half-mile sprint, down to the edge of the sea, and into the water, which as a rule she was reluctant to enter unless somebody went with her.

Were there two sets of splashes or only one?

That night when they got back to the house Harriet flung herself down on the hearth-rug and slept like a worn-out dog, not even stirring and twitching with dreams as she usually did. And the moment she woke next morning she dashed outside, looking alertly about as if she expected somebody; she seemed rather puzzled

and crestfallen at the emptiness of the salty, sunny village
street.

'I suppose you'll have to wait till this evening, Harriet,'
Toby told her. 'Till Mr Brooman blows his whistle. But
we can go up to the church and have a look at old stone
Toby, if you like.'

They walked up to the church with Mrs Knight when
she went to do her daily chapter. There lay stone Toby,
basking in the April sunshine, but Harriet was not interested in him. The Toby she expected must be somewhere
locked inside the stone, or else already down below
searching for his master on the sunswept wind-swept
beach.

Just in case he was somewhere inside, Toby sat down
for a moment with his arm round stone Toby's neck, and
murmured into the fringed clever uplifted ear:

'Good boy then, good old boy! Don't you worry, Toby,
I'm sure he's waiting for you, down there in the sea. And
Lady Swaye and the children will be there too. You'll have
to learn to be a water-dog, Toby.'

Motionless, apparently deaf to this consolation, stone
Toby went on gazing vigilantly towards the east. But
Harriet, jealous and impatient, barked and pranced from
side to side, and tugged at her master's sleeve until he got
up and followed her down the steep and slithery sand
path which led on over the headland and back to the
beach. Ghost-Toby did not join them there; it seemed
that wherever he was, he would only come out to play

when summoned by Mr Brooman's whistle. But that never failed. Dusk after dusk the four of them went along at their varying paces over the wet sand, live dog and ghost-dog racing ahead, Mr Brooman limping, helped by his stick, telling stories of Malta and Gibraltar, of the dogs of Hong Kong and the plains of Yugoslavia where he had carried the Olympic torch, while Toby the boy listened and watched Harriet's antics, and sometimes raced ahead, alongside of her and her unseen companion, practising for the four-hundred-and-forty yards, which was his next ambition.

When the Knights came back in the summer, Toby with a silver cup to show off proudly to Mr Brooman, stone Toby was still up there on the headland. And as in the spring, he joined them invisibly on their walks in the long twilit evenings.

'Sometimes, nowadays,' confided Mr Brooman, 'he'll come right along the village street, right up to the 'ouse with me. But I never yet got him to come inside. 'E always stops outside the door.'

It was a happy summer. The long salty sunlit days stretched in a peaceful shining chain, one after another, each exactly like the one before, and yet all as different as the shells on the beach; time seemed to have slowed down. Toby's father fished, and his mother wrote, and stone Toby drowsed in the sun all day, up on his headland, waiting for Sir Bertrand, and came down in the evenings to race and play.

'Well, well,' said Mr Brooman rather sadly when September came, and it was time for the Knights to leave, 'I'll miss you, young Toby, and Harriet, when the nights draw in and the winds get a-blowing. It seems a long time to spring. I'm not getting any younger, and that's the truth.'

Looking carefully at Mr Brooman, Toby saw that it *was* the truth. Somehow, unnoticed by him, the old man seemed to have shrunk in the course of the summer; the skin hung more loosely on his face, and his limp was more pronounced.

'It's good that you've got Crusader's Toby to keep you company. Maybe when it gets to be real winter you'll be able to persuade him into your house.'

'Ah; maybe I will,' said Mr Brooman thoughtfully, and Toby felt a sudden queer pang of anxiety – was it for the old man or for stone Toby up there on his headland? Would they be able to look after each other through the storms of the coming winter?

'I'll try to get Mum and Dad to come down at Christmas,' he said. 'I've often asked them and Dad did promise that some year we might.'

'Ah, you do that! Swaycliffe's grand in winter, when the sea piles up and roars for days on end, and the sky gets black as ink and the beach is all white with the snow. It's worth seeing, that is.'

By hard pleading, Toby did manage to convince his parents that they should come back to Swaycliffe in the winter holidays. All the time they were packing the car with food and warm clothes and extra bedding, Toby was on edge with expectation. During the drive down on Christmas Eve he longed for the sight and smell of the sea, all winter-wild, and for the company of Mr Brooman and Crusader's Toby. A gale had been lashing the north-sea coast all the week before Christmas. Would Toby be all right? Would he still be there, up in the church?

As soon as they had arrived and unpacked the car, Toby ran along the snowy lane to Mr Brooman's. But the house was dark, shut and locked. Full of worry, he went on to the Post Office to ask Mrs Grimes if the old man had gone away.

'Ah, dear, then you hadn't heard?' she said, giving her eyes a wipe. 'Well, to be sure, it was only ten days ago, I daresay you wouldn't have. Poor old gentleman.'

'What happened, Mrs Grimes? Did he get ill?'

'No, 'twasn't like that. It was all along of that there crusader's dog up in the church.'

'What happened?' Toby asked again, anxiously.

'Well, Mr Brooman was very upset, dreadful upset he was, on account of the Historical Monuments Depart-ment, or some such, sent an inspector along and then they decided as how the old dog shouldn't be left here an' allowed to fall into the sea like all the rest o' the bits from the church, but was to be took off and put into York Museum. Oh, he argued about it terrible, did Mr Brooman, an' ast the vicar and even writ to the Council, but they wouldn't take no notice of him, said it was best that the dog should be preserved because it was a uncommon example of twelfth-century work.'

'Oh my goodness.' Toby's heart sank dreadfully. He could imagine how Mr Brooman must have felt. 'Did – did they take the dog away?'

'Well, they was all set to. A couple of chaps come out with hammers and chisels and a council van, an' they took the old dog off his base and put him in a crate an' fetched it down here to the village. 'Twas a desprit cold arternoon, snow and wind, an' it must ha' been a sharp old job prying that heavy stone thing loose, up there on the headland. So when they was done they went into the Old Ship for a quick warm-up. And you'll never guess what Mr Brooman did.'

'What did he do?' Toby asked, though he thought he *could* guess.

'Why, he must ha' fetched out his old garden barrer – for bits of it was washed up along the shore next day – an' (no one knows how he done it, all on his own, wi'out help) he must ha' got that crate out o' the van an' into his wheelbarrer and wheeled it down to the sea – wheeled it right *into* the sea. And Doctor Motkin reckons that musta give him a heart-failure – for he'd had one or two bad turns with his heart already, this last two-three months – anyway, he never come back.' She wiped her eyes again. 'Washed up, he was, next morning, half a mile down the shore. But they say his face was ever so peaceful. Maybe he was glad to go. Arter all, 'tis a long time since his missis died, poor old soul,'

'What about Tob— what about the dog? Did they find him?'

'Never a trace. There's a big undertow here, you know – special when summat's heavy – it must ha' gone right down deep. The Ancient Monuments people were mad about it; terrible put out they were. But there was naught that anyone could do.'

No there wasn't, thought Toby, and he felt proud for old Mr Brooman, battling his way down to the sea through snow and gale. He thought of the old man's voice saying, 'Things that come from the village ought to stay here.'

He thanked Mrs Grimes and went out into the street.

He knew that he ought to go home and help his mother – who would be wondering where in the world he had got to – unpack and make the beds and decorate the Christmas tree. But he hadn't the heart to do that, quite yet.

He turned into the biting wind, followed by Harriet, who was rather subdued, and walked along the short snowy street to the beach.

Dusk was falling. As far as the eye could see the beach curved away to right and left, an unbroken sweep of white. And the sea mumbled and muttered, inky black, far out, with a pale frill of foam at its edge. Nobody, nothing was stirring. Even the birds were silent.

But out on that windswept emptiness Harriet's spirits

suddenly picked up, and she went bounding off, lifting her feet ridiculously high, with a rocking curvetting motion, like a painted dog. Down to the water's edge she galloped, and splashed in.

Toby raced after her, as fast as he could go – faster – much faster – swallowing great gulps of burning cold air. And as he ran, the sorrow for Mr Brooman's death fell away behind him, and a feeling of freedom and triumph streamed through him – as if he had been joined by the happy spirits of Crusader's Toby and Mr Brooman, old no longer but light and strong as on the day when he had raced with the Olympic torch across the plains of Yugoslavia.

The Gift Pig

Once there was a king whose queen, having just presented him with a baby princess, unfortunately died. The king was very upset at this, naturally. But he had to go on with the arrangements for the christening just the same, as court etiquette was strict on this point. What with his grief and distraction, however, and the yells of his daughter, an exceedingly lively and loud-voiced infant, the invitations to the christening were sent out in a very haphazard manner, and by mistake two elderly fairies were invited who were well known to loathe one another, so that when they met there was bound to be trouble, though when encountered separately they were pleasant enough.

The day of the christening arrived and at first all went well. The baby princess was christened Henrietta and behaved properly at the ceremony, crying a little but not too much. Then the whole party of relatives and guests strolled back from the royal chapel to the throne room where the reception was being held; the king noticed with alarm that the two elderly fairies were walking side by side. They seemed to be nodding in the most friendly way, but when he edged nearer to them he heard one say,

'How very well you are looking, darling Grizel! One wouldn't – by artificial light – take you for a day over two hundred.'

'Hardly surprising since I celebrated my hundred-and-eightieth birthday last week. But how are *you*, dear Bella? Do you think it was wise to attend the service in that draughty chapel? You walk with such a limp these days.'

'I am perfectly well, thank you, my love. And one does have one's social duty.'

'Especially when there is a free meal attached to it, tee hee!'

'But I confess I hardly expected to see you here – I understood the king's friends were all intelligent and – well, you know – *creative* people.'

'Creative, my angel? In that case, do tell me how *you* qualify for admission?'

Shuddering, the poor king made haste to cut the cake and circulate the sherry in hopes of sweetening these acid ladies. He wished that he could get rid of them before the visitors began to give their christening presents, but saw no way to.

Presently the guests, fairy and otherwise, having eaten every crumb of cake and drunk all the sherry, began depositing their gifts and taking their leave. The baby, pink and good in her cradle, was given whole rooms full of silver and coral rattles, shoals of shawls, bonnets and bootees by the bushel, mounds of matinee jackets and mittens, stacks of embroidered smocks and knitted socks. Besides this, she was endowed with good health, a friendly and cheerful nature, intelligence, and a logical mind.

Then the fairy Bella stepped forward and, smiling at the king, said,

'You must forgive me if my wish is not quite so pleasant as some of the preceding ones, but meeting – ahem – such very *odd* company in your palace has made me nervous and brought on a migraine. Let the princess rue the day that someone gives her a pig, for if ever that happens she will turn into a pig herself.'

'Moreover,' said the fairy Grizel, coming to the other side of the cradle, 'she will marry somebody with no heart and only one foot.'

'Excuse *me*, dear, I hadn't finished yet; if you could kindly give me time to speak. The princess will lose her inheritance—'

'I *beg* your pardon; I was going to say that there will be a revolution—

'*Will* you please be quiet, madam! There will *not* be a revolution – or at least, the princess herself will be lost long before that occurs – she will be poor and unknown and have to work for her living— She'll marry one who has spent all his life in the open—'

'Oh, for gracious' sake! Didn't I just say she would marry somebody with only one foot?'

'The two things are not incompatible.'

'You don't very often find agricultural workers with only one foot.'

'Ladies, ladies!' said the king miserably, but not daring to be too abrupt with them, 'you have done enough harm to my poor child! Will you please continue your discussion somewhere else?'

The feuding fairies took their leave (so exhausted by their exhilarating quarrel that they both went home, retired to bed, and died next day) while, left alone, the poor king hung with tears in his eyes over his beautiful pink baby wondering what, if anything, could be done to avert the various bits of evil fortune that were coming to her. All that seemed to lie in his power was strict censorship of her presents, so as to make sure that she was never given a pig.

This he managed successfully until she was five years old, when her cousin came to stay with her. Lord Edwin Fitzlion was a spoilt, self-willed boy of about the same age as the princess; he was the seventh son of a seventh son; his brothers were all much older and had gone off into the world, his father had taken to big-game hunting and hardly ever came home, while his mother, tired of looking after boys and attending to shirts, schools, boots, and bats, was away on a three-year cruise. Lord Edwin had been left in the care of servants.

He was very beautiful, with dark velvety eyes and black hair; much better looking than his fat pink cousin; he was inclined to tease her. One day he overheard two equerries discussing the prophecies about her, and he became consumed with curiosity to see whether she would really turn into a pig if she were given one.

There were considerable difficulties about bringing pigs into the palace, but finally Edwin managed to buy a small one from a heavily bribed farmer. He smuggled it in, wrapped in brown paper and labelled *Inflatable rubber dinghy with outboard pump attachment*. Finding the nursery empty he undid the pig and let it loose, then rushed in search of Henrietta. 'Henry! come quick, I've brought a present for you.'

'Oh, where?'

'In the nursery! Hurry up!'

With rare politeness he stood aside to let her go in first and heard her squeak for joy as she ran through the door,

'Oh, it's a dear little pig—'

Then there was silence, except for more squeaks, and when Lord Edwin looked through the door he saw two little pigs, absolutely identical, sniffing noses in the most friendly way.

Lord Edwin was sent home in disgrace to his father's

castle, where he proceeded to run wild, as his parents were still away. (In fact they never returned.) He spent all his time in the woods, riding his eldest brother's horse, Bayard, and flying his next brother's falcon, Ger. One day when far from home he saw a large hare sitting upright on the other side of a pool. Quickly he unhooded the falcon and prepared to fly her.

The hare said,

'You'll be sorry if you do that.'

'Oh, who cares for you,' said Edwin rudely, and he loosed Ger. But the falcon, instead of towering up and dropping on the hare, flew slantwise across the pond into some thick trees and vanished from view. Edwin's eyes followed the bird in annoyance and perplexity. When he looked back he saw that a little old man with an unfriendly expression was standing on the spot where the hare had been.

'You are a spoilt, ill-mannered boy,' the old man said. 'I know all about you and what you did to your cousin. You can stay where you are, learning a bit of patience and consideration, until a Home Secretary comes to rescue you.'

Nobody had been particularly fond of Edwin, so nobody missed him or inquired after him.

The king, of course, was heartbroken when he learned what had happened to his daughter. Numerous tests were carried out on the two little pigs, in an attempt to discover which one was the princess. They were put in little beds with peas under the mattresses but both rummaged out the peas and ate them in the course of the night. Dishes of pearls and potato-peelings were placed in front of them, in the hope that the princess would prefer the pearls, but they both dived unhesitatingly for the potato-peelings. The most eminent pig-breeders of the kingdom were brought in to scrutinize them, but with no result; they were two handsome pink little pigs, and that was all that could be said of them.

'Well,' said the king at length, 'one of them is my daughter, and she must receive the education due to a princess. Some day I suppose she will be restored to her proper shape, as she is to marry a one-footed man, poor dear—'

'The fairy didn't actually say a *man* with one foot,' pointed out the Lord Chamberlain.

'Use your sense, man. What else could it be? Anyway she must have a proper education. It would never do if when she reverted to human shape she knew no more than a child of five.'

So the little pigs sat seriously side by side on two little chairs in the schoolroom and were taught and lectured at by a series of learned professors and eminent school-mistresses. No one could tell if any of this teaching sank in, for they merely sat and gazed. If asked questions, they grunted.

One day when the pigs were nearly fifteen, the king came into the schoolroom.

'Hullo, my dears,' he said, 'how are you this morning?' He patted his daughter and her friend, then sat down wearily in an armchair to rest while they had their lunch. Affairs of state were becoming very burdensome to him these days.

A footman brought in two big blue bowls of pig-mash, one in each hand. The pigs began to give piercing squeals and rush about frantically, bumping into tables and chairs and each other. Their attendant firmly collared them one at a time, tied a white napkin round the neck of each, and strapped them into two chairs. The bowls were put in front of them and instantly there was such a guzzling and a slupping and a splashing and a slobbering that nobody could hear a word for five minutes until the bowls were empty. Then the little pigs looked up again, beaming with satisfaction, their faces covered in mash.

The footman solemnly stepped forward again and wiped their faces clean with a cloth-of-gold flannel. Then they were let out to play, and could be seen through the window whisking about the palace garden with tails tightly curled, and chasing one another across the flower-beds.

The king sighed.

'It's no use,' he said, 'one must face facts. My daughter Henrietta is *not* an ordinary princess. And her friend Hermione is a very ordinary little pig. I am afraid that no prince, even a one-footed one, would ask for Henrietta's hand in marriage after seeing her eat her lunch. We must send them to a finishing school. They have had plenty of intellectual education – at least I suppose they have – it's time they acquired a little polish.'

So the two pigs were packed off (in hampers) to Miss Dorothea ffoulkes' Select Finishing School for the Daughters of the Aristocracy and Nobility.

At first all went well. The king received monthly re-reports which informed him that his daughter (and her friend) had learned to walk downstairs with books on their heads, to enter and leave rooms, get in and out of motor cars with grace and dignity, play the piano and the harp, waltz, cha-cha-cha, embroider, and ride side-saddle.

'Well, I've always heard that Miss ffoulkes was a marvel,' said the king, shaking his head with astonishment, 'but I never thought anyone could teach a pig to ride side-saddle. I can't wait to see them.'

But he had to wait, for Miss ffoulkes strictly forbade the parents of her pupils to visit them while they were being put through her course of training. The reason for this was that she had to treat the girls with such frightful severity, in order to drill the necessary elegance and deportment into them, that if they had been given the chance they would have implored their parents to take them away. Letters, however, were always written to the dictation of Miss ffoulkes herself, so there was no opportunity of complaining, and at the end of her course the debutantes were so grateful for their beautiful poise that all was forgotten and forgiven.

Miss ffoulkes nearly met her Waterloo in Henrietta and Hermione though. She managed to teach them tennis, bridge, and how to dispose of a canapé stick, but she could not teach them flower-arrangement. The pigs had no taste for it; they always ate the flowers.

One day they had been spanked and sent into the garden in disgrace after it was discovered that they had eaten a large bundle of lilies and asparagus-fern which they were supposed to build into a decorative creation. Sore and miserable they wandered down Miss ffoulkes' dreary gravel paths. Simultaneously they were seized by the same impulse. They wriggled through the hedge at the bottom of the garden and were seen no more at the Select School.

Instead of a final report on deportment the king had a note from Miss ffoulkes which said,

'I regret to announce that your daughter and her friend have committed the unpardonable social blunder of running away from my establishment. The police have been informed and will no doubt recover them for you in due course. Since this behaviour shows that our tuition has been thrown away on them your fees are returned herewith. (Cheque for £20,000 enc.) Your very obdt. srvt. Dorothea ffoulkes.'

In spite of all efforts, the police failed to trace the two little pigs. Advertisements in newspapers, on television and radio, pictures outside police stations, offers of rewards, brought no replies. The king was in terror, imagining his daughter and her friend innocently strolling into a bacon factory. He gave up all pretence at governing and spent his time in a desperate round of all the farms in the kingdom, gazing mournfully at pig after pig in the hope of recognizing Henrietta and Hermione. But none of the pigs responded to his greetings.

As a matter of fact Henrietta and her friend had gone no farther than the garden of the house next door to Miss ffoulkes. There they had been rootling peacefully (but elegantly because their training had not been wasted) among the roses near the front gate when a young man in a white coat came out of the house, irritably listening to the parting words of a beautiful young lady with flowing dark hair.

'And don't forget,' she was saying earnestly, 'all your last experimental results are in the stack under the five-gramme weight, and the milk for tea is in the test-tube at the left-hand end of the right-hand rack, and the baby amoeba wants feeding again at five. Now I really must fly, for my fiancé becomes very annoyed if he is kept waiting.'

'Goodbye, Miss Snooks,' said the white-coated young man crossly, and he slammed the gate behind her. 'Why in the name of goodness do all my assistants have to get married? Not one of them has stayed longer than three months in the last three years.'

Then his eye fell on the two pigs, who were gazing at him attentively.

'Pigs,' he mused. 'I wonder if pigs could be taught to do the work? Pigs might not be so prone to become engaged. Pigs, would you consider a job as research assistants?'

The pigs liked his face; they followed him into the house, where he instructed them in the research work he was doing on cosmic rays.

'I shall have to teach you to talk, though,' he observed, 'for I can't put up with assistants who grunt all the time.' He laid aside all his other work and devoted himself to teaching them; at the end of a week he had succeeded, for he was the most brilliant scientist and philosopher in the kingdom. In any case, nobody had ever considered teaching the pigs to talk before.

When they could speak the professor asked their names.

'One of us is Henrietta and one is Hermione, but we are not sure which is which,' they told him, 'for we were muddled up when we were young.'

'In that case I shall call you Miss X and Miss Y. Miss X, you will look after making the tea, feeding the amoeba, and filing the slides. Miss Y, you will turn away all visitors, keep the cosmic ray tuned, and polish the microscope. Both of you will make notes on my experiments.'

The two pigs now found their education of great value. They could carry piles of books and microscope slides about on their heads, curtsy gracefully to callers as they showed them the door, write notes in a neat little round hand, and play the piano and the harp to soothe the professor if his experiments were not going well. They were all very happy together, and the professor said that he had never before had such useful and talented assistants.

One day after about five years had passed in this manner, the professor raised his eye from the microscope, rubbed his forehead, looked at Miss Y, industriously taking notes, and Miss X, busily putting away slides, and said,

'Pigs, it occurs to me to wonder if you are really

human beings turned into your present handy if humble form?'

'One of us is,' replied Miss Y, tucking her pencil behind her ear, 'but we don't know which.'

'It should be easy to change you back,' the professor remarked. 'I wonder I never thought of it before. We can just switch on the cosmic ray and rearrange your molecules.'

'Which of us?'

'You can both try, and I daresay nothing will happen to one of you.'

'Should we like that?' said the pigs to each other. 'You see we're used to being together,' they told the professor.

'Oh, come, come,' he exclaimed impatiently. 'If one of you is really human, it's her plain duty to change back, and the other one should not stand in her way.'

Thus admonished, both pigs walked in front of the ray, and both immediately turned into young ladies with pink faces, turned-up noses, fair hair, and intelligent blue eyes.

'Humph,' remarked the professor, 'that ray must be more powerful than I had allowed for; we do not seem to have advanced matters much farther.'

As the young ladies still did not know which of them was which, they continued to be called Miss X and Miss Y, and as they were very happy in their work they continued to help the professor.

One day Miss Y noticed a number of callers approaching the front door. Though she curtsied politely and did her best to turn them away, they insisted on entering the laboratory.

'Professor,' said a spokesman, 'we are the leaders of the Revolution, and we have come to invite you to be the first president of our new republic, since you are undoubtedly the wisest man in the country.'

'Oh good gracious,' said the professor, very much taken aback and frowning because he hated interruptions to his work, 'whatever possessed you to revolt, and what have you done with the king?'

'We revolted because it is the fashionable thing to do – all the other countries have done it ages ago – and the king retired last week; he has taken to farming. But now please step into the carriage which is waiting outside and we will escort you to the president's residence.'

'If I accept,' said the professor, 'it is understood that I must have unlimited time to pursue my research.'

'Yes, yes, you will need to do very little governing; just keep an eye on things and see that justice and reason prevail. Of course you can appoint anybody you choose to whatever government positions you wish.'

'In that case I shall appoint my two assistants, Miss X and Miss Y, to be the Home and Foreign Secretaries. I am certain that no one could be more competent.'

The new president's residence turned out to be none other than the castle of the Baron Fitzlion, long since deserted. Here the republican government was set up, and as none of the old officials had been removed from their posts, everything proceeded very smoothly, and the professor and his two assistants found ample time to continue their research on cosmic rays.

They were now investigating the use of the professor's ray projector on plant life; one day Miss X took a small portable projector into the woods nearby, proposing to make notes about differences in the ray's effect on coniferous and deciduous trees.

While scribbling in her notebook she heard a sneeze, and looked up to discover that a larch in front of her had developed a head. Two handsome black eyes gazed at her mournfully.

'Are you the Home Secretary?' the head inquired.

'Why, yes,' replied Miss X, controlling her natural surprise at such a question being put to her by a tree.

'In that case would you be so extremely kind as to liberate the rest of me with your camera, or whatever it is?'

'I'm afraid this portable projector isn't strong enough for that – it only runs off a battery. We shall have to build a larger one beside you and connect it to the mains; that will take two or three weeks.'

He sighed. 'Oh well, I've been here fifteen years, I daresay I can wait another three weeks. No doubt I deserved this fate for turning my poor little cousin into a pig, but I *am* so stiff.'

'Did you turn your cousin into a pig?' said Miss X with interest. 'I suppose that might have been me.'

'Were you turned into a pig?'

'Somebody was; we cannot be sure if it was my friend Miss Y or myself. You see, we are not certain which of us is which.'

'Henrietta was to lose her inheritance and go through a revolution.'

'So she has.'

'And be poor and unknown and earn her living.'

'We both are and do.'

'And marry a man with one foot. I'll tell you what,' said Lord Edwin, who had rapidly developed a tremendous admiration for Miss X's cheerful pink face and yellow hair – such a refreshing contrast to the leaves and branches which were all he had had to look at for the last fifteen years – 'I've only got one foot just now, you're standing on it; so if you marry me it will prove that you are the princess.'

'That's true,' she said thoughtfully, 'and then I shall be able to go and see poor Papa and tell him that I am me; there didn't seem much point in disturbing him until I had some more data.'

So the marriage ceremony between Lord Edwin and Miss X was performed while they were building the full-size cosmic ray projector nearby, and as soon as the bridegroom had been released they went to see the king, who was very contented on his farm and had no wish at all to resume governing.

'I have acquired a fondness for pigs after looking at so

many,' he said. 'I am sure you young people can manage very well without me.'

So Lord Edwin became Prime Minister (having learned thoughtfulness and civilized behaviour during his long spell in the woods). Miss Y, who was now known to be Hermione, married the professor, and they all governed happily ever after.

The Rain Child

Once there was a boy who lived far away from any town, with an old woman, in a little hut that stood on the edge of a huge apple orchard. In front of the hut a great flat plain stretched away into the distance, as far as the eye could see, and much farther; and behind the hut were these hundreds and thousands of acres of apple trees. In winter the branches were bare and black; in spring they covered themselves with pale green leaves, and then came the pink and white flowers, which changed, after a while, to tiny green apples; the apples grew larger, red or yellow according to their kind; and the best time of all was in the autumn when the leaves of the trees turned gold or scarlet and the apples were ripe, ready for picking. Then one day the pickers would arrive in wagons from many miles away, with their baskets and their ladders, and for a short time the whole orchard would be alive with jokes and laughter, shouting and songs, while the men climbed up and down the ladders and the apples were picked and packed into rush baskets.

The boy loved that time; he liked to help the pickers and he would run from tree to tree, talking to the men and listening to their jokes; and the old woman, though she grumbled at the noise, would bring them jugs of cold tea with slices of cucumber and lemon floating on top. But then, one day, the men and the apples would all be gone, the birds would fly away southwards, and silence would settle down over the orchard again. The boy loved that time too; he enjoyed the silence, and he knew the whole orchard so well, every tree by its different looks, that he could wander for miles down the avenues of trunks, and never lose himself.

The old woman he lived with was not his mother; she was much too old for that. He did not know how they had come together; she had always been there, looking after him. He called her sometimes 'Ana' and sometimes 'Foster-mother'. She called him 'Child', or 'Little one', or 'You young devil', depending on her mood. The boy had never heard his name.

Long ago, when he was a baby, he could remember how, when he had woken to cry on a stormy night, hearing the rain beat on the roof or the wind thresh among the orchard trees, old Ana would take him from his cradle and hold him on her lap, rocking him and singing.

She always sang the same song:

Sleep, child, on my knee
Your mother is an apple tree
Your father is a shower of rain –
Sleep, child, sleep again.

Over and over again she used to sing the song, time after time, through the long windy winter nights. Because of this, the boy never wondered about his parents; he never asked who were his mother and father, or why they never came to see him. He knew that his father was in the sky, in the rain, and he knew that his mother was an apple tree. When he became big enough to wander out among the trees by himself, he sought among them all until he found the one which, he felt certain, was his mother. This tree was not one of the largest in the orchard – but it was not one of the smallest, either. It was not right in the middle of the orchard – but not very close to the edge. It had a very beautiful regular shape, with branches rising in gentle curves, like fingers from the palm of a hand; the trunk was smooth and quite free from cracks or lumps; and, at harvest time, this tree was always covered with apples which were a light yellowish-green, streaked with red, not too big, but not small, not too sweet, but not too sharp, and always very juicy.

The boy fell into the habit of visiting this tree, every day, right through the year, in spring, summer, autumn, or winter. And he would talk to it.

'Were you awake, Mother, last night, when that gale

was blowing?' he might ask. 'It was a very fierce wind: the last of your leaves has blown off today. Never mind! They will all grow again in the spring. Listen, I have learned a new poem – shall I say it to you?' And then he would recite the poem. Or he would sit down and tell his tree some story out of a book he had just learned to read, or say over his multiplication table until he had it right – for although there was no school within a hundred miles, the boy did lessons; the old priest from the tiny church out in the middle of the plain used to ride over on a mule twice a week and teach him.

'Listen, Mother, now I am going to tell you about the Romans,' the boy might say, sitting cross-legged on the dry grass, and over his head all the leaves would rustle and whisper, as if the tree were murmuring its interest in what he told it.

Sometimes, in winter, when the wind roared day after day, and the snow lay piled deeper and deeper under the bare trees, the boy would wake at night and worry: 'Is my mother warm enough? Is she safe in this gale? Can her branches bear this wind without breaking?'

In the morning he would slip on his snowshoes, which were big and flat, made from woven willow-wands, designed to slide over the surface of the snow, however deep it lay, and then he would hurry between the black lines of bare trees until he came to where his own tree stood, sturdy and unharmed, although the snow rose up almost to where her branches began.

'Oh, I am so glad that you are safe!' the boy would cry, lovingly running his hand along a slender bough, rubbing off the crust of snow.

Old Ana told him that snow was good for apple trees.

'They need the winter cold, they need a rest after all the trouble of bearing apples,' she said. 'And the snow keeps their roots warm in the ground, and the frost kills off harmful pests that spoil their apples and nibble their leaves. Trees need the winter-time.'

Then, in the spring, how beautiful his tree was! How happily he spent whole days under her dazzling canopy of pink and white petals, while the bees hummed in and out, filling up their sacks with nectar. The boy would lie learning his lessons, murmuring his words aloud like the bees, while the snowy-piled tree listened and attended. Or so he felt.

And when it rained, when day after day in grey November the sky hung thick and dark and water poured down, or when a summer storm beat on the leaves until they dangled straight as soaked clothes on a line, the boy would think to himself, 'Now my parents are talking together; now she is telling him about me—' while he listened to the splash and patter of the raindrops.

The boy never thought it strange that his father should be a rainstorm, his mother an apple tree; it was so; that was all; and he loved the tree quite as much as if she had been a person. I am the tree's son, he thought; I am the rain child; they are both looking after me.

In spring-time when the grass was thick with daffo-dils, and then buttercups, and then big white daisies, he used to weave the flowers into garlands to hang on the branches of his tree; and in the autumn he decked her with chaplets of red berries.

If ever he had any unhappinesses – if the old priest scolded him for not knowing his lesson, if Ana rapped him on the knuckles for breaking a dish, if his kitten fell sick or a plant in his garden died – he would run through the orchard to his tree, throw his arms round her smooth trunk, and pour out all his troubles to her. And her branches would murmur overhead, her leaves would rustle; he was soothed by her silent sympathy and would begin to feel better.

So time went softly by – days and weeks and years; the boy learned to ride on a pony, he learned to shoot with a bow and arrow, he learned the names of the birds and the stars and the lands of the distant world, and there came a day at last when the old priest said,

'I have taught you all I know. Now you must learn from others.'

More weeks went by, and then a cavalcade of men came riding to the orchard. These were not apple-pickers: they were soldiers, escorting a grave elderly man who had a grey beard and wore a furred cloak of purple cloth. He said to the boy,

'We have come to take you away.'

The boy was aghast.

'Why? This is where I live! This is where I have always lived. This is where I belong!'

'Not so,' said the bearded man. And he added, 'Do you know who you are?'

'I am the tree's child. I am the rain child.'

'But what is your name?'

'I don't know,' said the boy, and then he fell silent. He had never pondered before about the fact that Ana simply called him 'Child', while the old priest addressed him as 'You'.

'Your royal name is Nicholas Alexander,' the bearded man told him. 'Yesterday you were Prince Nicholas Alexander. Today you are king. You are king and emperor of this country.'

And he knelt down and kissed the boy's hand.

'Now,' he said, 'you must ride with us to your capital city and take charge of all that is yours.'

A fear came over the boy. He said,

'I don't understand. *Why* am I king? *Why* was I prince yesterday and king today? And why has nobody ever told me this before?'

The bearded man said,

'Ever since you were born our country has been ravaged by the armies of an invader for thousands of miles. The war has raged for year after year. This was the only corner of the land they never reached, and this was the only place where you could be safe; so orders were given that you must be brought up here in secrecy, that nobody, not even you yourself, must know who you were, or enemies would surely have learned that you were here and sent assassins to kill you. But now at last our enemies have been defeated – they have all been driven back to their own lands, and their own cities have been sacked; there is no more danger from them.'

'But why,' repeated the boy, 'was I prince yesterday and king today?'

'Because,' said the grey-bearded man, 'your gracious mother, who was queen and empress of all this country, died last night. So now you are king.'

'But I thought—' said the boy. 'I understood—' Then he fell silent, for what he had been about to say suddenly sounded foolish. 'And my father?' he said instead.

'Your father the king died in battle many years ago. That is why your mother was so concerned for your safety.'

The boy said,

'Excuse me. I must think about this.'

And he left the hut, where they had been talking, and walked outside. There he saw Ana, pegging out some washing on the line. She curtsied to him, with a respect she had never shown before.

'Is this true?' he asked her. 'Is it true, what that man said? Was I the prince? Am I now the king?'

'Yes, my lord, it is true,' said Ana.

'Why did you never tell me?'

'I was forbidden.'

'But you said—' His throat was tight with grief. He

found it hard to bring out the words. 'You sang the song to me – that said my mother was an apple tree—'

'Oh, that,' said Ana. 'That was only a rhyme, to send you to sleep when you were a baby, when you were fretful.'

And she picked up her peg basket and went indoors. The boy stood staring at the nearest trees, but as if he hardly saw them.

'Come, sire,' said the grey-bearded man presently. 'We must set out, for we have many miles to ride before dark. Here – I have brought you clothes more suitable for your station.'

He unfolded a suit of scarlet cloth, embroidered with gold, and a fur-lined cloak; he had brought a gold chain for the boy's neck.

'Wait, now,' said the boy, when he had put these on. 'I have something else to attend to. Wait for me here. I am going into the orchard. I shall not be gone long. I wish to be alone.'

And he set off, running, between the lines of trees. It was the time of early summer, when they were all covered with downy green leaves and the last of the blossom. The boy ran straight to the tree which he had taken to be his mother; he thought that she had never seemed more beautiful, with tiny clusters of green apples, and a few flowers still scattered here and there.

He knelt down and put his arms around the trunk, his cheek against the bark. His trouble was too deep for tears, but after a while he whispered,

'I was wrong. You are not my mother. You have never been my mother. I had a real mother – but she cannot have loved me, for she sent me away, and now she has died without ever speaking to me. But *you* have always cared for me and listened to me and looked after me and helped me; and I love you best in the world. You are my mother more than that woman who was queen. And now they are going to take me away from you – and I don't know how I can bear it. Help me again. Please help me!'

At all the former times when the boy had come to tell his troubles, the tree had listened in silence, except for the rustle of its leaves. But this time, as he knelt with his arms around the trunk, he felt a deep, deep trembling go through the tree's whole frame, from the roots to the branches, as if it were most profoundly moved. For many minutes the boy knelt in silence, and felt the tree quiver in his embrace, like somebody who is too grieved to speak.

Then in the distance he heard the bearded man shouting:

'Your grace! Please to make haste!'

Slowly, he stood up. He felt calmer now; sad, but collected.

He said, 'I know that I have to go. But I shall come back; however far they take me, I shall certainly come back. Remember me. Oh, please remember me!'

And, taking off the gold chain from his neck, the boy twined it carefully round and round one of the apple tree's slender branches. Then, breathing in sharply as if he had a sudden pain too bad to bear, he turned and ran blindly through the orchard until he came to where the men and horses were waiting, with old Ana mounted on a mule, for she was coming too.

Soon after the start of their journey they passed the old priest's house, and the boy stopped to say goodbye to him.

'Yes – you have learned all I could teach you,' the priest said. 'You have enough in you to fit you for kingship. Go now, with my blessing.'

'I am going, but I shall certainly come back,' the boy said.

'Why, what should bring you back here?' the old man exclaimed. 'No, child, no – you will find plenty of duties waiting for you out in the world. There will be no reason for you to come back to a flat plain and a thousand apple trees. Goodbye, highness, and may heaven smile on your work.'

They rode on and when, at the day's end, they stopped to eat and sleep at an inn, and the boy laid aside his furred cloak, the bearded man inquired severely,

'Where is the gold chain I brought, which is the badge of your kingship?'

The boy answered, with haughty composure,

'I have given it to someone I love. You will have to find me another.'

Next day they reached a city where they left their horses and transferred to great gold-painted carriages, quilted inside with velvet. And, after another week's travelling, they came to the capital of the land, where, with great and elaborate ceremony, Nicholas Alexander the Sixteenth was crowned king and emperor.

People said of him,

'He is so young – but what dignity he has already! Although he was brought up in poverty and obscurity, anybody can see that he is of the blood royal, and that those who had charge of him were accustomed to courtly ways. He has been taught all that a prince should know.'

Nonetheless there was much for the boy to learn, and more to do – new laws to make for a land that had so long been racked and torn by war, new towns to build, ruined towns to restore – countless tasks and problems which the new young king had to solve as he came to them. His days were very full.

'He has a thoughtful heart,' the people said. 'The old queen was a brave and shrewd ruler, but she was cold-hearted – the right leader in war, not so good in time of peace. We are lucky to have our young king now.'

Everybody loved him, in spite of his grave manner, for he worked so hard and took such pains.

In the autumn he said to his prime minister, 'I need a rest. I am going away.'

'To the sea, your majesty? To the mountains?'

'No, I am going back to the orchard where I spent my childhood. I need peace and silence. I want nobody with me – except old Ana; she can come to do the cooking.'

This greatly scandalized the prime minister, but the king had his way; off he went, driving himself in a light carriage with Ana beside him. And after a week's travel they arrived at the little hut. Ana set to work at once, airing and cleaning it, while the young king walked off into the orchard.

All the trees were loaded down with apples; in a few days the pickers would arrive, for their annual three weeks of laughter and hard work. But just now all was silent and calm; waiting. The king walked straight to the tree which he had taken to be his mother.

To his astonishment and fear he found, as he approached her, that she bore no fruit; unlike the other trees, which were loaded down by the heavy burden of an excellent crop, her branches appeared to carry not a single apple. – No, there was one: on the branch around which the king had fastened his gold chain, he discovered a single fruit. It was a large apple, bigger than his two fists doubled together. And it shone brilliant yellow – it appeared to be made of pure gold. The branch on which it grew drooped down pitifully, almost cracked by the weight; and the whole tree looked peaked and ailing; its leaves were few and pale; they dangled limply as if they were ready to fall. As the king reached the tree, the golden apple fell heavily to the grass, and lay at his feet. He picked it up and almost staggered under its weight; he could not bear to keep it in his hands for more than a moment.

'Oh, my poor dear!' he cried out in bitter self-reproach. 'What a dreadful burden you have been carrying!'

He knelt down and wrapped his arms round the trunk of the tree.

'I asked too much of you,' he told it. 'I laid more on you than a tree should have to bear. I am sorry – I am sorry. Forgive me! Now that I have been king, I know more about what can be borne and what cannot. I will not ask any more of you. I shall always love you – to the end of my life – but you must go back to being only a tree again.'

As before, he felt the tree tremble in his arms; a few of its sad pale leaves fluttered past him and drifted on to the grass. Gently the king stroked a smooth branch, and then he picked up the massive gold apple.

'I have come back to rest here,' he told the tree, 'but you need rest even more. Winter is coming – the cold and the silence will be good for you. They will heal you of this trouble.'

He kissed the tree's bark and went away to the hut.

Next day the pickers arrived, with their laughter and jokes and songs, and, as in other years, the king helped them. When all the apples were picked and carted away the men left, and the king left too, with old Ana.

But first he went to kiss his tree goodbye. 'I shall come back sometimes,' he said, 'to rest here, and to tell you about being a king.'

As they left, a light autumn rain began to fall, pattering on the leaves and grass; the drops of rain ran down the king's cheeks like somebody else's tears. He thought, as he had so often when a child,

'Now they are talking to each other. Now she is telling him about me. I need not worry about her. She will not be lonely.' And the rain comforted him, as he drove along the narrow straight road, which seemed to lead on for ever across the plain.

Next autumn, when he came back to the orchard, his tree was covered with fruit – real apples, not fruit of gold; and so it was every year after that, until the king died at a great age. Then his tree went into mourning; all the leaves fell from her branches; and in a month she, too, was dead.

The Faithless Lollybird

Far away to the north, in a small hut in the middle of a large forest, there lived a weaver whose name was Luke. All this happened not long ago as the clock ticks, but a long way off as the crow flies.

In his hut, Luke had a loom, taking up most of the floor space. And every day, on his loom, he wove the most beautiful cloth – material for coats and cloaks and carpets, for sheets and shirts and shawls, for towels and tablecloths and tapestries, for babies' blankets and bishops' aprons. Some of the things he made seemed almost too good for everyday wear and tear. They were so beautiful that it seemed wrong to do anything but hang them on the wall and gaze at them. But everything he made was really meant to be used.

And to help him with his weaving, Luke had a bird, a Lollybird. When he had strung up his loom ready to start, with the woollen, or cotton, or silk threads going longways – the warp – Luke would tie another length of wool to a shuttle and hand it to the Lollybird, which up to that moment would have been sitting very still on the chimney-piece, or a corner of the loom, or Luke's shoulder, carefully watching all that he did, without moving a single feather.

However, as soon as he handed the shuttle to it, this Lollybird would begin to fly with the most amazing speed back and forth, in and out, up and down, among the strings on the loom, going so fast that nothing of it could be seen at all except a blur of colour as it shot to and fro. The Lollybird itself was just a little grey creature, but as it worked it would snatch one thread and then another from Luke. Sometimes dropping the shuttle entirely it would wind a scarlet strand round its neck and a green one round its stomach, it would carry a pink thread in its beak and clutch a silver one in its claws, so that if it had ever stopped, if you could have caught a glimpse of it, you would have thought it was a travelling Christmas tree, all sparkling and rainbow-coloured. But it never did stop, until the work was finished, and the last knot made, the last thread pulled tightly into place. Then with a final swoop and a last flash of its wings it would come to rest on Luke's shoulder, or the top of his head, and together they would take a careful look at the piece of cloth they had just woven.

Perhaps it was a coronation robe for a king, all scarlet

and gold, with fur round the border and a roaring lion in the middle. Or perhaps it was a carpet for a cathedral with angels and lilies and harps, all in blue and green and silver. Or maybe it was a curtain for some great gallery in a Lord Mayor's house, with a picture of unicorns roaming through a forest and butterflies fluttering among the apples on the branches. Or it might be a tablecloth for a children's school, with cats and dogs, and the sun and moon, and birds and fish, and letters and numbers, to give the children something to look at as they were eating their dinner.

Whatever the piece of cloth was that they had just woven, Luke and his Lollybird would carefully inspect it, making sure there were no rough edges, or lumpy places, or loose threads anywhere. But there never were.

Then Luke would give a sigh of satisfaction, and say,

'Well, I think we did a good bit of work that time, my dear Lollybird,' and the Lollybird would cock its head on one side in approval and say,

'Certainly can't see anything wrong with that little job, master,' and the two friends would stop work for a short time.

Sometimes, in these spells off between jobs, Luke might play on his flute, while the Lollybird chirped a little song. The Lollybird had no voice to speak of, and its song sounded like somebody scratching a twig down the side of a nutmeg grater. Indeed, the Lollybird was a little embarrassed about its lack of singing ability, but Luke didn't mind. He had a mandolin as well as the flute and sometimes the Lollybird, hopping to and fro on the mandolin's strings, would scratch them with its claws and fetch out a faint thread of tune while Luke softly whistled a few matching notes. Then, if the day was a fine one, they might go for a walk in the forest, the Lollybird sitting on Luke's shoulder or flying ahead of him through the great trunks of the trees.

On these walks they searched for the leaves and flowers and roots which Luke needed to dye the silk and wool that he used in his weaving. There was a plant with golden flowers whose root gave a beautiful yellow, and a purple flower that dyed red, and a kind of toadstool which, pounded to a pulp, produced a fine dark orange, and the bark of a tree which could be ground up to make a deep rose-pink. Wild spinach gave them bright green, and certain nuts and berries were good for browns and crimsons. The only colour they could not get from any plant in the forest was a blue to satisfy them; for that, Luke had to send away many hundreds of miles. A kind of shellfish, only found in southern seas, gave a beautiful clear dark blue, but Luke often grumbled because the loads of shellfish, which had to be brought through the forest by sledge, took a long time on the way, and sometimes, if a pattern they were working on used a lot of blue, they might have to wait for a new supply to arrive.

'I wish we could find a decent blue close at hand,' Luke would say.

On their walks through the wood the two friends also found tufts of coloured moss and flower petals, bright leaves, flakes of glossy bark, gay feathers dropped by birds, even small sparkling stones and chips of rock, which they wove into their fabrics, so that often the lengths of material they made were quite dazzling and seemed to shine and ripple the way a brook does when it catches the sun's light.

Because the things he made were so beautiful, Luke's fame began to spread all over the world. More and more people wanted to buy his work. Customers came from farther and farther away, in ships and on camels, by sledge and bicycle and caravan, in lorries and balloons, on horseback and in helicopters. So that presently, after a few years had passed, Luke and his Lollybird had to work harder and harder if they were to keep up with all the orders that poured in.

'I never get a chance to sit in the sun any more,' complained the Lollybird. 'We haven't had time for any music since the last new moon. We don't even get a breath of fresh air.'

Lately Luke had hired two boys to hunt for his dye-plants and mosses. The ones they brought back were not always so good, but there was no time for Luke and his Lollybird to go into the forest. They had to work all the hours of daylight. By the time night came the Lollybird was tired out, and would fall asleep perched on the loom with its head tucked under its wing.

'You should refuse to take any more orders,' it said to Luke one morning.

'It would be wrong to disappoint people,' said Luke. 'Specially when they have come all this way. Why, only today we had the Emperor of Japan, wanting a new dressing-gown, and the Mayor of New York, needing a carpet for his town hall, and the Queen of the Windward Islands, with an order for a screen to keep the wind off, and the manager of the Milan Opera, about a new stage curtain for his opera house, and the President of Finland, ordering new tapestry for the Finnish—'

'Finnish? We never *shall* finish!' wailed the Lollybird, and it snatched up a shuttle and darted angrily between the warp strings of a beautiful white and silver christening shawl which they were making for a little princess in Denmark. '*She* wouldn't know the difference if they wrapped her in an old bath towel,' it muttered as it flew back and forth.

'It would be wrong to disappoint people,' repeated Luke.

'What about me? *I'm* disappointed if I don't have a bit of music, or get out for my evening stroll,' said the indignant Lollybird.

Matters became even worse. For now a railway was built through the forest, with a station right beside Luke's hut, so that more and more people would come to order things, and to watch the weavers at work. The visitors stood around, and picked up the shuttles, and tangled the wool, and were a dreadful nuisance all day long. In the evening they invited Luke out to the café which had been built just down the road, and they talked to him and praised his work and asked him how he planned his patterns. He quite enjoyed all the company and cheerfulness. It made a change from the long quiet evenings he had spent alone with the Lollybird, after it grew too dark to go on weaving, when he had had nothing to do but play his flute, not very well, while the Lollybird sang its little scratchy song, like a pencil being scraped down a nutmeg grater.

The Lollybird did not enjoy all this extra company at all. It never took part in the conversation, or went out to the café. As soon as the light was gone it would retire to the back of the loom and go to sleep there, hidden among dangling hanks of wool, with its head under its wing. And, even during the day, when the Lollybird was working, very few people noticed it flashing to and fro under the strands of the warp, for it went faster than their eyes could follow. Many people, in fact, did not realize that the Lollybird even existed. If they praised the work and Luke said,

'Oh, it is partly the Lollybird's doing too, you know,' they believed that he was joking, and laughed politely.

So by and by he gave up mentioning the Lollybird.

One morning the Lollybird said, 'Master, it's spring. The cuckoos have come back to the forest, and the swallows are here, and the storks are building their houses, and the wild geese keep flying past, and I need to go out and stretch my wings.'

'Rubbish,' said Luke. 'You have quite enough healthy exercise flying up and down inside the loom. And we are two days late on the set of flags for the new Mandolian Republic. Hurry up and get to work.'

The Lollybird got to work, but it was sulking dreadfully as it flew backwards and forwards with the red, black, and yellow silk threads for the Mandolian flags; indeed it clutched some of the threads so tightly in its little hot angry claws that, although they did not snap immediately, the very first time that the flags were flown in a hurricane (and hurricanes are very common in Mandolia) several of them tore in half.

Now this was the first time that the Lollybird had ever done bad work. At the end of the day it felt guilty and miserable and sulkier than ever.

That evening a group of admirers called in to sit round Luke and look at the work half-finished on the loom, and praise it. They brought a bottle of wine, and presently they all began drinking and singing songs.

'Don't you keep a bird in here?' one of them said presently. 'Wouldn't the bird sing us a song?'

'Oh,' said Luke carelessly. 'It will be asleep by now. And in any case it's only a working-bird, not a songbird. Its song is no better than a frog croaking.'

Now the Lollybird had not been asleep. The voices and talk and laughter had kept it awake. And at these words of Luke's its heart swelled inside it with shame.

One of the visitors had left the door open a crack and,

under cover of the noise and singing, which had started up again, the Lollybird crept to the end of the loom and then flew swiftly and silently out through the crack of the door, although it was black dark in the forest and none but night creatures were stirring.

The Lollybird had never been out at night. It was not accustomed to flying in the dark, and bumped into several trees. Soon it was lost. Nevertheless it flew on listening to the songs of the nightingales and envying their voices. Presently it reached a wide open space. This was an airstrip, for now Luke had his blue shellfish flown in by plane, and there was the freight-plane sitting in the middle of the space.

'What an enormous bird,' thought the Lollybird, which had not had a chance to fly out that way since the plane began coming.

Just then the Lollybird itself nearly came to a sudden end, for a large horned owl, which had noticed it bumping among the trees and followed out of curiosity, swooped down to grab this clumsy stranger and missed it by no more than the flutter of a feather. The Lollybird saw two great golden eyes coming faster than a train and nipped out of the way with a skilful twist learned from years of flying up and down inside the loom.

The owl thumped against the plane's wing, and the terrified Lollybird flew straight through an open hatchway and into the plane itself.

'Hoooo! Ha!' shouted the owl outside. 'I can see you,

you miserable little beggar! I'm going to eat you up in one mouthful. Come out of there!'

In fact he couldn't see the Lollybird at all, and presently he gave up and flew off in search of other prey. But the Lollybird didn't know he had gone and stayed trembling in its dark corner for a long time.

After a while the pilot arrived, climbed in, slammed the door, and started up the engine. Now the Lollybird was even more frightened, but what could it do? Nothing at all. The plane took off, circled round, climbed higher, flew and flew through the black hours of night, until they were many many thousands of miles from the airstrip, and the forest, and Luke's little hut.

At last morning came, and the sun rose, and the plane landed, and the pilot opened the door and got down and walked away.

Then at last the Lollybird dared to creep stiffly out of its hiding-place and scramble through the hatchway into the noise and light and muddle of a great airport.

There were so many things to see that it saw nothing at all. By pure good luck it escaped being run over by a truck, or squashed flat by a crane, or squeezed in a pair of automatic doors. Avoiding a Boeing 707 and a fire-wagon, and a limousine, it darted between two taxis and flew straight into the open doorway of a bus, which immediately started up and sped off along the wide straight road that led into the middle of London.

'My goodness!' thought the Lollybird, hanging upside

down by one claw from the luggage rack and gazing out with astonishment at all the houses and supermarkets and cats and dogs and people whizzing past. 'To think there was all this in the world and I never knew it!'

In Piccadilly Circus the bus came to a stop. By this time dusk was falling, and nobody noticed the Lollybird, which flew out and perched on a windowsill where it looked at the dazzling lights of the advertisements and the many-coloured cars and the people in their gay clothes and the stalls selling apples and pears and strawberries and the brightly lit windows of the restaurants and the police cars and ambulances with their flashing blue beacons and the fire engines all red and gold rushing along ringing their bells.

'My goodness,' thought the Lollybird again, 'I wish Luke could see this. If we had our loom here, what a picture we could weave.'

But then it remembered how angry it was with Luke. 'Anyway I can manage without him,' it thought. 'All I have to do is string a web from those prongs.'

The Lollybird began to bustle about, collecting threads and strands, of which there were plenty to be found in the untidy streets. First it drew out a long streamer of the smoke trailing from a car's exhaust pipe and wound it into a spiral, then it snatched a string from a boy's balloon, and twitched a length of raffia from a woman's shopping-basket. Here it tweaked a dangling end of wool from a girl's shawl, there it snatched a spare hair from a man's beard. All these and many other things were threaded with wonderful skill between the TV aerials that sprouted from the roofs.

Now the Lollybird really began to enjoy itself. It picked up coloured ribbons and bits of tissue paper, metal foil, orange-peel, tufts of fur from poodles, silvery rings from Coke cans, and long shining strands from the tails of police horses. Everything was woven into a huge and sparkling canopy which presently dangled all over the top of Piccadilly Circus like a beautiful tent.

'Oh, what a clever Lollybird I am!' cried the Lollybird with great enthusiasm, and it flew off to do the same thing somewhere else.

But meanwhile poor Luke was in a dreadful state without his Lollybird.

He had just managed to finish the job they had been working on when the Lollybird left home, but he found that he was quite unable to start anything else. He had no idea how to set about it. His fingers were too clumsy, he kept dropping the shuttle, his patterns got into a muddle, and in less than two days the inside of his hut was one complete tangle of wool, so that nobody could so much as get through the door.

At first Luke was very angry at the Lollybird's disappearance.

He went stamping through the forest, bawling and shouting.

'Lollybird! Hey, you Lollybird! Where are you? Come back at once!'

But there was no answer.

All night he called and called. 'Where are you, you naughty Lollybird? Where are you, you faithless Lollybird?'

But still there was no answer.

Then Luke began to wonder if some owl or eagle had caught the Lollybird, and to worry, and feel sorry. Then he began to remember that he had not always treated the Lollybird very well, that he had made it work when it wanted to fly out into the forest, that sometimes he had given it nothing but dry biscuits to eat for days on end, when he was too busy to stop and cook the millet porridge that the Lollybird liked best. And sometimes, he remembered, he had insisted on finishing a job of work when the Lollybird was tired and stiff, when it was yawning into its wing and having difficulty keeping its eyes open.

'Oh my dear Lollybird! Where are you? Come back, come back and I won't make you work so hard.' But still there was no answer.

By this time most of the people who had come with orders for more work, or to watch and wonder at the weaving, had become impatient and gone back home again. The forest was empty and silent. But somebody, just as they left, reported that somebody else had been told that yet another person thought he had heard tell that someone else had seen the Lollybird climb into a plane and fly off in it.

'In that case the Lollybird may be anywhere in the

world,' thought Luke. 'How shall I ever find it again? But there's no use staying here, that's certain.'

So Luke shut up his hut and climbed on to the last shellfish plane and flew to London.

When he reached London, one of the first things he heard was a story of a wonderful bird which had spread a sparkling web all over the top of Piccadilly Circus.

'Oh, that must be my Lollybird!' cried Luke, and he leapt into a taxi and told the driver to go as fast as possible to Piccadilly. Luckily Luke had plenty of money; all these years he had never spent a hundredth part of what he and the Lollybird earned between them. When he reached Piccadilly Circus he looked about for the beautiful canopy. But it was gone. The Westminster City Council Cleaning Department had come with brooms and mops and suction cleaners and had swept it down and tidied it all away.

But now Luke heard stories about a wonderful bird which had spun a cover like a huge egg-cosy, only bigger, all glittering and rainbow-coloured, over the dome of St Peter's church in Rome.

'That must, that must be my wandering Lollybird!' he cried, and he took another plane and flew to Rome. But when he got to St Peter's he found that the Rome City Council had sent helicopters with mops and hoses and had removed the wonderful cover.

'Oh,' cried Luke sorrowfully, 'where, where shall I find my wayward Lollybird?'

But now he heard tales of a marvellous bird that was

weaving a multi-coloured canopy over the elephant house in the Berlin Zoo.

He sent a telegram: PLEASE, PLEASE DO NOT STOP THE BIRD, and jumped into another plane and flew to Berlin.

When he reached the Berlin Zoo everybody was watching in admiration as the tiny bird flew darting about, snatching a hank of wool from a llama, catching a plume from the tail of an ostrich, gathering a tuft of black fur from a gorilla, whisking up a dropped peacock's feather, and a bright scale that some fish had cast off, and weaving them all into its beautiful sparkling web, while a whole ring of elephants stood underneath and gazed at it spellbound with uplifted trunks.

'Oh,' cried Luke in rapture, 'it is, it must be, my faithless Lollybird!'

And the Lollybird heard his voice among all the other voices in the crowd and answered him,

'Yes I am, I am your faithless Lollybird!'

'Come back, come back, you naughty thoughtless Lollybird! I can't manage without you!'

'No,' said the Lollybird, 'you can't manage without me, but I can manage very well without you. Goodbye, I'm off to London again.'

And it flew tauntingly away with a flip of its tail.

'Come back, come back, you disobedient Lollybird!'

'Goodbye, goodbye! You can't manage without me, but I can manage very well without you.'

Poor Luke had to follow as best he could. There was no plane just then, so he caught a boat. When it came chugging up the Thames he saw that the naughty Lollybird had woven a glittering web across Tower Bridge, all made of straw wine-bottle-vases, and scraps of polystyrene, and bus tickets, and milk-bottle tops.

But when Luke stepped off the boat, just too late, the vagrant Lollybird flew gaily away, crying,

'You can't manage without me, but I can manage very well without you!'

'Come back! Come back to your proper work, you wicked Lollybird!'

'Not yet! Not yet! Maybe never at all. Not till you have called me a hundred, hundred times, not till you have found a blue dye in the forest, not till I can sing as well as the nightingales, not till you promise never to overwork me ever, ever again!'

'I promise now!' cried the sorrowful Luke.

'Promises cost nothing. You'll have to prove you are telling the truth before I believe you,' replied the uncaring Lollybird, and away it flew.

Luke didn't know what to do. He rented a room with a telephone, he rang up the police, he put advertisements in all the papers, saying, 'LOST! My faithless Lollybird. Large reward to finder.'

Many people had seen the elusive Lollybird, and rang up to say so, but wherever it had been seen, by the time Luke arrived, the bird was always gone. Luke wandered through the streets of London by day and night, calling and crying,

'Where are you, you mocking Lollybird? Where are you, you thankless Lollybird?'

Then Luke began to hear that the bird had been seen at concerts, and at musical instrument shops, and at schools where pupils were taught singing.

One night Luke went to a concert at the Royal Festival Hall. Sure enough, there was the Lollybird, perched on the conductor's rostrum, listening hard to the music. After a while, though, it couldn't resist beginning to flit about and pick things up here and there, a gold thread

from a lady's evening cape, a white hair from the conductor's head, a fern frond out of a pot of growing plants,
a tie from a flute-player's neck, a length of spaghetti from
a plate in the restaurant. Then it began to weave a web
across from the bows of the violinists to the boxes on the
opposite side of the hall.

The violinists couldn't play with their bows tied down,
the music came to a stop, and Luke cried out,

'Lollybird! You are behaving very badly. Come back to
your master!'

'Not yet! Not yet! I'm having far too good a time to
come home!' replied the teasing Lollybird, and away it
flew, through a window and across the Thames, into a
great hotel where it tied all the table-napkins into a fluttering string and knotted them round the chandelier.

Then it flew all the way down the river, snatching
up strings of streetlights and trailing them in the water
behind it.

Luke was tired out and went back to his room to bed.

But by now the provoking Lollybird had learned how to
use the telephone. Luke had no sooner gone off to sleep
than the phone would ring and when he picked up the
receiver he heard a shrill voice calling in his ear,

'Hullo, hullo, hullo, hullo, this is your faithless Lollybird!'

Night after night the Lollybird woke him in this way
until Luke grew pale and thin and had great black circles
under his eyes from want of sleep.

'Come back! Come back, you heartless Lollybird,' he cried into the telephone.

'Not yet! Not for a long time yet!'

The Lollybird was taking singing lessons from a famous opera singer. In exchange for the lessons it was weaving her a beautiful cloak from brown paper and string and bits of tinsel and pine-needles and photographers' flash-bulbs. The Lollybird wove its web, and the singer sang scales, and the Lollybird repeated them; its voice was growing louder and sweeter with every lesson. And at the end of each lesson it would borrow the singer's telephone to ring up Luke and call,

'Hullo, hullo, hullo, hullo! This is your faithless Lolly-bird.'

'Come back home! Come back and do your proper work!'

'Not till you have called me a hundred, hundred times,' replied the wayward bird, and it sang like a snatch of music from The Magic Flute, and plunked down the receiver.

Now, by chance, Luke heard tell of a famous echo, in a cave in a valley in Derbyshire, an echo that would repeat the same word for half an hour at a time, throwing it from one side of the valley to the other. So he took a train, and a bus, and a taxi, and went to the cave. The Lollybird was piqued and inquisitive at being left behind, and it flew after Luke secretly to see what he was up to, and perched on a bush outside the entrance to the cave.

'Lollybird!' cried Luke inside the tunnel. 'Come back, come back, come back to your proper work, you teasing Lollybird!'

A hundred times he called it, and each word was repeated by the echo a hundred times, so that the whole valley was filled with Luke's voice calling Come back, come back, come back!

'Well, well, perhaps I will, some day,' said the Lollybird, darting about the valley, listening to all the echoes, and cocking its head on one side to count them. 'But not just yet, not just yet, my dear master!'

And away it flew.

Not just yet, not just yet, not just yet, repeated the echoes in the valley, as Luke came out of the cave and saw the Lollybird, a tiny speck, flying farther and farther away over the distant hills.

After this Luke became very discouraged. He began to feel that he might grow into an old man before the runaway Lollybird decided to come back, that he might as well give up hope of trying to persuade it.

So, very sadly, he went back to the airport and took a plane (he had to charter one specially, for no planes flew that way any more, and this took the last of his money) and he returned to his forest.

The hut was dark and cold, half fallen down, and it was still full of a dreadful tangle of knotted wool and yarn and silk and cotton. Luke was too tired to do anything about the tangle that night, and he had no oil for his lamp, so he lay down in the dark in the middle of it all and went to sleep. But next day he slowly and clumsily set about the disagreeable task of unknotting all the knots and unsnarling all the snarls, winding up all the different lengths of wool and silk, and setting the hut to rights.

But when he had finished it was still empty and cold and silent. The people who had once come to see him weave had long ago left; the railway was closed down and grass grew along the track; no planes flew that way any more; winter was coming and the birds were quiet in the forest.

Luke walked slowly through the trees. The silence lay thick as mist. He remembered how the Lollybird used to fly out with him, looking for plants and mosses.

Oh,' he cried sadly, 'oh how very much I miss you, my dearest Lollybird.'

He remembered how helpful the Lollybird had always been, and how cheerful, how much it enjoyed inventing new patterns and finding new bits of stuff to weave with, how lively it woke in the mornings, how willingly it worked long hours, and how much, when work was done, it had liked to sing its little grating song and pick out a tune on the strings of the mandolin.

'I am sorry I was unkind about its voice,' he thought.

Then he remembered the Lollybird's declaration that it would never return till Luke had found a blue dye in the forest.

'But even if I did find one, how would it ever know?' he

thought, and as he wandered along the forest track, tears ran down his face and fell among the withered leaves beside the path.

At last it grew too cold to stay outside any longer, and he went back to the hut.

But, to his astonishment, he saw a light shining in the window. And when he went in, there was his Lollybird. It had lit the lamp, and kindled a little fire, and set a saucepan full of millet porridge on the hob. And it was looking at the empty loom, and the stacked-up shuttles and skeins of wool and yarn, very disapprovingly, with its head on one side.

'Am I dreaming?' said Luke. 'Are you a dream, or are you really my Lollybird come back at last?'

'No, I'm not a dream,' said the Lollybird, giving the porridge a stir.

'Oh, my dear friend, my long-lost Lollybird! How very, very glad I am to see you!'

'It's plain I've come back none too soon,' said the Lollybird tartly. 'For you don't appear to have done a stroke of work since I left home. We'd best have our supper quickly and go to bed, for we'll need to get started early in the morning.'

Luke was too happy to ask any questions that night. But, next morning, when they had started work, and the Lollybird was flashing to and fro across the loom with a strand of rose-pink wool in its beak and another under its wing, he did venture to ask timidly,

'I thought you said that you wouldn't come back till I'd found a blue dye in the forest. Why did you change your mind?'

'Oh well,' said the Lollybird looking down its beak with a casual air, 'if I'd waited for *that*, I've no doubt I'd have had to wait a mighty long time. And to tell the truth I was getting a little bored flying about the world.'

All day they worked, weaving a curtain that was rose-coloured and black and blue and olive-green. When it was done Luke took a thoughtful look at it and said, 'I reckon that's the best bit of work we ever did, my dear Lollybird,' and the Lollybird, also after a careful scrutiny and tweaking all the strands with its beak to make sure that none were loose, replied, 'No, I can't see anything wrong with that little job, master. Who did we make it for?'

'I really forget,' said Luke. 'But I daresay it'll come in handy for something. Now, how about a bit of music?'

He fetched out his old flute and played a tune. And because of all its lessons the Lollybird was able to sing him arias from all the greatest operas, in a voice that any nightingale might have envied.

Never again did Luke make his Lollybird work too hard or too long. They took no more orders than would keep them busy for a reasonable part of the day; and when work was over they would go off into the forest, looking for feathers and bright stones, shining petals and gaily coloured leaves.

Next spring, to Luke's astonishment, a new flower came

up under the trees, a flower that he had never seen before, which, when picked and dried and powdered, gave them a most beautiful blue dye, a blue as dark and clear as the middle of the ocean on a fine winter day.

'I wonder where the seeds can have come from?' Luke said. 'Maybe some bird dropped them as it flew over. What a mysterious thing!'

But the Lollybird knew that the flowers had sprung up from Luke's tears, as he wandered sadly along the forest path, crying, 'Oh, how very much I miss you, my dearest Lollybird.'

The Dog on the Roof

Not many years ago there was an old lady living in Washington Square, New York. Her name was Mrs Logan, and she lived right in the park; she hung her clothes on a tree, on coat hangers, and ate her breakfast sitting on a bench. She lived there with her cab-horse, Murphy – and her cab too, of course.

They are not there now. This is the story of why they lived there, and why they left.

At the time I am speaking of, there was also a poet, called Paul Powdermaker, living in a fourth-floor studio in a house in Twelfth Street, five minutes' walk from Washington Square.

Living with Paul was a Labrador dog called Bayer. Bayer was big, with a thick black shiny coat and thoughtful brown eyes. Paul had taken charge of Bayer when his previous owner moved to Patagonia. Paul was not accustomed to dogs, but he had a very kind nature. Bayer was good-natured too, as black Labradors mostly are, and the two got on well. (Poets and dogs nearly always do get on well; they speak the same language.)

Bayer had only one bad habit: of course he did not consider it bad, but some people might. His previous owner had trained him to howl at the sound of a Salvation Army band – or any music played in the street. At the first sound of a transistor, or people singing, or drums, or guitars, Bayer would start to bark and howl and carry on, making as much noise as he could to drown the music.

Paul had one fault too: he never took Bayer out for a walk. He didn't realize that dogs need adventures.

Luckily in the studio they shared there was a door that led out on to the roof. So, five or six times a day, Bayer would pad over to this door and give a short, polite bark; then Paul would get up, pen in hand, open the door, shut it again behind Bayer, and go on with his writing, which he did for twenty hours a day.

Once outside, Bayer would suddenly change from being a rather fat, slow, sleepy, lazy indoor dog to a keen, alert, active (but still rather fat), outdoor one.

First he would rush to the edge of the roof and look down to see what was going on in Twelfth Street. Then he would bark hard, about twenty times, just to announce that he was observing everybody in the street and keeping an eye on everything. There were trees along each side of the street, and birds in them, and sometimes a cat or two in the front gardens, and pigeons and blue jays on the roofs, and a few people strolling or walking briskly.

Sometimes there would be another dog down in the street; then Bayer would bark extra loud. And Bayer had a friend, called Rackstraw, who lived in the basement area of the house along at the corner; so some of his barks were for Rackstraw, and meant, 'Good morning! How are you down there? I'm all right up here. Isn't it hot/cold/fine/rainy/frosty/snowy today?'

We shall come back to Rackstraw later.

When Bayer had finished his barking, he would take off like a champion hurdler and race right along the block all the way from one end to the other and then back, several times. The roofs were not all flat. Some sloped up to parapets; some were two or three feet higher than their neighbours; here and there, studio skylights stuck up like big triangular boxes; or there were clusters of chimneys like giants' fingers, or water tanks on legs which looked like pointed rockets about to take off.

Bayer knew all this landscape of roof as well as most dogs know their backyards, and he went bounding along, clearing the walls like a greyhound, nipping among and through the chimneys like a polo pony, skirting around the water tanks and studio skylights like a St Bernard on the slopes of the Alps. Bayer had a very good head for heights, and, though he often dashed right to the edge of a roof and barked so hard that he looked as if he were going to bark himself right off, he had never done so yet.

When he had breathed in enough fresh air, he would return to his own door, and let out another short polite bark, and Paul Powdermaker would let him in.

Though he worked so hard at it, Paul did not earn a very good living from his poetry writing. Very few poets do. He wrote hundreds of poems, and sent them to dozens of magazines, but hardly any of his poems were printed. And the payment for those that were printed was not high. So, as well as poetry, Paul wrote fortunes for the fortune cookies used in Chinese restaurants. He was paid for this work not in money but in big boxes of free fortune cookies; and these were what he and Bayer mostly ate. Bayer had become very expert at eating the cookies and spitting out the slips of paper with the fortunes printed on them.

One sharp December evening Paul had just let out Bayer, and was writing a fortune for a cookie: 'Never hide inside a teapot. Someone might pour boiling water on you.' At this moment he heard Bayer up above on the roof, barking much louder than usual.

Paul opened the window, leaned out, and looked down to see what was causing Bayer's agitation.

Down below on the sidewalk, clustered around a little ginkgo tree, he saw a group of carol singers with two guitars and a drum. They were singing 'The Holly And The Ivy' and, up above, Bayer was accompanying

them by howling as loudly as he could. They weren't a
Salvation Army band but, so far as Bayer was concerned,
there wasn't a lot of difference. He stood right on the
edge of the roof and made a noise like a police siren
with hiccups, jerking himself backward and forward with
every bark.

The carol singers didn't mind Bayer; they thought he
was joining in out of Christmas spirit; in any case he
didn't sound so loud to them, four storeys down, because
they were making a good deal of noise themselves.

In the midst of all this commotion, old Mrs Logan
drove slowly along the street in her horse-drawn cab.
Mrs Logan was not really driving the cab; she was asleep.
Her horse, Murphy, knew the way home perfectly well.
So Mrs Logan was inside the cab, having a nap, while
Murphy plodded thoughtfully along, taking his time.
They were returning from their usual day's inactivity,
spent outside a big hotel, the Plaza, waiting for customers
who might wish to drive around Central Park or along
the main shopping streets in an open horse-drawn cab.
Very few customers *did* want to at such a cold time of
year. And if by any chance they felt like a cab ride, they
hardly ever picked Mrs Logan's cab, because Murphy, a
brown horse the colour of gingerbread, was so terribly
thin that his ribs resembled a rusty radiator; they looked
as if you could play a tune by running a stick across
them. Murphy looked as if his maximum speed would be
about half a mile per hour.

So customers generally picked cabs with fatter, stronger horses. And tonight, as on nearly all other evenings, Murphy and Mrs Logan were coming home to their sleeping quarters in Washington Square without having had a single fare all day. Mrs Logan would then wrap Murphy in a lot of old quilts she kept folded up in a cardboard box; and she would wrap herself up in a lot more; and they would share a supper of half-eaten rolls, ends of pretzels, bits of sandwiches, and other food that Mrs Logan had picked out of garbage cans early that morning. Then they would go to sleep, Murphy standing, Mrs Logan sleeping in the cab, which would be parked under a big stone arch, the Washington Arch.

No policeman ever bothered Mrs Logan.

The first time she spent a night in Washington Square a policeman called O'Grady said to her, 'Ma'am, you shouldn't be camping here, you know.'

'Ah, now, have a heart, dear boy,' said Mrs Logan. 'I'm from way back in the country, from the lovely little town of Four Corners, New Hampshire – and the sight of the green leaves and the squirrels in this park will be easing the sadness of my poor homesick heart. I tell you what, Officer O'Grady,' she said, 'I'll be singing you a song now.'

So she sang him a beautiful song that went:

When an Irish Robin
Hops into your waistcoat pocket
Won't your ould heart shoot up

Like a fine skyrocket?
Remember the nest
In the Isle of the Blest
With four beautiful eggs of blue
Where an Irish Robin
Is waiting and singing
For you!

Officer O'Grady was so charmed by this song, which
Mrs Logan sang in a very sweet voice, thin as a thread
but dead on the note, that he immediately gave her
leave to stay under the Washington Arch just as long
as she liked, and furthermore he told all his friends in
the Sixth Precinct office that Mrs Logan was not to be
bothered.

So all that any of the other policemen did was to
pass the time of day and keep a friendly eye on her, and
sometimes ask her to sing the song about the Irish Robin,
which she always did for them.

Just as Mrs Logan and Murphy drew abreast of the
carol singers (who had now got to 'The First Noel'),
Bayer, up above on the roof, became so overexcited
that he did something he never had before: he barked
himself right off the roof, and fell like a heavy black
plum, down, down, four storeys, until, as luck would
have it (and very fortunately), he landed on the canvas
hood of Mrs Logan's cab. This worked as well as a
trampoline; Bayer bounced on it a couple of times, then

he tumbled into the cab itself, not hurt at all, but a trifle surprised.

Mrs Logan was surprised too.

'Musha!' she said. 'Will ye be believing it now, dogs falling from the sky! What next, at all?'

Bayer politely removed himself from the cab, and jumped to the ground.

'Are you hurt?' inquired Murphy, who was just as surprised as Mrs Logan, but not given to exclaiming.

'No, thank you, not at all,' said Bayer. 'I hope I didn't frighten your driver.'

'Oh, very little frightens Mrs Logan. She is quite a calm person,' said Murphy, and he went on plodding in the direction of Washington Square.

Bayer felt that, now he was down in the street, he might as well take advantage of the opportunity. It was a long time since he had had the chance to run about and sniff all the delicious smells at ground level, and he was fairly sure that Paul would not begin to worry about him for some time. So he loped along companionably beside Murphy, slowing his pace to the horse's tired, stumbling walk.

When the cab came to a stop under the Washington Arch, and Mrs Logan wrapped up herself and the horse, and divided a handful of crusts and pretzel-ends between them, Bayer was rather shocked.

'Don't you have a proper stable?' he asked the horse. 'And is that *all* you get for supper?'

Compared with this, Bayer's own quarters in the

fourth-floor studio and his supper of fortune cookies seemed comfortable, even princely.

'How long have you lived here?' he asked.

'Nine or ten years, I suppose,' said Murphy.

'Can't you find anything better?'

'Mrs Logan hasn't any money,' Murphy explained, and then he told the story of how they came to be living under the Washington Arch.

'We come from a little town many hundreds of miles from here,' he said, heaving a sigh that went all along his bony ribs, like a finger along the keys of a piano. 'It is called Four Corners, New Hampshire, and there *are* only four corners in it – and the train station of course. We used to wait at the station, and as ours was the only cab, we made a good living. Mrs Logan lived with her brother, who has a farm. But one day four men got off the train and asked if we would take them all the way to New York. They offered eighty dollars for the ride. I've begun to think, lately, that perhaps they were robbers. On the way down (which took several days) they talked a lot about banks, and money, and the police.

'When we reached New York they said they hadn't any cash on them, but if Mrs Logan would be outside the Plaza Hotel next morning at ten, they would be there to pay her the eighty dollars. So we spent the night here and went to the Plaza next day; but the men never turned up with the money. And, though we have gone back there each morning at ten ever since, we have never seen them again.'

'What a set of scoundrels!' exclaimed Bayer. 'Maybe they never meant to pay you at all.'

'That is what I begin to think,' agreed Murphy sadly. 'But Mrs Logan still believes they will turn up one of these days; she thinks they must be having a little difficulty earning the money.'

'Why don't you both go back to Four Corners?'

'Oh, Mrs Logan would never do that. She would think that looked as if she didn't trust the men to keep their promise. But,' said Murphy, sighing again, 'I am growing very tired of the city – though it is so grand – I often wish I was back in my own stable at Four Corners – especially on a cold night like this one.'

That night was bitterly cold; the stars shone bright as flares, and the moon was big as an ice rink. Far away along Fifth Avenue the pointed tower of the Empire State Building glowed pink and green and blue against the night sky. All the squirrels of Washington Square were curled up tight in their nests; the rollerskaters and skateboarders and the Frisbee-slingers had long gone home to bed. Mrs Logan and Murphy and Bayer were the only live creatures there, standing patiently under the Washington Arch.

'Well, I think it's a shocking shame,' said Bayer, and then he trotted away, thinking hard as he went. He was going home, but first he intended to consult another acquaintance of his who lived in the basement area at the end of Twelfth Street.

This was a skunk named Rackstraw. Bayer and Rackstraw often held conversations, from roof to street, but up till now they had never met face to face.

Rackstraw had not been in Twelfth Street very long. He had arrived one day in a Rolls-Royce car; Bayer wanted to know more about him.

The basement area of the end house held several trash cans, a box or two, a stone trough containing laurel bushes, and a Styrofoam picnic basket lined with newspaper.

The carollers were now singing 'Good King Wenceslas' at the other end of the block, so Bayer went, a little warily, down a couple of the stone steps that led to the basement door, and called, loud enough for the skunk to hear over the music, 'Rackstraw? Are you at home?'

Instantly Rackstraw's handsome black and white head poked out of the picnic basket.

'Good heavens, Bayer! Is that you? What in the world are you doing down in the street?'

'Oh, I just jumped down,' Bayer said carelessly. 'There was no problem about it, I landed on the roof of Mrs Logan's cab.'

'My stars! I wouldn't dare do a thing like that!' said Rackstraw. He spoke with an English accent. Bayer had noticed this before; he recognized the English accent because Paul Powdermaker had an English friend called Lord Donisthorpe.

'Do you come from England?' Bayer inquired. 'I didn't know there were English skunks.'

'I was born and brought up in an English zoo,' explained Rackstraw. 'But my mother always told me that I ought to return to the land of my ancestors, if I could. The zoo where I lived was in a large park, where there were a lot of other entertainments as well – outdoor plays, and opera, and circuses. Last month an opera was being performed, and the audience ate picnic suppers by their cars in between the acts. I was hidden in a bush munching a piece of smoked salmon I had managed to pick up when I heard American voices. Somebody said, 'We'll drive the car on board the ship tomorrow.' I thought, Now's my chance! So, while they were eating, I climbed into the luggage compartment of their car (which was a Rolls-Royce) and hid under a rug. The next day the car was driven onto a ship, which sailed to New York. The trip took five days.'

'And you were in the luggage place all that time?' Bayer was greatly impressed. 'Didn't you run out of air and food?'

'There was plenty to eat, because they had left the remains of the picnic – bread and cheese and salmon and fruit and salad and plum cake. And the trunk was a big airy place. When we reached New York and they drove away from the dock I waited for my chance, and as soon as they opened the lid of the trunk I shot out. This was where they stopped, on Twelfth Street, so I have lived here ever since. It isn't bad – the people in the house are quite kind and give me fried potatoes; but in the spring I shall move on.'

'Where to?'

'Back to the place my mother and father came from. There are some cousins still living there. It is Mount Moss-crop, a hill in New Hampshire near a little town called Four Corners.'

'Why!' exclaimed Bayer, amazed, 'that's where Murphy comes from!' and then he told Rackstraw the story of Mrs Logan.

Rackstraw said thoughtfully, 'If only we could persuade Mrs Logan to go back home, I could ride with her as a passenger.'

'You could if you promised—'

'Promised what?'

All this time, Bayer had been keeping at a careful distance from his neighbour. Now he said, rather hesitantly, 'Well – er – I was brought up in the city, I never met a skunk before, personally, that is. But, well, I always heard – I was told that skunks – that you were able to – that is to say—'

'Oh,' said Rackstraw, 'you mean the smell?'

'Well – yes,' apologized Bayer, moving back onto a higher step, lest the skunk had taken offence. But Rackstraw did not seem annoyed.

'My mother trained me not to, except in emergencies,' he said. 'People in England are very polite; they don't like it. And my mother was very particular about manners. "Never, never do it," she used to say, "unless you are in great danger." So I never have.'

'It never happens by accident?'

'I suppose it might – if one were to sneeze violently – but it never has to me. Now, let's think how we can persuade Mrs Logan to return to Four Corners.'

Just then they heard the voice of Paul Powdermaker, who was walking slowly along the street, whistling and calling: 'Bayer? Bayer? Where are you?'

'We'll talk about this again,' said Bayer hastily. 'It's good to have met you. See you soon. Take care!'

'Good night!' called Rackstraw, and he slipped back into his cosy, insulated nest.

Bayer ran along Twelfth Street with his master, and climbed the seventy-four stairs back to their warm studio, where he had a late-night snack of fortune cookies. One of them said: 'A bone contains much that is noble. And L is for love.'

'Did you write that?' Bayer said to Paul. 'I don't think much of it.'

'One can't hit top notes all the time,' said Paul, who was hard at work on a long poem about the ocean. 'Don't distract me now, there's a dear fellow. And, next time you want to go into the street, warn me in advance; I nearly dropped dead of fright when I saw you jump off the roof.'

Bayer apologized for causing Paul so much anxiety, and

climbed into his basket. But it was a long time before he slept. He kept thinking of Mrs Logan and Murphy, out in the bitter cold, under the Washington Arch, waiting for morning to come.

After that day, Bayer always kept his ears pricked for the sound of Murphy's hoofs slowly clopping along the street. When he heard them, he would bark to go out on the roof. Mrs Logan formed the habit of putting up the hood of her cab when she drove along Twelfth Street, and Bayer would jump down onto the hood, bounce once or twice, and then either ride on the box with Mrs Logan, or run in the street beside Murphy. Paul grew accustomed to this, and stopped worrying. Bayer made himself useful helping Mrs Logan hunt for edible tidbits in trash cans – he was much better at it than the old lady – and he spent many days in town with the pair, talking to Murphy and keeping an eye out for the four men who owed Mrs Logan eighty dollars.

'One of them was tall and thin, with glasses,' Murphy told Bayer, 'one was little and round with a red nose; one was very pale, white-haired and blue-eyed; and one was dotted all over with freckles and had red hair. They rode with us for so many days that I had plenty of time to get to know them.'

Mrs Logan's cab was parked outside the Plaza Hotel. She nodded sleepily in the sunshine, while Bayer and Murphy watched all the well-dressed people pass by. As

Christmas was near, there were several men dressed as Santa Claus, ringing bells and collecting money for charity. Whenever they rang their bells, Bayer barked, but not so loudly as he would have three weeks ago; these days, Bayer didn't bark so loudly or so often, and since he was getting more exercise, he was not so fat.

He found a chunk of pretzel in the gutter and offered it to Murphy.

'How about you?' said the horse. 'Wouldn't you like it?'

'Oh, I'll be getting my fortune cookies later on.'

'Well – thanks, then.'

'What's your favourite food?' Bayer asked, as Murphy hungrily chewed the pretzel.

'Spinach,' answered Murphy when he had swallowed. 'Mrs Logan always buys me a bag of spinach if we earn any money. Up at Four Corners,' he said sighing, 'I used to be given as much spinach as I could eat; I had bushels of it. Mrs Logan's brother grew fields and fields of it, and I used to do the ploughing for him.'

'Spinach?' cried Bayer. 'I never heard of anybody liking *that* stuff!'

That evening, when Bayer was back at home, he sat beside Paul and laid a paw beseechingly on the poet's knee.

Paul wrote:

The ocean, like a great eye
Stares at the sky.

Then he stopped writing and stared at the dog.

'What's the trouble, Bayer? Do you want another fortune cookie?'

'No,' said Bayer, 'I need a whole lot of spinach.'

'*Spinach!*' exclaimed Paul, just as Bayer had earlier. 'What do you need that for?'

'For a friend.'

'Spinach – spinach—' Paul began to mumble, coming out of his poem slowly like a mouse out of a cheese. 'Now let me think – I read something about spinach in the paper – two or three days ago it was—'

Paul had *The New York Times* delivered every day, and there were piles of newspapers lying about all over the floor. He rummaged around in these untidy heaps, and it took ever so long before he found what he wanted.

'"*Load of Spinach Goes Begging,*"' he read aloud to Bayer. '"A freighter packed to the portholes with spinach is lying at anchor off the Morton Street pier, waiting for somebody to buy up her load. The asking price is twenty dollars. The ship met with such severe gales on the way to New York from Florida that the usual two-day run was extended to eight. Consequently the cargo has deteriorated, and New York greengrocers are not keen to buy. The owner will probably accept a giveaway price if anyone is prepared to take his load off his hands. Come along, Popeye, here's your chance!"'

'*Twenty dollars,*' thought Bayer sadly. 'That's a terrible lot of money. But a whole load of spinach would certainly set Murphy on his feet again, and make him fit for the trip back to Four Corners.'

The next day at seven, Bayer was out on the roof although it was still dark and bitterly cold. The street-lamps down below glimmered like Christmas oranges in the bare trees of Twelfth Street. Bayer heard the slow clip-clop of Murphy's hoofs coming along, and he jumped down as usual, bouncing lightly off the canvas hood onto the road below. He trotted beside the cab, and was about to tell Murphy of the boatload of spinach off the Morton Street pier when a most unexpected thing happened.

Around the corner of the street marched fifty-seven Santa Clauses.

They were wearing Father Christmas costumes. Some carried sacks, and some had bells. Many held Christmas trees. They marched in rows: five rows of ten, and one row of seven.

Mrs Logan, who had been dozing on the box, woke up and stared with astonishment at the sight.

'Glory be to goodness!' she murmured. 'That's enough Santa Clauses for every week in the year, so it is, and five more for luck!'

Then she looked more closely at the last row of Santa Clauses, who were breaking rank to pass the cab, and she cried out, 'Divil fly away with me if those aren't the fellas that rode with us down from Four Corners, New Hampshire! Will ye be after giving me my eighty dollars now, if ye please?' she called to them.

Murphy recognized the men at the same instant, and he whinnied loudly; Bayer, catching the general excitement, barked his head off. Rackstraw bounced out of his nest.

Most of the Father Christmases seemed mildly surprised at this; but four of them dropped their Christmas trees and bolted away, as if they had suddenly remembered they had a train to catch.

Murphy did his best to chase them; but he was far too thin and tired to keep up more than a very slow canter for a couple of blocks, and the men easily got away from him;

very soon they were out of sight. Bayer and Rackstraw followed a few blocks farther, but they, too, lost the men in the end. One of the men, however, had dropped a wallet in his fright; Bayer pounced on that and carried it back in triumph. Inside were four five-dollar bills. Twenty dollars!

The owner of the freighter anchored off the Morton Street pier was greatly astonished when a shabby old cab, drawn by a skeleton-thin old horse, drew up on the dock by his ship, and an old lady, waving a handful of green paper money, offered to buy his load.

'Certainly you can have it,' the owner said. 'But where will you put it? The Port Authority won't allow you to leave it on the dock.'

'Ah, sure, then, they'll let me keep it there for a night or so,' said Mrs Logan hopefully. 'And in the meanwhile old Murphy here will eat a great, great deal of it.' So the load of spinach was dumped out on the dock. It was in a very limp and wilted state, but even so it made a massive pile, twenty feet high and thirty feet long. Murphy gazed as if, even now he saw it, he could hardly believe his eyes.

'Go on then, ye poor ould quadruped,' said Mrs Logan. 'Eat your head off, for once.'

Murphy didn't wait to be told twice. After ten minutes he had made a hole as big as himself in the green mountain of spinach. Then Mrs Logan packed as much spinach as she could into the cab.

Murphy reluctantly stopped eating – 'Best ye don't gobble too much all at once,' Mrs Logan warned him, 'or 'tis desperate heartburn ye'll be getting—' and they started slowly back towards Washington Square.

Lifting the spinach and packing it into the cab had been a hard, heavy job, and it made a heavy load to pull; Bayer could see that Mrs Logan and Murphy were not going to be able to shift very many loads before night-fall. And a Port Authority inspector was walking up and down, looking disapprovingly at the hill of spinach.

Bayer galloped back to Twelfth Street to consult with Rackstraw.

Greatly to his surprise, when he reached the door of his own house, he saw, parked at the kerb, the very same white Rolls-Royce that had brought Rackstraw to the city. And on the doorstep Paul Powdermaker was enthusiastically shaking the hand of his English friend, Lord Donisthorpe.

'Oh, please, oh, please, Paul, dear Paul, we need your help and advice very badly!' exclaimed Bayer, bounding all around Paul in his agitation.

Lord Donisthorpe, who was a thin elderly English gentleman with a tuft of grey hair like a secretary-bird and a long nose, and a pair of spectacles which were always halfway down it, gazed with a mild dreamy interest at Bayer. Lord Donisthorpe knew a great deal about animals; in fact he was the owner of the zoo from which Rackstraw had escaped.

'Gracious me, my dear Paul! How very remarkable and touching! You and the dog are in verbal communication! You talk to one another! That is remarkably interesting. I shall certainly write a paper on it, for the Royal Society.'

'Oh, it's nothing,' said Paul, rather shyly and shortly. 'Poets and dogs generally understand one another, I believe. Well, Bayer, what is it? Can't whatever it is wait for a few minutes? Lord Donisthorpe has just arrived from his Mexican trip—'

'Oh, no, Paul, it can't, you see it's that mountain of spinach by the Morton Street pier that Mrs Logan wants to move to Washington Square – the spinach has to be moved today or the Port Authority will tell the sanitation trucks to take it away. But we need a car or a truck – Mrs Logan and Murphy can't possibly manage it all on their own.'

Paul – whose mind was still half on his ocean poem – could not make head or tail of this at first, and it needed endless repetitions before he managed to understand what Bayer was talking about. By that time Lord Donisthorpe had also grasped the nature of the problem; and the sight of Murphy and Mrs Logan doggedly plodding along Twelfth Street with another load of spinach finally brought it home to both men.

Lord Donisthorpe ran out into the street and took hold of Murphy's bridle. Murphy came to a relieved stop.

'My dear ma'am! Excuse me – ahem – I am not usually

one to meddle in other people's affairs – but I own a zoo, in England – I do know quite a lot about animals – and that horse, my dear ma'am – really that horse is too thin to be pulling a cab so laden with spinach. What he needs, if you will forgive my saying so, is about twenty square meals.'

'Man, dear, don't I know it!' said Mrs Logan. 'And there's about a hundred square meals waiting for the blessed crayture; if only we can get the stuff shifted to Washington Square.'

The end of it was that Paul Powdermaker and Lord Donisthorpe spent the rest of the day shifting spinach from the dockside to Washington Square in Lord Donisthorpe's Rolls. They had just delivered the last load before darkness fell. In the middle of Washington Square there is a paved area; all the spinach was piled here in a huge mound, the height and shape of an outsize Christmas tree.

Mrs Logan and Murphy passed the day resting; Mrs Logan thought long and hard, while Murphy ate. Bayer ran back and forth alongside the Rolls, and greatly enjoyed himself.

Police Officer O'Grady had long ago been moved on from that precinct; but another policeman called O'Brien walked by at dusk and thoughtfully surveyed the huge pile of spinach.

'I doubt ye won't be allowed to keep that there, ma'am,' he said mildly.

'Ah, glory be! Where else can I keep it, at all?' said Mrs Logan.

'Well, maybe it can stay there till just after Christmas,' said O'Brien.

'In that case there's no call to worry; Murphy will have ate it all by then.'

Indeed, during the next few days Murphy munched so diligently at the great pile that it shrank and shrank, first to the size of an up-ended bus; then to the size of Lord Donisthorpe's car; and finally to no size at all. Meanwhile, Murphy, from all this good nourishing food, grew bigger and bigger; his coat became thick and glossy; his head, which had hung down like a wet sock, reared up proudly; his mane and tail grew three inches a day, and even his hoofs began to shine. He took to trotting, and then to cantering, around and around Washington Square, among the rollerskaters; he even frisked a little, and kicked up his heels.

During this time Lord Donisthorpe and Paul Powdermaker had many conversations with Mrs Logan over cups of tea and muffins in a coffee shop in University Place.

'If I were you, ma'am,' said Lord Donisthorpe, 'I would wait no longer, hoping to get your money back. I fear those wretches who deceived you are gone for good. If I were you, I should take that fine horse of yours, and go back to Four Corners, New Hampshire.'

Mrs Logan needed a lot of convincing. But in the end

she did agree. 'Isn't it a sad thing there should be so much wickedness in the heart of man?' she said. ''Tis the city folk that are bad, I'm thinking. True enough, I'll be glad to go back to Four Corners.'

'What will you do for food along the way?' said Paul. 'It's not so easy to pick up broken pretzels and sandwich crusts in the country.'

Mrs Logan had an idea about that.

'Now Murphy's in such grand shape, I reckon we'll be entering for the Christmas Day cab-horse race. If we win, 'tis a five-hundred-dollar prize; that money would buy us journey food back to Four Corners, and leave plenty over for a Christmas gift for my brother Sean, who must have thought me dead these ten years.'

'Christmas race?' said Lord Donisthorpe. 'If Murphy wins that – and I really don't see why he should not – it will be a fine endorsement for my Spinach Diet Plan for horses. I shall write a paper about it for the Royal Society ...'

So it was agreed that Murphy and Mrs Logan should enter for the race.

Paul and Lord Donisthorpe polished up the cab, and the brass bits of Murphy's harness, checked the reins, saddle soaped the leather, and waxed the woodwork, until the cab looked – not new, but a bit better than it had before. And they tied a big red rosette on Murphy's headband.

*

But meanwhile there was trouble brewing in Twelfth Street.

At this time of year, people had naturally been buying Christmas trees and taking them home, putting them in pots and decorating them with tinsel and lights.

But after a couple of days in warm houses, many of the trees began to smell truly terrible.

A meeting of the Twelfth Street Block Association was held.

'It's that skunk living at the end of the street!' people said. 'We always knew that having a skunk in the street would lead to trouble. That skunk has to go.'

Paul Powdermaker argued that this was unfair and unreasonable. 'That skunk – whose name is Rackstraw, I might inform you – has never been near any of your Christmas trees. He has not touched them. How could he? He lives outside in his picnic basket; the trees are inside. There has been no connection. Furthermore he is a very well-behaved skunk; my dog – who ought to know – informs me that Rackstraw never gives offence, in any possible way.'

But just the same, the Block Association decided that Rackstraw must be removed to the Central Park Zoo.

Only, nobody quite knew how to set about this. Whose job is it to remove a skunk? First they called the Sanitation Department and asked them to send a garbage truck. The Sanitation Department said it was no business of theirs. The police said the same thing.

The Central Park Zoo said that they would take Rackstraw, if somebody would deliver him; but they were not prepared to come and fetch him.

'You had better stay in my studio till all this blows over,' Paul said to Rackstraw. But Rackstraw said that he was not used to living indoors; he would prefer to spend a few days with Mrs Logan in her cab. So that is what he did.

On Christmas Day large crowds assembled in Central Park to watch the cab race.

For this event the cabs had to race three times all around the park – a distance of eighteen miles. During the morning no traffic was allowed on the streets alongside the park.

All the contestants lined up outside the Plaza Hotel – there were thirty of them, cabs polished to a brilliant dazzle, and gay with ribbons, tinsel, and holly. The horses were in tiptop condition, bouncing and eager to be off. Mrs Logan's cab was certainly not the smartest; but no horse looked in better shape than Murphy. His coat gleamed like a newly baked bun; and he was snorting with excitement.

Lord Donisthorpe was staying with the friends with whom he had crossed the Atlantic. They lived in a top-floor apartment overlooking the park, so after he and Paul had wished Mrs Logan well, they went up to the penthouse garden, where they would have a grandstand view of the whole race.

The starter's gun cracked, and, after a couple of false starts, the competitors clattered off, whips cracking and wheels flashing.

During the first lap, Murphy drew so far ahead of all the others that it hardly seemed like a race at all. Galloping like a Derby winner, with Bayer racing at his side barking ecstatically, he tore up Central Park West, turned east along 110th Street, crossed the north end of the park, and came racing down Fifth Avenue. All the other contestants were at least half a mile behind.

Then, as Murphy approached the Plaza Hotel, ready to turn the corner and begin his second lap, something unexpected happened. There were four men in Santa Claus costumes outside the Plaza, and, as Murphy came racing along, he had a clear view of their faces. With a loud neigh of recognition, he swung off the racecourse, and started chasing the men, who fled down Fifth Avenue with Murphy thundering after them.

'What's got into that horse?' yelled the crowd of watchers. 'Has he lost his way? Has he gone mad? Murphy, Murphy, you took a wrong turn!'

Mrs Logan had also spotted the men in Santa Claus costumes and she was shouting, 'Musha, wisha, come back, ye spalpeens! What about my sixty dollars?'

(As they had spent the twenty dollars from the wallet on spinach, she reckoned that the men owed her only sixty.)

Before, the men had easily escaped from Murphy. But

now they hadn't a chance. Mrs Logan leaned out with her whip and her umbrella, and hooked them into her cab one by one – helped by enthusiastic people along Fifth Avenue.

Just outside the Forty-Second Street library she grabbed the last Santa Claus. The stone lions in front of the library were roaring their heads off, because it was Christmas; and Murphy whinnied joyfully; and Bayer barked his loudest.

Rackstraw, curled up in the back of the cab, had been rather startled when the thieves were hauled in. For a moment, indeed, he felt tempted to disobey his mother's rule. But he restrained himself. 'Politeness always pays, Rackstraw,' he remembered his mother saying. So he contented himself with biting the swindlers, who seemed to him to have a terrible smell already.

'Now I have the lot of ye!' said Mrs Logan. 'And it's over to the polis I shall be handing ye, for now I see that ye were a lot of promise-breaking raskills who niver intended to pay me back at all.'

By now the police had arrived with sirens screeching and were grouped around the cab waiting to handcuff the Father Christmases. It seemed they had reasons of their own for wanting these men.

So, although Mrs Logan and Murphy didn't win the Central Park cab race, they did earn the gratitude of the State of New Jersey.

Why? Because these men were Christmas tree thieves,

who had been cutting down cedars and spruces along the scenic parkways of New Jersey. But the evergreens had been sprayed by the Highways Department with deer-repellant chemicals, which, when the trees were taken into a warm room, began to smell far, far worse than any skunk. So the stolen trees – and the men who had taken them – were easily identified.

And the grateful Highways Department paid Mrs Logan a handsome reward.

'I knew the smell of the trees had nothing to do with Rackstraw!' said Bayer.

Rackstraw looked very prim. 'I never disobey my mother's rule,' he said.

The friends were all back in Washington Square, helping Mrs Logan and Murphy prepare for their journey.

The cab was stuffed with spinach and pretzels, fried potatoes for Rackstraw, and bottles of root beer for Mrs Logan.

'How about coming along?' said Murphy to Bayer.

Bayer was deeply tempted. But he said, 'I can't leave Paul. He has been very kind to me, and he might be lonely, all on his own.'

But inside him Bayer thought sadly how much he would miss his three friends. Poets are poor company, even if they do understand dog language.

'Goodbye, then,' said Murphy.

'Goodbye! Goodbye!' called Rackstraw and Mrs Logan.

All Mrs Logan's police friends had come to the square to wave her goodbye – and a big crowd of other people as well. Newspaper cameras flashed. It was a grand send-off. Mrs Logan sang her Irish Robin song for the last time; then they started.

As Bayer watched the cab roll away, a huge lump swelled up in his throat. In a moment he knew that a terrible anguished howl was going to come out.

Just then Paul Powdermaker pushed his way through the crowd.

'Bayer,' he said, 'Lord Donisthorpe has invited me to travel to England and spend a year in his castle. I'd like to go – but if I take you, it means you will have to spend six months in quarantine kennels. The English are very strict about that. So I was wondering if you'd care to go to New Hampshire with Mrs Logan and Murphy—?'

Bayer turned his head and saw that the cab was out of sight. Murphy had broken into a gallop and was whirling Mrs Logan out of New York faster than any crack stagecoach.

'I'd never catch up with them now,' said Bayer.

'Nonsense, my dear dog!' exclaimed Lord Donisthorpe. 'What's a Rolls for, may I ask? A good goer Murphy may be, but I never yet heard of a horse who could outrun a Rolls-Royce ... Jump in, and we'll soon be up with them.'

Bayer and Paul leaped into the white Rolls – which still had a certain amount of spinach clinging to its grey tweed upholstery – the motor came to life with a soft purr, and the great car lifted away like a helicopter.

Just the same, Murphy had gone forty miles before they caught up with him.

So that is why, if you go to Washington Square, New York, you won't find Mrs Logan hanging her dresses on a tree and singing about the Irish Robin, or Murphy the horse standing under the Washington Arch. They are back in Four Corners, New Hampshire, and Bayer the Labrador and Rackstraw the skunk are with them.

The Midnight Rose

There's a village called Wish Wintergreen in the county of Somerset, just where the Mendip hills slide down into the marshes. Not a large village – only forty houses, or thereabouts, set round in a square, but with all that's needed – one church, one pub, one school, bank, butcher, baker, builder, plumber (who also does TV repairs), chemist, jail, fish-and-chip shop, court-house, post office; outside the square of houses, and their long green gardens full of apple trees and roses and cabbages, there are eighty-nine green mounds, set round in a ring. How big are the mounds? About as high as a double-decker bus. The children roll down them in summertime, and toboggan down them in winter. What's under them? Nobody knows. Canon Godliman, grandfather to the present vicar, started digging into one of them a hundred years ago; he was struck dumb for a month; then he couldn't stop talking, night or day, for another month. His wife couldn't decide which was worse. What did he talk about? All kinds of queer things – unicorn teams, the city of Neksheb, the evil spirit of the north who plays his gloomy strains in Swedish waters, the three frivolous battles of Britain, Roman soldiers who carried bundles of nettles to keep them warm, Doll money, and the wake of Teanley Night. No one could make head or tail of such stuff. At the end of the second month he died, worn out; but he was eighty-nine, so it might have happened anyway.

One day, in the gloomy month of January, this tale begins. The village was very quiet that day. Wish Wintergreen is a quiet place at all times, the natives don't talk a lot, but that day it was extra quiet. Christmas had long gone by, but spring was nowhere yet in sight. Not a soul in the road or on the green. In the village school the teacher, Miss Clerihand, was saying: 'Well, children. We all know what's going on in the court-house today, and we can't help thinking about it. So there's no use trying to do sums or spelling. We'll do history instead. Barbie, where was the land of Dilmun?'

'On the edge of the world, miss.'

'What was there, Paul?'

'A beautiful garden, with cucumbers and apples and grapes in it.'

'What else, Sammy?'

'In that garden, the raven utters no cry,
The lion kills not.'

'What else, Tom?'

'In that garden, the wolf snatches not the lamb,
The sick man says not "I am sick."'

'What else, Ted?'

'In that garden the old woman says not "I am an old woman,"
The old man says not "I am an old man."'

'Who lived there, Cecily?'

'Our great-grandmother Eve.'

'What was her other name, Harold?'

'Ninmu, the lady who makes green things grow.'

'Who came to the land of Dilmun, Ellen?'

'A gipsy, one of the wandering tribe of the Tchingani.'

'His name, Sarah?'

'Duke Michael.'

'What did he do, Paul?'

'Told the lady Eve's fortune. Said she would have two beautiful babies.'

'What did she give him, Chris?'

'A basket of earth with a root in it.'

'Where did he go, Sammy?'

'In a boat, down one of the four rivers flowing out of the land of Dilmun.'

'And where then, Tom?'

'Half around the world to Somerset, the Land of Summer.'

'What did he do there, Barbie?'

'Built himself an island and planted a garden.'

'And in the middle of it,' chorused all the children, 'he put the basket of earth and the root.'

'What happened then?'

'He grew old and died.'

'What did he say before he died?'

'Ten thousand years from today, on a night midway between winter and spring, the rose shall blossom at midnight,' all the children said.

'Who will be there to behold it?'

'Whoever is there to behold it, they shall remember the beginnings of the world, and shall also see forward to the ending of the world. And in their power shall it be to make that ending a ruin or a victory.'

'Good,' said Miss Clerihand. 'What became of Dilmun, Sammy?'

'It was swept away in the Great Flood.'

'Where to, Tom?'

'It floated off into space.'

'Where is it now, Barbie?'

'Become one of Saturn's moons.'

'Right. And when is the night that the rose shall blossom?'

'Between now and St Valentine's Day!' they all shouted.

'And where will it blossom?'

'Here! Right here! In our own village.'

'Right,' said Miss Clerihand again. 'And we don't want any strangers coming here to dig up the rose and take it away to the Science Museum or the National History Museum, do we?'

'No, *that* we don't!'

'Good,' said the teacher once more. 'You know your history well. I think we'll take a break now and play Up Jenkins. Joe,' she said to one boy, who had not answered any of the questions, but sat quiet and pale in the back row, 'Joe, you may go outside if you like, for a breath of air.'

Joe nodded without reply, slid from his seat, put on his duffel jacket, and ran outside. His face was marked by the tracks of two tears which had rolled down in spite of all his efforts to keep them in.

When he left the classroom, Joe walked out of the school porch and crossed the village green, where a great dead elm stood and a new young oak had been planted. He stood listening outside the grey stone court-house, where some cars were parked. No sound came from inside, and he did not dare go in. So instead he walked very slowly, kicking the frosty ground, to the high-arched bridge over the Wintergreen brook, which ran very clear, deep, and rapid here, over white pebbles, with watercress growing in clumps.

Joe sat on the parapet of the bridge, his shoulders hunched, his face downcast, chewing on a stem of water-cress and listening to the silence.

Presently along rolled a Landrover, which looked as if it had been driven over mountains and through deserts and maybe through the Red Sea as well – every inch of it was rusty, there were shreds of palm leaves and coconut fibre and seals' whiskers sticking out of the cracks, and in the dust on panels and windscreen rude remarks had been scrawled in dozens of foreign languages.

The vehicle slowed to a halt beside Joe and the motor stopped as if it meant never to start again. The driver jumped out.

'Where's everybody?' he asked. He was a tall, bronzed man, with a harsh, beak-nosed face, and sparkling black eyes, and bushy black eyebrows; his hair must have been black once, too, but had turned white as snow, what remained of it; Joe noticed that a curved metal plate had been patched over part of his bald crown. And down his left cheek ran a great dried scar.

'Where's everybody?' he asked again.

'Indoors,' said Joe shortly, 'watching the trial on TV.'

'What trial?'

'The one that's going on in there,' and Joe jerked his head towards the court-house.

'Why don't they watch it live?'

'They'd sooner stop at home.'

'Who's being tried? And for what?'

Joe paused and swallowed, began to speak and stopped. At last he said, 'The man who dug up the trowel.'

'What trowel?' The stranger's deep eyes flashed.

But Joe said, 'How did your head get hurt, mister?'

'In a fight,' answered the man absently, 'in the Valley of Gehenna. But a Persian doctor put this silver plate in for me, to replace the missing piece of bone.'

'Must be hot when the sun shines on it, mister?'

'Then I wear a hood. The silver plating picks up sounds and echoes very well,' said the traveller, tapping his head with the car key which he held; the silver surface gave out a faint ringing sound, like a glass tapped with a fork.

The stranger asked again: 'What trowel did the man dig up?'

'An old wooden one. Ten thousand years old, the professor from the London Museum says it is.'

'Why should they try a man for digging up a wooden trowel?'

'Because he won't give it to the museum people. He buried it again, just where he found it. And he won't tell them where that is. So they say he'll be sentenced to prison for ten years for disobeying a Court Order and refusing to hand over important historical objects.'

'When will the trial end?'

'Today or tomorrow. Or the next day.'

'Who is this man?'

Slowly and reluctantly the boy said, 'He's my father.'

'What's his name?'

'Joe Mathinwell.' The boy nodded towards a small builder's yard with a painted sign over the gate: 'Joseph Mathinwell, builder, plumber & undertaker'.

'Where *did* he dig up the trowel?' asked the traveller inquisitively, but Joe, turning to give him a clear steady look out of slightly red-rimmed eyes, answered, 'If he had told me, do you think I would tell *you*?'

'No,' said the traveller. 'No, I can see that you would not. It is plain that you are a brave, trustworthy boy.'

Joe made no reply to that.

The stranger walked across to the shop of Mrs Honeysett, Baker & Confectioner, went in, and bought a rock cake. The old lady observed that when he put his hand down to the tray with buns in it, the rock cake jumped right up into his hand.

'Do you know,' asked the traveller, 'whereabouts in this village the Midnight Rose is expected to bloom?'

Mrs Honeysett shook her head. 'Reckon the only fellow who could answer that question is Joe Mathinwell, father of that poor little mite out there. Ah, and his mum dead two years past, of the jaundice, and his dad liable for a ten-year sentence! But I've told Joe I'll keep the lad and look after him, if things fall out according.'

The traveller left her shop and went into that of Mr Chitterley the butcher, where he bought a slice of ham. As he moved towards the cash desk a large china pig that stood above it fell to the floor and was smashed to pieces.

'Can you tell me,' asked the stranger, 'whereabouts in this village the Midnight Rose will bloom?'

'No I can't,' snapped the butcher, looking with annoyance at his shattered pig. 'And if I could, I wouldn't. We can keep a secret in these parts, mister.'

The traveller went into the Somerset and West Country bank, where he cashed a traveller's cheque. As he wrote his name a great looking-glass on the wall behind the counter fell down and cracked clean across. And the big crystal chandelier that hung in the middle of the ceiling let out a faint secret hum, which was echoed, even more faintly, by the silver plate on the traveller's head.

'Can you tell me,' he asked, handing in his cheque, 'where the Midnight Rose will bloom?'

'Certainly not,' was the manager's short answer, as he counted out pound notes. 'That is not the kind of information we are required to divulge to customers. *Good* day to you.'

The traveller went on to the chemist, Mr Powdermaker, where he bought fivepence worth of powdered ginger, to the TV repair shop, fish bar, post office, and to the church (where he looked up rather warily at the stone griffins and dolphins which grinned down at him from the corners of the tower). At each place he asked the same question, and everywhere received the same answer.

The vicar was more polite about it than his parishioners.

'Really, my dear sir, it's impossible to say where Joe Mathinwell might have dug up the trowel. Mr Mathinwell is such a very busy man. Why, in this past week he has laid two new floorboards in the school, repaired a piece of paving in the south aisle of the church, cleaned out Mrs Honeysett's drains, unblocked Mr Chitterley's slaughter-house outlet, renewed the wiring at the bank, installed damp-proofing in the pub cellars, dug out a cavity for Mr Powdermaker's new boiler, laid a cement floor in Farmer

Fothergill's pigsties, repaired Mr Porbeagle's basement stairs, and mended a crack in the post office counter. So you see he might have come across the trowel in any one of those places.'

'And where he found the trowel, there the rose is, d'you reckon?' eagerly asked the traveller.

The vicar at once began to look extremely absent-minded.

'Ah well, maybe, maybe, who can say?' he replied guardedly. 'I know, myself, when I am gardening, that I tend to drop my tools in all kinds of odd places, not necessarily just where I have been working. But now excuse me, excuse me, my dear sir, I must go and write a sermon this very minute,' and he hurried away, his shabby coat tails flying.

The traveller ended up at the pub, The Rose Revived, where he was able to obtain a room for the night. But Mrs Bickerstaff the landlady was not able to give him lunch. 'I've my hands that full with cooking a meal for the lawyers and the judge,' she explained. 'Not but what I wouldn't object to drop a spoonful of arsenic in that old Tartar's Windsor soup! But business is business. I can make you a sandwich, though, sir.'

'A sandwich will be enough. How long is the trial expected to continue?'

'Another two-three days, maybe. 'Tis to be hoped as the rose'll bloom before sentence is passed, and then Joe Mathinwell, poor soul, won't need to hold his tongue no longer.'

'Do you know where the rose will bloom, Mrs Bickerstaff?'

'Ah,' she replied, 'that'd be telling, wouldn't it?'

After he had eaten his sandwich, the stranger went into the court-room to hear the trial of Joseph Mathinwell taking its course. But the arguments back and forth between the lawyers were very dull; they seemed to be about what grounds the government had for considering that it had a claim to the trowel which Mr Mathinwell had dug up, and why Mr Mathinwell ought to have obeyed the Court Order to produce the trowel. Nothing about where he had found it.

Mr Mathinwell himself sat calm and quiet. He was a thin pale man with a tussock of darkish hair on the top of his head. He kept his eyes steadily on his joined hands, and never looked up at the stranger sitting in the public benches. The old judge brooded at his high desk: Jeffreys, his name was, Mrs Bickerstaff had told the traveller, Lord Roderick Jeffreys, descended from that same wicked old Judge Jeffreys who had conducted the Bloody Assizes in the neighbouring county of Dorset; and had the same kind of reputation, took pride in sentencing offenders to the maximum penalty. He looked like that too: bitter mouth shut like a rat-trap and deep-sunk eyes like holes out of which something nasty might suddenly pop.

By the afternoon's end matters were no farther advanced, and the judge stumped out to his Bentley and had himself driven away to Mendip Magna, where there was a three-star hotel.

School was over for the day; children were catapulting from the grey stone building and across the bridge over the Wintergreen brook; the stranger began asking them questions.

'Do any of you know where this Midnight Rose is expected to bloom? In the post office, maybe? Or the laundrette?'

Laughing and chattering they surrounded him.

'My dad says it'll be in the British Legion Hall!' 'No – in Farmer Tillinghast's barn!' 'No – down the Youth Club!' 'Not there, glue-brain – at the wishing-well! You come with me, mister – I'll show you!' 'No, mister – you come with *me*!' 'With me!' 'With me!'

This way and that they dragged him. Deciding that the wishing-well sounded the likeliest site, he pulled himself from a dozen hands and followed Cissy Featherstone, who had promised to conduct him to it.

Meanwhile young Joe Mathinwell had been allowed a few words with his father by the kindly Serjeant of the Court, who at other times was Fred Nightingale the sexton.

'Only five minutes, now, mind!'

They were in the front office of the little jail, which had two cells, one for males, one for females. This was the first time in living memory that it had been used.

'Dad!' said young Joe urgently. 'There's a stranger in the village and he's asking around everybody and all over for where the rose is going to bloom!'

'Is he a newspaper reporter? Is he offering money?'

'I didn't hear, but he asked Mrs Honeysett, and Sam Chitterley, and Mr Moneypenny, and Mr Powdermaker and Mr Godliman and lots of others.'

'So? Did they tell?' asked Joe's father with a keen look.

'I reckon not. So now he's asking the kids.'

'Well,' said Mr Mathinwell, 'I reckon they won't tell him either.'

'Who d'you think he is, Dad?'

'Oh,' said Joe's father wearily, 'who can tell? Best take no chances. Maybe he's one o' them scientific foundations wishful to get hold of the rose and *measure* it. Or a film company a-wanting to film it.'

'Would that be so wrong, Dad?'

'There's things,' said Joe Mathinwell, 'ought to be kept private and quiet. Remember what it says in the good book: "And after the fire, a still, small voice." Do you think that still small voice would 'a' been heard if there'd been thousands of folk camping and shuffling around, and dozens of TV cameras? "He that contemneth small things shall fall," it do say in Ecclesiasticus. Don't *you* do that, Joe.'

'No, Dad, but—'

'Time's up, Joe, son,' called Fred Nightingale, keeping watch at the street door.

'Joe,' said his father quickly, 'that rose oughta be watered. See to it, will ye?'

'Yes, Dad,' said Joe, gulping. 'How much water?'

'Not too much. Just a liddle – just as much as it asks for.'

The Mathinwell garden had the best roses and the biggest cabbages in Wintergreen; Joseph, his neighbours said, could talk to green things through the tips of his fingers.

'What kind of water, Dad?' said Joe urgently.

But Mr Nightingale firmly shooed the boy out.

'Mrs Honeysett taking good care of 'ee?' called Joseph senior with anxious love in his voice.

'Yes, Dad ... ' Then Joe was out on the frosty, twilit green, his eyes brimming with tears, and his mind with worry.

The stranger had now returned from the wishing-well, and the various other false goals offered him by the village children (the way to the wishing-well had been a particularly long and slippery track along the side of a cowy valley); he was not angry at being fooled, but he looked thoughtful. He began to walk towards Joe, who broke into a desperate scamper, nipped through Mrs Honeysett's side gate, along to the back of her garden between the bee hives, through Mr Porbeagle's allotment, and so out among the great grassy mounds that encircled the village. (The Sleepers, they were called, no one knew why.) Icy, frosty dusk was really thickening now; the mounds had turned dove grey and did look very much like curled-up sleeping beasts.

'Don't let him find me,' Joe whispered to them as he ran dodging among them; by and by he was fairly certain that he had shaken off the stranger's pursuit, but in order to make even more certain he took the road to Chew Malreward and walked along it for a couple of miles, then circled back by a bridlepath. The moon climbed up, and then slid behind a bank of black cloud; but before it did so, a wink of something bright in the hedge-bank caught Joe's eye: bright, a small circle of light, it was, and he put his hand into a tussock and pulled out a wineglass, with a round bowl and a stem the length of his two middle fingers placed end to end.

'Well, there's a queer thing!' muttered Joe. 'Who could have been drinking wine out here in the middle of no-man's-land? And left his glass behind? Folk on a picnic last summer? Reckon I'll never know.'

The glass was neither chipped nor cracked nor broken; when he had cleaned out a few sodden leaves with a swatch of grass, it gleamed sharp as crystal. Mrs Honeysett would be pleased to have it, Joe thought, and checked a stab of pain, remembering the row of dusty tumblers unused on the shelf in his own home, locked now and shuttered.

Still, coming on the glass like that had someway light-ened his spirits; he felt hope rise in him as he trudged along, clasping the stem of the glass, holding it in front of him as if it were a flagstaff. Hope of what? He hardly knew.

When the rain began, first a few drops, then a drench-ing downpour, he held the glass even more carefully upright, for a question had slid into his mind: would there be enough rain, before he reached the village, to fill the glass right up to its brim? Perhaps there might, he thought; just perhaps. Heaven knows *he* was wet right through his duffel jacket to his skin, and his boots scrunched with water as he walked. One good thing, in such weather as this, most probably the stranger would have given up his prying and his prowling, and would be shut away snug in the bar parlour of The Rose Revived.

By the time that Joe made his way over the hump-backed bridge, the glass was brim full. Not another drop of rain would it hold. Maybe it doesn't matter about the stranger after all, Joe thought joyfully; and so he went straight to the school, let himself in by the little back door, which was never locked, and watered the rose.

At ten minutes to midnight Lord Roderick Jeffreys's limousine softly re-entered Wish Wintergreen; it glided over the hump-backed bridge and came to a stop in the shadows by the church. The night was wild now; huge gusts of wind roared and rollicked; as the chauffeur got out and stepped to open the car door for his master, a massive stone griffin dislodged itself from the cornice of the church and came crashing down on to the car roof, trapping the man inside, who yelled with agony.

'Saunders, Saunders! Get me out of here! I think my leg's broken! Get me out!'

'I can't, sir,' gasped the driver, wrestling with the smashed door-lock.

'Well then phone the police! Phone for an ambulance! Ring somebody's doorbell. Knock somebody up! Bang on their doors!'

The chauffeur rang and knocked at house after house, but nobody seemed to hear his calls and tattoos. Either the inhabitants of Wish Wintergreen were a set of uncommonly sound sleepers – or else none of them was at home. Not even at the jail could Saunders raise any response. And the phone-box on the green was, as usual, out of order.

Doggedly, finding nothing better to do, the chauffeur began walking along the road to Mendip Magna.

And the wind began to drop.

In the village school, all was dark and silent. Not a shoe squeaked, not a corset creaked, not a bracelet clinked. Yet the whole population of the village was there, packed in tight and soundless, like mice in a burrow, intently watching: children breathless, kneeling, squatting and crouching in front, while their parents stood in a circle behind them. Fred Nightingale was there, and Joseph Mathinwell, his hands resting on the shoulders of his son Joe in front of him. All their eyes were fixed on one thing, the rose that was slowly growing out of a crack between two floorboards in the centre of the room.

It was a white rose; that they all remembered afterwards. But that was the only point on which their recollections did agree. About all else, their memories were at variance. Size? Big enough to fill the whole room.

Or tiny, no larger than a clenched fist; but every single petal clear and distinctly visible, though you could see clean through, like a print on a photographic negative. The flower cast a shadow of light, as other objects cast a shadow of darkness. Scent? The whole school was imbued with its shadow and its fragrance. Fragrance of what? Apples, cucumber, lilac, violets? No, none of those things. Like nothing in the world, but never to be forgotten. The leaves, in their tracery of delicate outline, of an equal beauty with the flower.

Now, as the flower itself opened wider and wider, the watchers found that their hearts almost stopped beating from terror. Terror? Why? Because how much longer could it continue to grow and expand its petals? How many more seconds had they left to marvel at this wonder? They clasped each other's hands, they held their breath. For all in the room five seconds, ten seconds, seemed to lengthen into a millennium of time. Then the church clock struck the first note of midnight, and, as it did so, swifter than a patch of sunlight leaving a cornfield, the rose was gone. Nothing remained but a faint fragrance.

Nobody spoke. *Think* they might, but their thoughts were locked inside them. Quiet as leaves, the villagers dispersed, each to his own home, children stumbling dreamily, clasping the hands of parents, lovers arm in arm, old and young, friends, grandchildren and grandparents lost in recollection.

Only Joseph Mathinwell paused by the jail door a

moment to exchange a few quiet words with the stranger, who had been there too, at the back of the group, as was proper for an outsider.

'You'll be taking it back then – the root, and the trowel? And the basket of earth? To where it came from?' Joseph sighed.

'Yes,' the stranger answered him. 'It should never have been brought away. For thousands of years I and my fathers before me have searched. The duty was laid on us. Now the search is over; restitution will be made. The gap will be filled. Farewell then, my friend, Joseph Mathinwell.'

'Farewell, Duke Michael.'

The prisoner turned and walked back into the jail; Fred Nightingale locked him in.

The trial of Joseph Mathinwell had to be adjourned because of the injuries to Judge Jeffreys, who had two broken legs. But before a new judge was summoned, the prisoner had agreed to reveal where he had found the wooden trowel. It had been under the floor of the village school, he said. When officials from the London museum visited the school, however, it became plain that someone had been there before them. One cubic metre of earth, approximately, had been removed from beneath the floorboards. Mathinwell obviously could not have done it, for he had been in jail; nobody else in the village could throw any light on the matter. The prisoner was duly released, and went about his business. The school smelt faintly of roses, and does to this day.

The inhabitants of Wish Wintergreen, never a chatty lot at any time, walk about even quieter these days, with a solemn, happy, inward, recollected look about them. Sometimes, at night, they may glance up at the planet Saturn, in a friendly recognizing way, as if they looked over the hedge at the garden next door. They do not speak about these things. They are used to keeping secrets. But if anything at all hopeful is to happen in the world, there may be a good chance that it will have its beginnings in the village of Wish Wintergreen.

In that garden, the raven utters no cry,
The lion kills not.
In that garden, the wolf snatches not the lamb,
The sick man says not 'I am sick' . . .

The Gift Giving

The weeks leading up to Christmas were always full of excitement, and tremendous anxiety too, as the family waited in suspense for the Uncles, who had set off in the spring of the year, to return from their summer's travelling and trading: Uncle Emer, Uncle Acraud, Uncle Gonfil, and Uncle Mark. They always started off together, down the steep mountainside, but then, at the bottom, they took different routes along the deep narrow valley, Uncle Mark and Uncle Acraud riding eastward, towards the great plains, while Uncle Emer and Uncle Gonfil turned west, towards the towns and rivers and the western sea.

Then, before they were clear of the mountains, they would separate once more, Uncle Acraud turning south, Uncle Emer taking his course northward, so that, the children occasionally thought, their family was scattered over the whole world, netted out like a spider's web.

Spring, summer would go by, in the usual occupations, digging and sowing the steep hillside garden beds, fishing, hunting for hares, picking wild strawberries, making hay. Then, towards St Drimma's Day, when the winds began to blow and the snow crept down, lower and lower, from the high peaks, Grandmother would begin to grow restless.

Silent and calm all summer long she sat in her rocking chair on the wide wooden porch, wrapped in a patchwork quilt, with her blind eyes turned eastward towards the lands where Mark, her dearest and first-born, had gone. But when the winds of Michaelmas began to blow, and the wolves grew bolder, and the children dragged in sacks of logs day after day, and the cattle were brought down to the stable under the house, then Grandmother grew agitated indeed.

When Sammle, the eldest granddaughter, brought her hot milk, she would grip the girl's slender brown wrist and demand: 'Tell me, child, how many days now to St Froida's Day?' (which was the first of December).

'Eighteen, Grandmother,' Sammle would answer, stooping to kiss the wrinkled cheek.

'So many, still? So many till we may hope to see them?'

'Don't worry, Granny, the Uncles are *certain* to return safely. Perhaps they will be early this year. Perhaps we may see them before the Feast of St Melin' (which was December the fourteenth).

And then, sure enough, sometime during the middle weeks of December, their great carts would come jingling and trampling along the winding valleys. Young Mark (son of Uncle Emer), from his watchpoint up a tall pine over a high cliff, would catch the flash of a baggage-mule's brass brow-medal, or the sun glancing on the barrel of a carbine, and would come joyfully dashing back to report.

'Granny! Granny! The Uncles are almost here!'

Then the whole household, the whole village, would be filled with as much agitation and turmoil as that of a kingdom of ants when the spade breaks open their hummock; wives would build the fires higher, and fetch out the best linen, wine, dried meat, pickled eggs; set dough to rising, mix cakes of honey and oats, bring up stone jars of preserved strawberries from the cellars; and the children, with the servants and half the village, would go racing down the perilous zigzag track to meet the cavalcade at the bottom.

The track was far too steep for the heavy carts, which would be dismissed, and the carters paid off to go about their business; then with laughter and shouting, amid a million questions from the children, the loads would be divided and carried up the mountainside on muleback, or on human shoulders. Sometimes the Uncles came home at night, through falling snow, by the smoky light of torches; but the children and the household always knew of their arrival beforehand, and were always there to meet them.

'Did you bring Granny's Chinese shawl, Uncle Mark? Uncle Emer, have you the enamelled box for her snuff that Aunt Grippa begged you to get? Uncle Acraud, did you find the glass candlesticks? Uncle Gonfil, did you bring the books?'

'Yes, yes, keep calm, don't deafen us! Poor tired travellers that we are, leave us in peace to climb this devilish hill! Everything is there, set your minds at rest – the shawl, the box, the books – besides a few other odds and ends, pins and needles and fruit and a bottle or two of wine, and a few trifles for the village. Now, just give us a few minutes to get our breath, will you, kindly—' as the children danced round them, helping each other with the smaller bundles, never ceasing to pour out questions: 'Did you see the Grand Cham? The Akond of Swat? The Fon of Bikom? The Seljuk of Rum? Did you go to Cathay? To Muskovy? To Dalai? Did you travel by ship, by camel, by llama, by elephant?'

And, at the top of the hill, Grandmother would be waiting for them, out on her roofed porch, no matter how wild the weather or how late the hour, seated in majesty with her furs and patchwork quilt around her, while the Aunts ran to and fro with hot stones to place under her feet. And the Uncles always embraced her first, very fondly and respectfully, before turning to hug their wives and sisters-in-law.

Then the goods they had brought would be distributed through the village – the scissors, tools, medicines, plants, bales of cloth, ingots of metal, cordials, firearms, and musical instruments; then there would be a great feast.

Not until Christmas morning did Grandmother and the children receive the special gifts which had been brought for them by the Uncles; and this giving always took the same ceremonial form.

Uncle Mark stood behind Grandmother's chair, playing on a small pipe that he had acquired somewhere during his travels; it was made from hard black polished wood, with silver stops, and it had a mouthpiece made of amber. Uncle Mark invariably played the same tune on it at these times, very softly. It was a tune which he had heard for the first time, he said, when he was much younger, once when he had narrowly escaped falling into a crevasse on the hillside, and a voice had spoken to him, as it seemed, out of the mountain itself, bidding him watch where he set his feet and have a care, for the family depended on him. It was a gentle, thoughtful tune, which reminded Sandri, the middle granddaughter, of springtime sounds, warm wind, water from melted snow dripping off the gabled roofs, birds trying out their mating calls.

While Uncle Mark played on his pipe, Uncle Emer

would hand each gift to Grandmother. And she – here was the strange thing – she, who was stone blind all the year long, could not see her own hand in front of her face – she would take the object in her fingers and instantly identify it.

'A mother-of-pearl comb, with silver studs, for Tassy . . . it comes from Babylon; a silk shawl, blue and rose, from Hind, for Argilla; a wooden game, with ivory pegs, for young Emer, from Damascus; a gold brooch, from Hangku, for Grippa; a book of rhymes, from Paris, for Sammle, bound in a scarlet leather cover.'

Grandmother, who lived all the year round in darkness, could, by stroking each gift with her old, blotched,

clawlike fingers, frail as quills, discover not only what the thing was and where it came from, but also the colour of it, and that in the most precise and particular manner, correct to a shade.

'It is a jacket of stitched and pleated cotton, printed over with leaves and flowers; it comes from the island of Haranati, in the eastern ocean; the colours are leaf-brown and gold and a dark, dark blue, darker than mountain gentians—' for Grandmother had not always been blind; when she was a young girl she had been able to see as well as anybody else.

'And this is for you, Mother, from your son Mark,' Uncle Emer would say, handing her a tissue-wrapped bundle, and she would exclaim,

'Ah, how beautiful! A coat of tribute silk, of the very palest green, so that the colour shows only in the folds, like shadows on snow; the buttons and the button-toggles are of worked silk, lavender-grey, like pearl, and the stiff collar is embroidered with white roses.'

'Put it on, Mother!' her sons and daughters-in-law would urge her, and the children, dancing around her chair, clutching their own treasures, would chorus, 'Yes, put it on, put it on! Ah, you look like a queen, Granny, in that beautiful coat! The highest queen in the world! The queen of the mountain!'

Those months after Christmas were Grandmother's happiest time. Secure, thankful, with her sons safe at home, she would sit in a warm fireside corner of the big wooden family room. The wind might shriek, the snow gather higher and higher out of doors, but that did not concern her, for her family, and all the village, were well supplied with flour, oil, firewood, meat, herbs, and roots; the children had their books and toys; they learned lessons with the old priest, or made looms and spinning wheels, carved stools and chairs and chests, with the tools their uncles had brought them. The Uncles rested, and told tales of their travels; Uncle Mark played his pipe for hours together, Uncle Acraud drew pictures in charcoal of the places he had seen, and Granny, laying her hand on the paper covered with lines, would expound while Uncle Mark played:

'A huge range of mountains, like wrinkled brown linen across the horizon; a wide plain of sand, silvery blond in colour, with patches of pale, pale blue; I think it is not water but air the colour of water; here are strange lines across the sand where men once ploughed it, long, long ago; and a great patch of crystal green, with what seems like a road crossing it; now here is a smaller region of plum-pink, bordered by an area of rusty red; I think these are the colours of the earth in these territories; it is very high up, dry from height, and the soil glittering with little particles of metal.'

'You have described it better than I could myself!' Uncle Acraud would exclaim, while the children, breathless with wonder and curiosity, sat cross-legged around her chair.

And she would answer, 'Yes, but I cannot see it at all, Acraud, unless your eyes have seen it first, and I cannot see it without Mark's music to help me.'

'How does Grandmother *do* it?' the children would demand of their mothers.

And Argilla, or Grippa, or Tassy, would answer, 'Nobody knows. It is Grandmother's gift. She alone can do it.'

The people of the village might come in, whenever they chose, and on many evenings thirty or forty would be there, silently listening, and when Grandmother retired to bed, which she did early, for the seeing made her weary, the audience would turn to one another with deep sighs, and murmur, 'The world is indeed a wide place.'

But with the first signs of spring the Uncles would become restless again, and begin looking over their equipment, discussing maps and routes, mending saddle-bags and boots, gazing up at the high peaks for signs that the snow was in retreat.

Then Granny would grow very silent. She never asked them to stay longer, she never disputed their going, but her face seemed to shrivel, she grew smaller, wizened and huddled inside her quilted patchwork.

And on St Petrag's Day, when they set off, when the farewells were said and they clattered off down the mountain, through the melting snow and the trees with pink luminous buds, Grandmother would fall into a silence that lasted, sometimes, for as much as five or six weeks; all day she would sit with her face turned to the east, wordless, motionless, and would drink her milk and go to her bedroom at night still silent and dejected; it took the warm sun and sweet wild hyacinths of May to raise her spirits.

Then, by degrees, she would grow animated, and begin to say, 'Only six months, now, till they come back.'

But young Mark observed to his cousin Sammle, 'It takes longer, every year, for Grandmother to grow accustomed.'

And Sammle said, shivering, though it was warm May weather, 'Perhaps one year, when they come back, she will not be here. She is becoming so tiny and thin; you can see right through her hands, as if they were leaves.' And Sammle held up her own thin brown young hand against the sunlight, to see the blood glow under the translucent skin.

'I don't know how they would bear it,' said Mark thoughtfully, 'if when they came back we had to tell them that she had died.'

But that was not what happened.

One December the Uncles arrived much later than usual. They did not climb the mountain until St Mishan's Day, and when they reached the house it was in silence. There was none of the usual joyful commotion.

Grandmother knew instantly that there was something wrong.

'Where is my son Mark?' she demanded. 'Why do I not hear him among you?'

And Uncle Acraud had to tell her: 'Mother, he is dead. Your son Mark will not come home, ever again.'

'How do you *know*? How can you be *sure*? You were not there when he died?'

'I waited and waited at our meeting place, and a messenger came to tell me. His caravan had been attacked by wild tribesmen, riding north from the Lark mountains. Mark was killed, and all his people. Only this one man escaped and came to bring me the story.'

'But how can you be *sure*? How do you know he told the *truth*?'

'He brought Mark's ring.'

Emer put it into her hand. As she turned it about in her thin fingers, a long moan went through her.

'Yes, he is dead. My son Mark is dead.'

'The man gave me this little box,' Acraud said, 'which Mark was bringing for you.'

Emer put it into her hand, opening the box for her. Inside lay an ivory fan. On it, when it was spread out, you could see a bird, with eyes made of sapphire, flying across a valley, but Grandmother held it listlessly, as if her hands were numb.

'What is it?' she said. 'I do not know what it is. Help me to bed, Argilla. I do not know what it is. I do not wish to know. My son Mark is dead.'

Her grief infected the whole village. It was as if the

keystone of an arch had been knocked out; there was nothing to hold the people together.

That year spring came early, and the three remaining Uncles, melancholy and restless, were glad to leave on their travels. Grandmother hardly noticed their going.

Sammle said to Mark: 'You are clever with your hands. Could you not make a pipe – like the one my father had?'

'I?' he said. 'Make a pipe? Like Uncle Mark's pipe? Why? What would be the point of doing so?'

'Perhaps you might learn to play on it. As he did.'

'I? Play on a pipe?'

'I think you could,' she said. 'I have heard you whistle tunes of your own.'

'But where would I find the right kind of wood?'

'There is a chest, in which Uncle Gonfil once brought books and music from Leiden. I think it is the same kind of wood. I think you could make a pipe from it.'

'But how can I remember the shape?'

'I will make a drawing,' Sammle said, and she drew with a stick of charcoal on the whitewashed wall of the cowshed. As soon as Mark looked at her drawing he began to contradict.

'No! I remember now. It was not like that. The stops came here – and the mouthpiece was like this.'

Now the other children flocked around to help and advise.

'The stops were farther apart,' said Creusie. 'And there were more of them and they were bigger.'

'The pipe was longer than that,' said Sandri. 'I have held it. It was as long as my arm.'

'How will you ever make the stops?' said young Emer.

'You can have my silver bracelets that Father gave me,' said Sammle.

'I'll ask Finn the smith to help me,' said Mark.

Once he had got the notion of making a pipe into his head, he was eager to begin. But it took him several weeks of difficult carving; the black wood of the chest proved hard as iron. And when the pipe was made, and the stops fitted, it would not play; try as he would, not a note could he fetch out of it.

Mark was dogged, though, once he had set himself to a task; he took another piece of the black chest, and began again. Only Sammle stayed to help him now; the other children had lost hope, or interest, and gone back to their summer occupations.

The second pipe was much better than the first. By September, Mark was able to play a few notes on it; by October he was playing simple tunes, made up out of his head.

'But,' he said, 'if I am to play so that Grandmother can see with her fingers – if I am to do *that* – I must remember your father's special tune. Can *you* remember it, Sammle?'

She thought and thought.

'Sometimes,' she said, 'it seems as if it is just beyond the edge of my hearing – as if somebody were playing it, far, far away, in the woods. Oh, if only I could stretch my hearing a little farther!'

'Oh, Sammle! Try!'

For days and days she sat silent, or wandered in the woods, frowning, knotting her forehead, willing her ears to hear the tune again; and the women of the household said, 'That girl is not doing her fair share of the tasks.'

They scolded her, and set her to spin, weave, milk the goats, throw grain to the hens. But all the while she continued silent, listening, listening, to a sound she could not hear. At night, in her dreams, she sometimes thought she could hear the tune, and she would wake with tears on her cheeks, wordlessly calling her father to come back and play his music to her, so that she could remember it.

In September the autumn winds blew cold and fierce; by October snow was piled around the walls and up to the windowsills. On St Felin's Day the three Uncles returned, but sadly and silently, without the former festivities; although, as usual, they brought many bales and boxes of gifts and merchandise. The children went down as usual, to help carry the bundles up the mountain. The joy had gone out of this tradition though; they toiled silently up the track with their loads.

It was a wild, windy evening, the sun set in fire, the

wind moaned among the fir trees, and gusts of sleet every now and then dashed in their faces.

'Take care, children!' called Uncle Emer, as they skirted along the side of a deep gully, and his words were caught by an echo and flung back and forth between the rocky walls: 'Take care – care – care – care – care – . . .'

'*Oh!*' cried Sammle, stopping precipitately and clutching the bag that she was carrying. 'I have it! I can remember it! *Now* I know how it went!'

And, as they stumbled on up the snowy hillside, she hummed the melody to her cousin Mark, who was just ahead of her.

'Yes, that is it, yes!' he said. 'Or, no, wait a minute, that is not *quite* right – but it is close, it is very nearly the way it went. Only the notes were a little faster, and there were more of them – they went up, not *down* – before the ending tied them in a knot—'

'No, no, they went down at the end, I am almost sure . . .'

Arguing, interrupting each other, disputing, agreeing, they dropped their bundles in the family room and ran away to the cowhouse, where Mark kept his pipe hidden.

For three days they discussed and argued and tried a hundred different versions; they were so occupied that they hardly took the trouble to eat. But at last, by Christmas morning, they had reached agreement.

'I *think* it is right,' said Sammle. 'And if it is not, I do not believe there is anything more that we can do about it.'

'Perhaps it will not work in any case,' said Mark sadly. He was tired out with arguing and practising.

Sammle was equally tired, but she said, 'Oh, it *must* work. Oh, let it work! Please let it work! For otherwise I don't think I can bear the sadness. Go now, Mark, quietly and quickly, go and stand behind Granny's chair.'

The family had gathered, according to Christmas habit, around Grandmother's rocking chair, but the faces of the Uncles were glum and reluctant, their wives dejected and hopeless. Only the children showed eagerness, as the cloth-wrapped bundles were brought and laid at Grandmother's feet.

She herself looked wholly dispirited and cast down. When Uncle Emer handed her a slender, soft package, she received it apathetically, almost with dislike, as if she would prefer not to be bothered by this tiresome gift ceremony.

Then Mark, who had slipped through the crowd without being noticed, began to play on his pipe just behind Grandmother's chair.

The Uncles looked angry and scandalized; Aunt Tassy cried out in horror: 'Oh, Mark, wicked boy, how *dare* you?' but Grandmother lifted her head, more alertly than she had done for months past, and began to listen.

Mark played on. His mouth was quivering so badly that it was hard to grip the amber mouthpiece, but he played with all the breath that was in him. Meanwhile Sammle, kneeling by her grandmother, held, with her own warm young hands, the old, brittle ones against the fabric of the gift. And, as she did so, she began to feel what Grandmother felt.

Grandmother said softly and distinctly: 'It is a muslin shawl, embroidered in gold thread, from Lebanon. It is coloured a soft brick-red, with pale roses of sunset-pink, and thorns of soft silver-green. It is for Sammle . . .'

THE KINGDOM AND THE CAVE

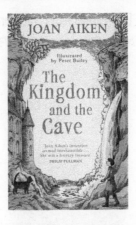

When Joan Aiken was just seventeen she wrote her first novel, *The Kingdom and the Cave*, a thrilling adventure about a cat and his boy.

'The Under People. They live in a huge Cave. They are thought to be boring upwards. Giant worms and flying ants. Underground magic.'

Mickle, the palace cat, knows the kingdom is in danger. He can feel it in his whiskers and he has found a mysterious note in the royal library . . . (Yes, of course he can read, and speak – if he chooses to!) Mickle and Prince Michael, with the help of their animal friends (and quite a bit of magic!), set out on a perilous quest to find the sinister Under People, discover their secret power and save the Kingdom of Astalon.

'Joan Aiken's invention seemed inexhaustible.
She was a literary treasure'
Philip Pullman

MOSSY TROTTER

By Elizabeth Taylor

With illustrations by Tony Ross

'We – that is, Herbert and I – want you, Mossy, to be our page-boy,' Miss Silkin said, staring hard at Mossy, as if she were trying to imagine him dressed up, and with his hair combed. Mossy went very red, and nearly choked on a piece of cake.

Mossy Trotter is almost eight, and when he moves to the countryside, life is full of adventure: there's the rubbish tip to explore for treasure, and the woods to get lost in. But every now and then his happiness is disturbed – chiefly by his mother's meddling friend, Miss Silkin.

'This book is delightful. Mossy is a totally realistic little boy, always trying to do interesting things that the grown-ups don't approve of. Taylor writes brilliantly from a child's point of view'
Kate Saunders

AN EPISODE OF SPARROWS
By Rumer Godden

Someone has been digging up the private garden in the
Square. Miss Angela Chesney is sure that a gang of local
boys is to blame, but her sister, Olivia, isn't so sure. She
wonders why the neighbourhood children – 'sparrows', she
calls them – have to be locked out: can't they enjoy the
garden too?

Nobody knows what sends young Lovejoy in secret search
of 'good garden earth'. Still less do they imagine where their
investigation will lead them – to a struggling restaurant, a
bombed-out church, and, at the heart of it all, a
hidden garden.

'A masterpiece of construction and utterly realistically
convincing ... Lovejoy, Tip and Sparkey were so real to me that
they have stayed alive in my head for more than fifty years'
Jacqueline Wilson

DISCOVER
Virago Classics

virago